OXFORD BLUE

Also by Veronica Stallwood and available from Headline

Deathspell
Death and the Oxford Box
Oxford Exit
Oxford Mourning
Oxford Fall
Oxford Knot

OXFORD BLUE

Veronica Stallwood

HEADLINE

First published in 1998 by
HEADLINE BOOK PUBLISHING

10 9 8 7 6 5 4 3 2 1

British Library Cataloguing in Publication Data

Stallwood, Veronica
Oxford blue
1. Detective and mystery stories
I. Title
823.9'14 [F]

ISBN 0 7472 2195 2

Typeset by Avon Dataset Ltd, Bidford-on-Avon, Warks

Printed and bound in Great Britain by
Mackays of Chatham PLC, Chatham, Kent

HEADLINE BOOK PUBLISHING
A division of Hodder Headline PLC
338 Euston Road
London NW1 3BH

For all my favourite residents of Vine Cottages,
past and present:

Leopold and Papageno
also
Alan and Robert
Jeremy and Stéphanie
Simon and Sarah

with love

1

The village of Gatt's Hill crouches along a ridge over-
looking the Thame valley. No, that isn't a misprint. This is
not the mighty River Thames which flows through the
country's capital, but a smaller, unimportant cousin of
his, lacking his grandeur, his history and his final *s*. For
most of the year our River Thame might be described as
a minor stream, and even in February, when the water
meadows are flooded and your car splashes through the
puddles that lie across the road by the narrow stone
bridge, you would hardly mistake it for its near-namesake.
And while the noble Thames was presiding over the great
changes in our nation's history, so our little river was
carrying local gossip chattering over its stony bed and
observing the small tragedies and triumphs of the villages
and hamlets that lie along its route.

Sometimes Kate Ivory walks down to the bridge and
leans on its lichen-spotted stone wall and stares into the
brown, chuckling water as though, if she stands and
stares for long enough, the stream will carry her troubles
away with the rest, down to the sea where they will
scatter and sink and be lost for ever. Today, perhaps
because the weather is grey and heavy, she does not
venture even that far, but stands by the gate of Crossways
Cottage and simply looks at the view.

An aged villager shambles past, a sour-looking, grey-
muzzled dog at his heels.

1

'Hello,' calls Kate in a friendly way. 'Looks like rain, don't you think?'

The man stares at her briefly, then turns his head away deliberately, muttering something that sounds like 'Mnerf,' but which is probably an adverse comment on Kate's intelligence.

The ridge on which Gatt's Hill sprawls is not high – maybe four hundred and fifty feet above sea level – but even so is sufficiently lofty to give some lucky villagers an uninterrupted view across to the Chilterns, some thirty miles away. On this day in September the distant hills are blue and lightly veiled by mist. To the left of centre rises a grey Norman church tower, artistically spotlit by a narrow ray of sunlight escaping from beneath a cloud. Over to the right, behind a stand of flimsy poplar trees, rise a number of small, humpy hills, each crowned with a bunch of trees like sprigs of broccoli. Across the landscape march straight files of pylons, converging on a single point as though illustrating a lesson in perspective, and fixing the position of Didcot power station beneath its plume of white vapour.

Kate Ivory breathed in the clean country air, sneezed at the smell of cow dung and listened to the sweet rural quiet of Gatt's Hill. In the distance a combine harvester chomped its way through a field of wheat. Above her, small aircraft growled across the sky, joined by the louder snarl of a helicopter. A group of children arrived on the recreation field opposite her cottage and started to argue over the swings. A yellow furniture van chugged down the hill towards the next hamlet. A small motorbike climbed up the same hill and vroomed out of sight along the single village street. No one took any notice of Kate.

This is what I need, she told herself: peace, quiet, and the chance to recover from the shocks of the past months. Oxford lay hidden behind the hill at her back. Even if she walked to the end of the garden, leant over the gate and craned her neck, she wouldn't be able to see it. Out of sight and, she hoped, out of mind.

After the tragedy, her friend Callie had suggested that she should leave her own house for a while.

'What you need is a holiday,' she had said, taking in Kate's pale face and the circles under her eyes. 'Take yourself off to the Bahamas, or go for a long walk in Nepal.'

'No thanks,' Kate had said. 'Normally, yes, those are the things I would like to do, but I seem to have lost all my energy. What's happened to me, Callie? I can hardly force myself out of bed in the mornings. I've done no work at all for weeks.'

'It's called grieving,' Callie had answered sensibly. 'You have to give yourself time to get over what happened. It might help if you distanced yourself from it, even by half a dozen miles. Please move into my cottage for a while. I shall be spending at least three months in New York, maybe more if things go well.'

'What about my own place?'

'Let it. Fill it with tenants. Put it in the hands of an agency. They'll do everything for you. You'll make a profit.'

'Why are you doing this for me?'

'I don't like leaving the cottage empty for all that time. You'll be doing me a favour. If another family takes over your house and lives in it for a while, it will exorcise the ghosts, stop the memories from being so vivid. And maybe the change of scene will perk you up a bit. Get your mind off things.'

'What do people do in the country? What will I do all day?'

'Go for long, muddy walks. Join in the exciting social life of the village. Paint a picture. Write a book. You're supposed to be a novelist, aren't you?'

And so Kate had allowed herself to be persuaded. Callie had disappeared off to New York and Kate had driven her ageing Peugeot up to Gatt's Hill with a couple of suitcases and her word processor in the back and had moved into Callie's cottage for an indefinite length of time. 'Until I feel better,' was the way she put it to herself.

Maybe she was feeling a bit better than when she arrived, but she was still far from her usual, lively self. She felt in her pocket and found a tissue. She wiped her eyes. It must be the wind that was making them water.

The village street was silent now except for the whining of the power cables overhead. Even the children in the recreation field had found some uncontentious game to play among the rubbish-strewn bushes. If the rural life seems a little dull at times, that's because I'm not used to it yet, she thought. She prodded at the earth in one of the flower pots. It felt dry and sandy. A couple of late-flowering geraniums struggled to survive her lack of care. Perhaps she should buy herself a basic guide to gardening before all Callie's plants died of neglect.

Or she could go for another walk.

A more vigorous gust of wind blew a handful of dust in her face and she turned to go back indoors. Crossways Cottage was quite charming, but in her current mood she was left cold by its white-painted walls, its mossy, tiled roof and tall brick chimney. 'It's the cold weather,' she told herself. 'I'll feel better when the spring arrives.' The

4

small, deep-set windows stared back at her, reserving judgement. She must stop frittering away her time. She could read a book, or make notes for her own new novel. She could listen to the radio or just sit and stare at the wallpaper.

Restlessly she wandered back outside. The rain clouds were clearing and the distant hills appeared much closer, the details of hedge and tree so distinct that she could have been looking at them through binoculars. But as the light altered, the surface of the earth wavered, and as she watched, the trees changed their shape and transformed themselves into the body of a man who sprawled face downwards in the middle of the field, his limbs crumpled, the rusty leaves of a hawthorn bush spreading from his head like a pool of blood. The trees and hedges, even the pylons, all the lines of the landscape seemed to point towards him. He grew, he spread over the whole field, he filled the entire countryside. The hot, metallic smell of blood filled the air. Kate felt the sky above her swing away in a dizzying arc and heard the rooks screaming their outrage in the treetops.

No. She shook her head to free it from the image. She wouldn't think about it. She concentrated on the foreground until the sky was still and the birds were silent again. The last children from the recreation field were trailing home to their tea and a magpie chattered in triumph over his reoccupation of the field. A grey-haired woman in wellies walked a dog. A young man in drab-coloured clothes and heavy boots strode past without glancing up at her cottage. He had a profile like a classical statue, all straight lines and well-defined planes, and shining blue-black hair combed back from his face and tied in a pony tail. His skin was deeply tanned, as though he spent most of his time in the open air. She watched him until he disappeared.

Out of sight, down the lane, she heard a car approaching. Kate recognized the unmistakable put-put of an old VW. You didn't see many of them around any more and she waited for it to come into view so that she could know she was right. Yes: egg-yolk yellow with traditional red rust patches and assorted dents. It coughed to a halt outside her cottage and the woman inside thumped the driver's door to open it and stretched long legs out on to the narrow grass verge. The legs were clad in opaque scarlet tights, the narrow feet in black suede boots, and they were soon followed by a dark purple skirt and a multi-coloured velvet patchwork jacket. When she stood up, Kate could see that the woman was tall and thin and had a lot of thick, curly brown hair. She gathered a large leather bag and a couple of plastic carrier bags from the front seat, walked towards Kate, then stopped by the gate of Crossways Cottage and examined each of her shoes in turn.

'I'd forgotten just how muddy it is in the country,' she said. 'It's buggered my favourite boots.' She had a low, dark voice – achieved, Kate assumed, by many hours of smoking and drinking in exotic nightclubs. She and Kate confronted one another for a moment. 'What on earth are you doing in a dump like this?' the woman enquired. Her skin was deeply tanned, so that the grey of her eyes seemed nearly colourless.

Kate said, 'Hello, Mother.'

2

'How did you find me?' asked Kate.

'That's not a very nice way to greet your long-lost mother. Aren't you going to ask me in?'

'I didn't lose you. You lost me. You disappeared years ago.' And then, remembering her manners, she said, 'Yes, of course. Come in. It's great to see you.' And, awkwardly, since they hadn't embraced for some ten years, she put her arms round her mother and gave her a brief hug.

'How are you?' she asked.

'I'm just fine.' It seemed as though they were stuck in a groove of banalities.

'I'm sorry about your boots. Put them by the back door and I'll brush them for you.'

'Never mind them now. How are you? You're looking a bit peaky, I must say.'

'Perhaps I'm just looking older.'

'Nonsense. There's no need to start looking older until you're well into your forties. Now, Kate, don't just stand there, come and help me unpack the car.' She followed her mother back out to the car, which stood at an odd angle, one wheel up on the verge, the others in the road. 'You take this,' said her mother briskly.

Kate looked down at the blue suitcase with its remnants of airline tags and a hand-printed label on the handle: *Roz Ivory*. How long was it since she'd last seen that name? She'd almost forgotten that she had such a thing as a mother, and this woman seemed an unlikely candidate for the post. In a daze, she carried the case into the house.

A minute later her mother brought in an even larger case, green this time, together with a faded cloth shoulder bag, dating from about 1970, and more plastic carrier bags. She dumped them on the floor next to the blue case. The heap was growing into roughly the size and shape of a young, recumbent elephant. Kate just stopped herself from asking how long her mother intended to stay.

'Well now, you'd better show me the way to the spare room,' said Roz.

Kate opened her mouth to say no, and what makes you think I want to see you after all this time, but then she closed it again, shrugged, picked up a suitcase and a couple of plastic bags and led the way to the narrow staircase. There were two rooms upstairs, one of them her own bedroom, the other, looking out across the Thame valley, she had intended to use as her workroom. On the table here she had placed her word processor and on the shelf, a few of her books. She hadn't done any work yet, but she certainly had the intention of doing some in the coming weeks. This, she supposed now, was the spare room.

'Very nice,' said Roz, looking around at yellow-painted walls, Swedish checks at windows and on the bed, and solid country furniture. She opened the third door off the tiny landing. 'Is this my bathroom?'

'This is the only bathroom,' said Kate. 'And up to now it's been mine.'

Somehow when her mother was around she had to spell out her territory in a way that made her despise herself. But she knew that if she didn't, she'd be pushed into a small corner of the cottage and made to feel like a visitor.

'There's no need to be so proprietorial,' said Roz. 'Didn't I teach you to share your toys?'

If they continued like this they'd be fighting in their old familiar way before the day was over.

'I expect you'd like to wash and so on,' said Kate. 'Would you like me to make some tea?'

'Is that the best you can manage for a celebration? Haven't you got any gin?'

At half past three in the afternoon? 'Possibly,' she said gingerly.

'Don't worry, I was only joking. And I've brought you a few bottles of duty free. We'll open them later. But for now, yes, tea would be lovely.'

Kate left her and went downstairs to make tea and to think. If her mother had bottles of duty free, then she had recently come from abroad. Where was it she had been when she last sent a postcard? Miami, perhaps. Or was it somewhere in Africa? From upstairs she heard sounds of splashing water, of the cistern flushing, of loud, tuneless singing. As she carried the tea and a plate of chocolate biscuits into the sitting room, Roz came downstairs. Everything the woman does seems charged with energy, thought Kate. Once, she had been like that herself; now it only made her feel tired to see it in someone else.

'Your friend has good taste,' said Roz, looking round. 'And money, by the look of it.'

'Yes.' Now that Roz had removed her pile of luggage to the spare room, they could see the sitting room properly again. As well as one or two classy pieces of furniture there were two deep, soft sofas, large enough to sit four slim people, or to allow one lazy one to stretch out at full length and kip for an hour or two in the afternoon. Curtains and covers were new enough not to look worn, but old enough to look comfortable, and in pale colours that made the most of the light that found its way in through the deep-set, small windows.

'I can't think why you want to live out here in the sticks, but this cottage is really quite civilized.'

Kate ignored the implied questions. 'Are you hungry? I can pop down to the supermarket and get us something for dinner.'

'A twelve-mile drive, and then all that frightful cooking and washing-up! Why don't we try the pub I saw as I drove into the village? Have you been inside it yet? What's it like? Full of yokels and tweedy types, I suppose.'

'I peered through the window on one of my walks. It looked all right. Rather self-consciously bucolic, but they do serve food.'

'That's settled, then. We'll eat there this evening. My treat.'

There was a silence, then Roz added, 'I suppose we could talk now. Have what they call a conversation.'

'If you want to.' She knew she sounded unfriendly, but she didn't want to rush into intimate revelations just yet.

'Do you want the story of my life?' asked Roz lightly. 'Or would you like to tell me yours?'

'Why don't you give me yours in reverse order, and then I can stop you when I've had enough. Start with how you found me here in Gatt's Hill.'

'I went to your house in Oxford. Agatha Street, I think it was. Who do you suppose Agatha was?'

'The builder's great-aunt, probably,' said Kate absently. 'Go on.' She had a chance to look at her mother properly now that she was actually sitting down in one place. Her skin was deeply tanned, presumably from years in the sun in Florida, or Kashmir, or wherever, and there were thin white creases radiating from the corners of her eyes. So she had been having a good time while she was away, having a lot of laughs. Had she missed her daughter at all? It was a question Kate didn't want to ask.

'Anyway, why have you moved?' asked Roz. 'What are those strange people doing in your place? They weren't at all helpful to begin with. I had to tell quite a large number of fibs before they would part with your new address. And why are you living here, in the middle of nowhere?'

'Such a long story,' said Kate.

'We have time, haven't we? You're not doing anything as far as I can see.'

'More tea?'

'No thanks. Would you like me to fetch the duty-free whisky now?'

'If you're desperate for a drink, I suppose you'd better.'

'I hardly ever touch the stuff, but I thought you looked as if you needed a pick-me-up,' said Roz crisply.

They glared at each other. Her mother had removed the velvet patchwork jacket and was wearing a patterned shirt and a long, designer knitted top. Her clothes looked foreign, fairly exotic, and they draped and swathed around her spare form. The colours were moodily autumnal, which suited her colouring. Her lipstick was a dark plum colour which made Kate aware that she was wearing no make-up at all and probably looked pale and washed-out.

'Where have you been all this time? Why didn't you keep in touch?' asked Kate.

'I've been abroad. All over the place. And I sent you a Christmas card.'

'Yes, but that was in 1994.'

'I'm sure it was more recently than that. 1996, surely?'

'1994. I kept it for a while. And what about my birthday?' She heard her voice, like a hurt child's.

'I thought you must have given up counting them by now. You wouldn't want to be reminded of your age, would you?'

'You're the one who stopped counting, not me. Look at you! Stuck in 1968!'

'Don't you like this top? You'd prefer to see me in a burka, I suppose. Tariq was very keen on that, I seem to remember. But so unflattering, I thought.'

'Tariq?' queried Kate, hoping for a clue to her mother's life.

'Oh, just a friend of mine,' said Roz dismissively. 'You wouldn't have liked him, I can tell.'

Kate could see from her mother's bland expression that she had no intention of revealing more about the mysterious Tariq. 'And just what is a burka?' she asked.

'One of those frightful long black garments, designed to prevent men from being distracted by female endowments.'

'No, not really your style,' said Kate.

'Maybe I should be wearing a nifty little suit from Agnès B?'

The thought was so ludicrous that they both collapsed into giggles.

'That's better,' said Roz. 'You looked as though you hadn't smiled for weeks. What on earth has happened to you? Do you feel like telling me about it?'

Kate didn't reply for a moment, but drank her cooling tea. 'I've been trying to forget about it, but with no success,' she said eventually. Roz nodded encouragingly and Kate continued, 'It's on my mind all the time. I had to get out of the house in Agatha Street because an old friend of mine, Andrew Grove, died there in the hallway. No, I'm avoiding the truth. He didn't just die, he was killed. Murdered. If he hadn't been there, in that place at that time, he would still be alive. I feel it's my fault. I'm to blame. Now do you understand why I ran away and why I'm hiding out here in the sticks?'

'No one can really understand, I imagine. But I do sympathize.'

'And I don't want to meet people, or go out and pretend to enjoy myself.'

'What sort of friend was he?' enquired Roz into the silence. 'How close?'

'You want to know if he was my lover? No, he wasn't. But he was a part of my life, knitted into its fabric. He found me work when I needed to earn money. He introduced me to his unsuitable girlfriends and I listened sympathetically when they dumped him. He took me to concerts. He fussed over me and cooked me meals.'

'Here, you'd better have this box of tissues.'

'Thanks.' She blew her nose, then went on, 'And he was killed because of me.'

'I imagine he was killed because of the evil in another human being.'

'That, too. But it doesn't make me feel any less guilty.'

'Did they find the person who did it?'

'Yes. He's in prison, on remand. I presume the trial will be in another few months. It seems to take for ever to put these things together.'

'Meanwhile you sit here brooding about it. I've never found guilt a very useful item of luggage. It's like depression: it robs you of energy and roots you to the spot.'

'You make it sound like laziness.'

'No. I don't think you're lazy. Laziness would be easier to deal with.'

'And how do you suggest I deal with guilt?'

'When did Andrew die?'

'What? Oh, three or four months ago, I suppose.'

'Well, much as I hate to say "snap out of it", I think that that's what you're going to have to start to do. Just look at you, Kate!'

'What's wrong with me?'

'When did you last visit a hairdresser?'

'I don't think there is one in the village.'

'I should hope not. I hate to think what era they'd be living in. But there are a couple of decent places in Oxford, surely.'

'I suppose so. Does my hair really look awful?' She pushed her fingers through her hair. It did feel a bit tacky.

'When did you last wash it? It's ratty and greasy.'

'Thanks! I'll wash it tomorrow, all right?'

There was silence for a while.

'Sulking never did suit you,' ventured Roz.

'I'm not sulking, I'm just offended.'

'Telephone your hairdresser before they close and make an appointment for tomorrow morning.'

And, as though she were still twelve years old, Kate went to do what her mother told her. Yes, they could fit her in at ten-fifteen, though it wouldn't be with her usual stylist. She had to admit that she felt better when she came off the phone, but perhaps that was because she enjoyed the stimulation of fighting with her mother.

'I think we should make a list of interesting things to do,' said Roz when Kate returned to her place on the sofa.

'As if it were the summer holidays,' said Kate.

'Half-term weekend, anyway,' said Roz. 'Tomorrow we go into Oxford.' She stopped when she saw Kate's expression. 'You have to face it some time,' she said. 'I'll drive you in to the hairdresser, and then we'll go looking for new clothes for you.'

'What's wrong with the ones I'm wearing?'

'They're all black, and they don't fit very well, and they don't suit you. We'll go on a shopping binge. It'll be great fun – just like the old days. And you needn't go anywhere near Agatha Street.'

'We could be back here in time for lunch,' said Kate.

'For tea, anyway.'

'Lunch,' insisted Kate.

'All right. At least it's a start. You must get out of this place. You look as though you've stretched out on that sofa watching television ever since you got here.'

'Sometimes I read a book.'

'That's what I mean. But from tomorrow things are going to be different.'

'In what way? I'll go into Oxford to get my hair done, but that's it. After that I'm staying put in this nice, safe, dull cottage.'

'I've only been here for a matter of hours, and already I'm screaming to get away. It's a lovely view out there, certainly, but don't you get tired of fields and trees, and acres of mud?'

'No,' said Kate firmly.

'Well I do, and I think you should, too. I think we should go for daily outings to London and Birmingham, and up to Edinburgh, maybe.'

'*Birmingham?*'

'Or we could try the new train that goes straight to Paris.'

'No thanks.'

'How far past the front gate *will* you go?'

'To the end of the village street,' said Kate.

'Did you know there's a copy of the village newsletter on the pinboard in the kitchen?'

'I vaguely noticed it was there. So what?'

'It's full of exciting things for us to do, right outside the front door. Since you won't go any further, we'll investigate the Countrywomen's Guild, the Parish Council meeting, and at the weekend we can join the other villagers picking up litter and making Gatt's Hill a place to be proud of.'

'Do we look like countrywomen? Is there a password? I don't believe they'll let us into their coven.'

'Personally I would rather explore the night-life of Paris, or, failing that, Oxford, but I can see that I'm not going to get you to move more than a few hundred yards from this sitting room. But any sort of activity has to be an improvement on your present state.'

Kate scowled. 'I've just realized that I've told you a lot about my recent life, but I still know nothing about yours.'

'It's really been very dull,' said Roz.

'You mean it's all disappeared in a cloud of cannabis smoke and absinthe fumes.'

'I don't know where you get these strange, old-fashioned ideas from.'

But before they could get properly settled in to another of their arguments, they were interrupted by a knock at the door. Roz got up to open it. Kate heard a murmur of voices and then Roz returned and said, 'Do you know anything about a gardener?'

'Nothing.'

'Are you sure? There's someone here who claims to

look after the garden at Crossways Cottage.'

'Oh, maybe Callie did mention something about it.'

'You should cut down on the wine consumption, it does dreadful things to the memory,' said Roz tartly, and returned to speak to the gardener. After a little more murmuring, Kate heard her mother say, 'Come in, then.'

3

It was surprising how deeply rooted her prejudices about the country were, Kate realized, as she saw Callie's gardener. Unconsciously she was expecting some grey-haired, rosy-cheeked ancient male stereotype, his trousers tied with string, who would pull his forelock and talk knowledgeably of mulching and staking and who would know how to recognize an ericaceous compost when he saw one.

'This is Donna,' said Roz.

Donna wore a skin-tight black top and black jeans glued on to her sparrow-thin legs. Her face might have sported a healthy country glow, but it was difficult to tell under the thick white make-up and black eye-liner.

'I'm your gardener,' said Donna, as though reading the disbelief on Kate's face. 'Didn't Miss Callan tell you about me?'

'She might have done, but I seem to have forgotten,' said Kate weakly.

Donna was small-featured, her cheekbones prominent, and with curly dark hair pulled back from her face with a black elastic band. Her neck and hands were suntanned, her fingernails iridescent violet. Her diamanté nose stud winked at Kate. Five gold rings of varying sizes decorated each of her ears. Kate shuddered in sympathy at the thought of the pain involved in all that piercing.

Donna smiled, showing uneven, coffee-stained teeth.

19

'I've taken my shoes off. I didn't want to make marks on the carpet.'

'Thank you. How thoughtful. I imagine it's the back garden you'll be working on, so let's go through to the kitchen,' said Kate, leading the way. Roz stood silently in the background, letting Kate get on with the discussion with the gardener. As they crossed the sitting room Kate noticed that the carpet was the colour of a new teddy-bear and would show every mark, certainly.

Donna padded after Kate in her yellow socks. 'That's nice,' she said, running her stubby finger over the smooth head of a small bronze figure.

'Yes, isn't it,' replied Kate. The bronze was modern, non-figurative, and had a silken, sensual feel when she touched it. She hadn't bothered to look at Callie's possessions in detail, other than to notice that they were pleasantly in keeping with the style of the cottage, but now she saw that there were one or two pretty pieces of furniture and some rather nice early Victorian water-colours on the walls.

'Aren't they by the man who always paints cows? What was his name?' asked Donna.

'I don't think I know him,' replied Kate, mystified.

In front of the log-burning stove Kate now noticed there glowed a red and blue Oriental rug. Callie's job in journalism must be bringing in good money. In the old days, she had lived in rented flats with the usual Ikea furnishings, but most of this stuff was way beyond that league.

'Yeah, she knows what she's on, does Miss Callan. Recognizes a genuine piece when she sees it,' said Donna, echoing her thought.

Opposite the front door, another door opened into the

kitchen, which was also large and square, with quarry tiles and colourful modern rugs underfoot. There was a pine table and a couple of chairs, and bright emerald and turquoise blinds to pull down in the evening. The back garden was framed neatly by the long window over the sink.

'Yes, that's it,' confirmed Donna. Kate couldn't tell from the expression in her brown eyes whether she was laughing at the ignorant townie or not. 'I've been off for a couple of weeks, and it looks like it needs some work doing out there.'

'I suppose it does.' Kate frowned, wondering whether she was supposed to issue coherent instructions.

Donna chewed at the corner of one of her sparkling fingernails. 'I just wondered if you wanted me to carry on with the garden. You was expecting me, wasn't you? If you don't want me here, I'll leave. I can get some other work somewhere, I expect.'

'No, don't go. Callie did mention something about it, I'm sure she did. But I was expecting someone ... different.'

'Don't worry,' said Donna, smiling as though she knew what Kate had been thinking. 'I do know what I'm doing, really. I used to help my Uncle Ken with his allotment. I used to go up there with him every afternoon after school. All the old buggers in the village went up there, hiding away from their wives and children, I suppose. They used to tell me what to do then sod off into their shed with a six-pack of beer. I just got on with it. I must have learned something. More'n I ever done at school, anyway.'

'Splendid,' said Kate. 'But what about your clothes? Won't you get dirty?'

'I keep my boots in the shed and put a work shirt on over the top of this lot.' She unlooped the pendant she wore round her neck and handed it to Kate. 'You look after this for me. I don't want to get it caught in the lawn mower, do I?'

'This is unusual. What is it?'

'A perfume bottle, just a little one. French, 1920s. It's chipped slightly here, see. It takes away from the value, but I still like it.' It was pretty: dark blue glass cut so that the light made it sparkle like sapphires.

'You can take the top off if you like,' she went on. 'Sniff it. You can still smell the old perfume.'

Kate sniffed at the glass dipper. At first she could smell nothing, then, as she concentrated, she could smell something, very faintly. It conjured up nightclubs, and jazz, and bright young things with bobbed hair and scarlet lips.

'It's like them old films,' said Donna. 'Do you watch them? *Casablanca. The Blue Angel.* I love all that stuff, the way it takes you back to the olden days. I'd like to wear clothes like that and have my hair sweeping across my face. Do you think I'd look good with black-pencilled eyebrows?'

Kate laughed. 'I'm sure you could look the part if you tried. You'll have to take your nose-stud out, though. I don't think they were fashionable in the 1940s.'

'Maybe I'll just stick with the perfume bottle for now.'

'I'll look after it for you,' said Kate. 'Don't worry about it. And now we ought to tackle the garden. Do you have any idea what needs to be done?'

'Miss Callan just lets me get on with it. I do two hours, twice a week in summer, once in winter. And you pay me five pounds an hour.'

Kate looked at the grey sky, searched vainly for a glimpse of the sun. 'Is this winter or summer?' she asked.

'Summer,' said Donna firmly. 'I'll be here again on Friday.' She looked pointedly at her watch. 'This first ten minutes is on you, all right?'

'Yes, of course.'

'And I have a break for a cup of tea and a biscuit halfway through.'

'I see. I'll join you.'

'Chocolate biscuits if you've got them.'

'I think we've eaten them all. But I'll pop down to the village shop,' said Kate obediently. The shop was expensive, had no great choice of goods and was staffed by teenagers more interested in listening to Radio 1 and chatting to their friends than in serving their customers, but still it was a better alternative to driving six miles to the big supermarket.

When Donna had disappeared towards the garden shed, Roz joined her daughter in the kitchen.

'Why did you leave it all to me? Do you know anything about gardens?'

'I do, yes. But I thought you were doing rather well, learning to cope all on your own.'

'You think I can learn how to tie my own shoelaces next?'

'If you're a good girl, yes.'

'I suppose we can trust her to know what she's doing,' said Kate, watching Donna entering the garden shed.

'She looks competent enough, in spite of all the metal inserts,' Roz agreed. 'The odder thing is that she seemed to know what she was looking at in Callie's sitting room. She knew more about Victorian landscape painting than you did.'

'I wonder where she learnt. She doesn't look as though she comes from that sort of background, but then, who can judge by appearances these days?'

'Someone taught her about keeping mud off the carpet. You think she might be the vicar's daughter? Or come from that elegant Queen Anne house at the bottom of the hill?'

'We ... ell.'

'No, I don't think so, either,' said Roz. 'And now you'd better go looking for those chocolate biscuits you promised her. I bet that little shop closes sharp at five.'

'What are you going to do?'

'Really, Kate, you're getting far too nosy. I shall sit, and think, and perhaps pass the time of day with a neighbour or two.'

'If you can get a more articulate response from one of them than "mnerf", you're doing well. Just keep out of trouble, OK?'

'Bossy little madam,' said Roz, but she spoke quite affectionately.

An hour later Kate, Roz and Donna were sitting at the kitchen table, drinking tea and making heavy inroads into the newly acquired packet of milk chocolate digestives.

'How did you qualify as a gardener?' asked Kate. 'Did you do a course?'

'Nah. I just watched the telly programmes and asked me uncle. I love putting in seeds and then seeing them come up and cover themselves with flowers, or vegetables and that. If you look after them, feed them and water them, cut off the dead bits and get them to grow thick and bushy, they do their best for you in return. I like that.'

'You reap what you sow, as our vicar might put it,' said Kate.

'You what? I dunno about that. I just like growing stuff. I soon had people begging me to do an hour or so in their gardens. We're like gold dust, they say.'

'Work must get a bit scarce in the winter.'

'I got me Giro.'

'Job-seekers' allowance?'

'Whatever. And me rent's paid. And then there's—'

'You are being nosy again, Kate,' warned Roz. 'Now, Donna, do tell us about your lovely blue pendant. Where did you find it?'

'I didn't find it,' said Donna sharply. 'I bought it – at an antiques fair. I like old perfume bottles, I'm collecting them. Well, I've got two or three now, anyway.' And she glared at Roz as though she, too, were asking too many questions.

'Every collection must start with two or three,' said Roz soothingly. 'I don't believe I've ever been to an antiques fair. Where do you find them?'

'They have them every week, thousands of them, all over the country,' said Donna. 'I often go. Me and . . .' But she didn't finish the sentence. 'You'll find a list of the local ones in the *Oxford Times* if you want to go.' She glanced at the clock. 'I suppose I'd better get on,' she said, and chased the last crumbs of chocolate around on the plate with a damp finger. 'I'm meeting someone later, so I mustn't be late.' A dreamy look came over her face and for a moment Kate felt a pang of jealousy.

'What's his name?' she asked, just to be friendly.

'Raven. That's what I call him. He's tall and he has great clothes and he drives a big car. We're not staying around in this shit-heap for ever. I'm going to get out, and Raven's going to help me. We got plans. He's brilliant,' said Donna, putting her boots back on and opening the back door. 'Dead sexy,' she added.

'He sounds ideal. Is he a gardener, too?'

'Nah. Course not. He's in business.'

Though what that meant in a backwater like Gatt's Hill, Kate had no idea. And Raven sounded very much like the product of a young girl's imagination. Still, she wasn't going to say that to Donna.

'Have a good mulch,' she said.

'I'll be cutting that bloody buddleia right back,' said Donna.

'Why? Isn't it the wrong time of year?' said Roz. 'I like to prune my buddleias in the spring.'

'I hope it's the wrong time. I hate buddleias. Untidy buggers, and seed themselves all over the place. With any luck it'll curl up and die.'

'So you like everything disciplined, do you?'

'Most things. Neat and in their place. And I like a nice tidy garden.'

Kate and Roz left her wielding a lethal-looking pair of secateurs and returned to the sitting room.

'How long will you be staying here, do you think?' Roz asked her daughter.

'I don't know. Callie was very vague about how long she'd be away. I have the cottage for an indefinite length of time. I thought I'd stay until I felt better.'

'You won't feel better unless you make an effort,' said Roz.

'Oh, shut up and leave me alone.' And Kate stretched out on the sofa and pretended to fall asleep. It was peaceful to be on her own again, and far from hanging heavy, time passed with no effort at all.

'You off in a dream again?' Donna had padded into the room in her yellow socks.

'She lives in a world of her own, that girl,' said Roz.

Kate realized she had wasted three-quarters of an hour in idle thought. 'Me, dreaming? I was thinking about work,' said Kate severely. 'Have you finished out there?'

'I've done my two hours.'

'Yes, of course you have. I wasn't doubting it.' Donna was scowling at her and Kate cast around for something to heal the gap that was widening between them. 'There are a few chocolate biscuits left. Would you like one?'

'Nah. It was time I got off.' She looked at Kate expectantly.

'Everything all right?'

'Of course.' She still looked at Kate, who suddenly remembered that she was supposed to pay Donna for her time. 'Money,' she said.

'Dosh,' confirmed Donna and looked relieved that this daft woman had at last got the message.

'Ten pounds,' said Kate, getting it out of her handbag.

'Thanks,' said Donna and stuffed it into the back pocket of her jeans. She put on her shoes by the front door and then went outside. Kate joined her in the small front garden.

'What do you think I should do with these?' she asked, indicating the sad-looking plants.

'You could try watering them,' said Donna, straight-faced. 'You get a wicked wind up here on this hill, and they soon dry out. Soak them properly, cut off the dead bits, talk to them occasionally. They'll soon perk up.'

'Thanks,' said Kate, resolving to turn herself into a green-fingered person.

'See ya,' said Donna.

'Friday?'

'Yeah.'

'Where do you live?' called Kate as she unlatched the front gate. She really ought to keep tabs on young Donna. She had seemed like a nice enough kid, but she also knew a little too much about the value of Callie's possessions.

'Down the Banks,' answered Donna.

'Is that in the village?'

'Yeah. I'd rather live down in Oxford, round by the Cowley Road, but the Council was having trouble with the old people's flats, so I got sent here instead.'

This made no sense to Kate, but at least she would know where to start looking if all Callie's valuable furniture disappeared overnight.

'Goodbye!' she called as Donna strode off down the village street. Her step was jaunty and she looked so alive, so part of this countryside, that Kate envied her. Donna might appear no bigger than a skinny twelve year old, but when Kate checked the back garden she found that the grass had been cut, the trees and shrubs looked tidier, things she thought must have been weeds had disappeared. Donna was a good worker, even if she did leave Kate with the uneasy feeling that she was being laughed at for her horticultural ignorance and lack of business acumen.

'Odd girl, that,' said Roz. 'But I think I rather like her. On Friday I shall find out more about her rich friend Raven.'

'I thought I was the nosy one who asked too many questions.'

'It's all a question of style. Some of us have it and some

28

of us,' she looked Kate up and down as she spoke, 'do not.'

4

Broombanks, the small council estate, lay at the far end of Gatt's Hill, as though the village had wished to distance itself as far as possible from the people who lived there. Not that the council tenants cared: they didn't want to know the likes of the snobby Hope-Stanhopes and the Fannings in any case. Their friends and relations, their lovers and the partners in their various business dealings, lived in the huge concrete estates on the eastern side of Oxford, not in the old stone cottages or the Grade 2 listed houses in the centre of the village. The different village factions met formally three or four times a year, to battle it out on the recreation field in mammoth rounders matches, or games of football, or in well-organized bonfire parties and pig-roasts (with vegetarian alternative for the inhabitants of the Old Rectory). Apart from that, they regarded each other with mutual contempt.

Donna reached the entrance to Broombanks just a few minutes after leaving Crossways Cottage. She passed the rusting cars parked in the roadway, and the snarling dog at number 3, listened to the row going on between Barry and Paula at number 5, sniffed appreciatively at the late-blooming roses in number 8's front patch, then turned into the small block of flats at the end of the cul-de-sac.

Up on the second floor she had a good view over the surrounding fields, and into her neighbours' back gardens. It was surprising how much you could learn about people just by looking into their gardens. Gary and Kev had stacked up a load of cartons next to their rusting motorbike and there were a few smaller boxes piled up in the old kitchen sink in their back yard. She wondered whether there'd be a visit from the police again soon, looking for some missing video recorders or microwaves. Paula's youngest, Lee, was peeing against Barry's new shed instead of braving the domestic violence going on inside the house. And Scott was admiring the row of leylandii he'd planted to annoy Mr Luckett in the house next door. The bad-tempered old bugger at number 7 had a good crop of sprouts coming along in his vegetable patch. She'd pop out one night and have them off him. That'd teach him to shout at her when she played her music too loud.

She pulled the curtains to frustrate the infant Peeping Toms, peeled off her clothes and had a quick shower. Then she settled herself in front of the mirror, and opened the drawer containing her make-up. Before she started work on altering it, she frowned at the young, pink-cheeked face that had emerged from under the layer of pale foundation.

'You look like you've just crawled out of some cabbage patch,' she told herself severely, and proceeded to paint shades of sophistication and world-weariness back on to the youthful image.

While she considered which of her large collection of clothes she would wear, she slipped a tape into the player, then turned up the volume, 'just to wake the old buggers up a bit'.

When she had zipped herself into a skin-tight black dress, she drew the curtains again and looked out of the flat's other window, down into the street. If the back gardens showed her the secret life of Broombanks, where loot was hidden and deals were made, and extra-marital affairs were planned, the street at the front was the public face of the estate. This was where you paraded when you had tarted yourself up. This, too, was where the estate's most spectacular rows took place between warring spouses. The kids from the problem family at number 4 were teasing the loony child from next door, and Kelly's two eldest, Jordan and Connor, were trying to run down their little brother with their mountain bikes. Situation normal. Nothing had changed since her own childhood. The street might be a different one but the games of aggression and survival hadn't changed.

Donna felt a strand of experience binding her to those kids in the street below. Somehow she would have to lean out of the window and cut it. Snip-snap. She wanted no connection to the poverty and hand-to-mouth living of Broombanks. She was going to be rich. She had her plans. She bought her lottery ticket on Wednesday and Saturday. She had six lucky numbers that would come up for her one day and send her off to Tenerife or the Bahamas with Raven. Or maybe the five scratchcards she bought every Friday would bring in more than the odd quid or two she'd won so far. Because she knew that she was not going to stay here in Broombanks much longer. She was going to escape, not to the toffee-nosed world of the Hope-Stanhopes and the Fannings, but to a life of sexy clothes and all-night clubs, of fast cars, very loud music and energetic sex that lasted through the whole of every afternoon. But even if her lottery numbers never came up, she knew she was going to make it. If Fortune didn't smile on them, she was going to get there from her own efforts.

Donna admired herself in the narrow wardrobe mirror and then considered what to put on her feet. She would like to wear the new stack-heeled shoes she'd bought last Saturday, but she wasn't sure she could walk in them as far as the place she was meeting Raven. For a moment she scowled. Why couldn't he drive his big, fast car up to her front door, scattering those scabby kids and leaving a shining band of black rubber on the roadway? He could blast the horn and play music through his quad speakers at top volume. Wake the bastards up. Everyone would sit up and notice her then.

But he'd told her that wasn't their style; they had to be discreet about their relationship, at least for now, and wasn't it time she grew out of childish amusements like that and learned to enjoy a more sophisticated lifestyle? Sod sophisticated, she grumbled, and why can't we enjoy spending some of the dosh we've made. But somehow she always ended by falling in with Raven's ideas. She scrunch-dried her hair in front of the electric fire, then she hung the blue glass pendant round her neck. It was her lucky charm and she never went out without it. One day she would replace it with a diamond as big as her fist, but for now she was happy with her perfume bottle. Finally, she decided to chance getting blisters from her new shoes, removed the thick socks which she wore in the flat instead of slippers and put on the shoes by the front door. If there was one thing she hated it was a mucky floor. She was humming a tune as she left the flat and clattered down the stairs.

She side-stepped Jordan and Connor, called a greeting to daft Kayleigh, who just gawped back at her. She managed a surreptitious kick on the rump of old Mr Luckett's dog, who had been scavenging in the Broombank dustbins and was now relieving himself against Kevin's D-reg Fiesta.

'Where you off to, then?' growled Mr Luckett, glaring at her suspiciously as the dog yelped off up the street.

'None of your bloody business.'

'You should wash your mouth out! Look at you! Dressed up like a tart. Deserve anything you get, you young girls.'

Donna gave him the finger and then was striding out of the Banks and away from its raw red-brick houses, towards her date with Raven. Tonight they'd be planning something exciting to amuse themselves with, she knew that.

In the Vicarage flat, the Reverend Timothy ('call me Tim') Widdows was also getting ready for an evening out. He had gelled his hair, admiring his new, cool haircut as he did so. He had ironed his stone-washed jeans and was looking through his collection of T-shirts to choose something suitable.

Not white, he decided, it didn't look good with the dog collar. And he'd give the chest-messages a miss for tonight, too. It was too easy to alienate people if you chose the wrong one. So, a plain colour. Dark blue, maybe, or wine red. He held the red up in front of the mirror. Did that make him look like a cardinal? He didn't want to be mistaken for a Papist. He settled for the blue, which drew attention to the colour of his eyes (forget-me-not) and away from that of his hair (carrot-red). He sniffed at the socks he had been wearing all day, wrinkled his nose and tossed them smartly and accurately into the laundry basket. He had a problem with his feet, he had to admit, and he scrabbled in his drawer for a clean pair of socks, finding some in pale blue to tone with his T-shirt. Then he laced on his sparkling new Reeboks, jogged up and down on the spot for a minute to show himself how fit he was, coughed and wheezed as he recovered, and wondered which jacket to wear. His anorak? Plebeian, which was good, but nerdish, which wasn't. He tried on his blazer, checked again in the mirror. No. Too middle class. He pulled on a black-and-silver baseball jacket instead, and wondered about the matching cap, worn backwards. Uh-huh. Too much. It looked as if – no, he corrected himself – it looked *like* he was trying too hard for street cred. He decided on the jacket and a bare head, hoping that no one would notice the thinning patch on his crown. Middle class was bad enough, but he certainly didn't want to look middle-aged as well.

It was no good, in this day and age, he told himself as he checked the money in his back pocket, expecting the congregation to come to you. Who wanted to spend their Sunday morning in a draughty old church when they could be polishing their motor or taking their kids for a swim? No, if you wanted to do God's work and spread His Word around, then you had to go to where the sinners were. Wasn't that what Christ Himself had done, after all? What you needed was the common touch, and Tim Widdows was quite sure that he had it in abundance.

The man Donna called Raven hadn't yet started to make any preparations for his date with her. For a start, he was slightly embarrassed by the name she had chosen for him, and found himself muttering 'Nevermore!' when she insisted on calling him Raven. For another thing, he was still at work, and although he looked forward to his time with Donna, he was also interested in the job he did during the day. The hours he spent with her, and the interesting things they did together, were just the spice in the soup, the icing on the cake, the guilt on the ginger-bread. And he laughed at the pun before turning back to the work on his desk.

The name she called him had one advantage, of course. No one was likely to associate it with him, and at least for the present he didn't want people to know about their relationship.

He had time to shower and change before he met her at their usual place.

At Crossways Cottage Kate got to her feet and said, 'I think you're right. I do need a pick-me-up. Why don't we go and suss out the pub now? I'm getting hungry, aren't you?'

'At my time in life I can ignore the baser aspects of my humanity,' said Roz portentously.

'You mean you concentrate on cigarettes and alcohol and don't bother with food,' said Kate rudely.

'Have you seen me smoke a cigarette? Has a glass of wine passed my lips?'

'Perhaps not. But there is still time,' said Kate darkly. 'But, anyway, what about our visit to the pub?'

'A good idea. But for goodness' sake do something to your hair and change your clothes before we go.'

'If you insist,' grumbled Kate, leaving the room.

'And put some make-up on,' called her mother.

Kate's response was, luckily, inaudible.

5

Oddly for a pub that found itself on top of a hill and several miles from the nearest canal, the one in Gatt's Hill was called The Narrow Boat. Its swinging sign looked like an old oil painting supplied to picturesque pubs by English Heritage.

'Rather heavily over-themed,' remarked Roz as they pushed their way through the etched and frosted glass doors.

Everything that could be decorated was painted with traditional pink roses and green squiggles. The walls were covered with framed photographs of canals, locks and barges. Brass gleamed. Whimsical watering-cans (painted green, decorated with pink cabbage roses) sat around on the tables, filled with bunches of cottagey-looking flowers.

'Plastic?' wondered Kate.

Roz sniffed at the nearest bunch. 'Not real, anyway,' she said.

'I wonder what the locals think of all this atmosphere,' said Kate, looking around.

Roz drew in a deep breath of beer and nicotine. 'I don't care about the locals, I just love the climate in here. I'm not used to all that clean country air I've been breathing all day. It's been doing dreadful things to my lungs.'

'What would you like to drink?' asked Kate, approaching the bar through the brown fog of cigarette smoke.

'The beers have names like Old Lame Rooster and Blasted Duck. They probably taste all right. Do you want to chance one?'

Although the bar was quite crowded, conversation had stopped when Roz and Kate entered, and twenty pairs of suspicious male eyes turned and looked them over, then returned to the contemplation of their pints of beer and their discussion of set-aside and subsidies. No one behind the bar attempted to take their order.

'You'll be more comfortable in the next room,' murmured a passing Australian waitress, indicating a door marked The Butty.

'Let's give it a try,' said Kate.

In this room there were tables, a misting of lower-tar smoke, and a bar displaying bottles of wine as well as the strangely named beers.

'A bottle of house white, two glasses and your menu, please,' said Roz as they settled themselves by a window (ruffled red gingham curtains, view of window box full of jostling, blooming geraniums, real this time). She stared unashamedly around the bar.

'Hm. Not too promising at first glance, but something might come in later, I suppose.'

'Are you thinking of a pick-up?' asked Kate.

'Someone will have to do something about your life, or lack of it.'

Kate wished their wine would arrive and kept a dignified silence.

Roz continued to study the other customers: two or three groups of youngish people, an elderly couple studying the menu with great care, a nondescript pair in their fifties, and a single man sitting at the bar.

'Junior management from British Leyland,' pronounced Roz of the youngish ones. 'Retired couple working out whether they can afford one course or two,' she said of the elderly couple. 'And I wonder who he is,' eyeing the man at the bar. As though he had heard her remark (and Roz had a clear, carrying voice, certainly) he turned and stared back at her. He gave her a friendly smile and looked as though he would like to join them.

'No!' hissed Kate. 'Don't you dare!'

'You're no fun to go out with. And apart from your friend Andrew, I haven't heard you mention any other men in your life,' said Roz. 'What's wrong with you, Kate? You used to be interested in men when you were younger.'

'Perhaps we haven't quite reached the stage where I want to tell you all my girlish secrets,' said Kate.

'Don't be silly. I'm your mother. Everyone wants to confide in their own mother. And I've noticed that the phone hasn't rung since I've been in the cottage, there have been no letters except junk mail and bills, and not a single postcard is propped on the mantelpiece.'

'When did I give you permission to go through my post?'

'It's on the table in my bedroom. I thought you wanted me to read it,' said Roz brazenly.

'Huh!'

'And there's no sign of anyone visiting,' continued Roz.

'You've checked the bathroom cabinet for razors and the laundry basket for male underpants, have you?'

'Don't be coarse.'

Before they could get properly stuck in to one of their arguments, the waitress arrived with the bottle of wine, and recommended the grilled salmon steaks.

'We'll both have the salmon, a green salad if we must, and lots of chips,' said Roz.

'Comfort food?' enquired Kate, when the waitress had left.

'You're the one who told me you're in need of comfort.'

'I don't remember saying that.'

'What you need is a man,' said Roz. 'How old are you now?'

Kate felt that the question was not rhetorical. Her mother really had forgotten how old her daughter was. 'Thirty-er . . .' she said. No point in being too specific if one's own mother didn't know the exact figure.

'That's what I mean. It's quite time you were thinking about marriage and babies and so on.'

'The two don't necessarily go together,' said Kate. 'And I'm tired of this subject.'

'Go on telling me about your life in Oxford,' said Roz soothingly. 'And how you came to leave it for the life of the country.' She poured them both a glass of wine. 'Why don't you carry on with the story while we wait for our food?'

'Somehow the house in Agatha Street had filled up with ties and commitments,' said Kate when she had drunk half a glass of wine and recovered her temper. 'There was the dysfunctional family next door, with their mother and three children. I acquired their eldest, Harley, to feed, and I made sure he did his homework. Then his dog, Dave, came to live with me when he was ejected by his mother's new dog-hating boyfriend. And then there was Susannah, my cat. Did you see her when you called in at Agatha Street?'

'A ginger animal with long legs? Yes, she looked quite happy, so you needn't worry about her.'

'She was a present from Paul, who also spent a lot of time at my place, and who disapproved of much of my lifestyle. He is a deeply conventional person and he wants me to settle down, and have a proper job, and get married, preferably to him, and produce children. Just the sort of person you'd approve of, I suppose. It was all too much, even before Andrew died. Are you still listening?'

But Roz had made eye contact with someone on the other side of the room and was smiling and lifting her glass.

'Well, you might at least pay attention when I'm un-burdening myself,' grumbled Kate.

'What? Oh, here's our food. This looks good.'

For the next few minutes they were silent while they sorted out who wanted salt and pepper and lemon for the salmon, and mayonnaise for Roz's chips.

'I don't know why you aren't the size of a house!'

'I burn it all off.'

'In a moment you'll tell me you live on your nerves.'

'Just get on and eat. You'll feel a lot better when your blood sugar has risen to a reasonable level.'

Kate ate, then noticed what her mother was doing. 'Stop making eyes at the bald man over there; his wife is just returning with a vicious green-eyed monster on her shoulder.'

'Pity. I've always found bald men attractive.'

Kate put down her knife and fork. 'Order me a vanilla ice cream with hot chocolate fudge sauce for pud,' she said. 'I'm going to suss out the Ladies.' And thus she took the opportunity to escape from her mother's intrusive questions and embarrassing interest in men.

'Shall I finish your chips for you?' Roz called after her.

'If you like.'

When Kate returned she found her mother had used the time to good advantage. There were now three strangers sitting at their table.

'Come and meet Alison and Ken Fanning,' said Roz.

'So pleased to meet you,' said Alison Fanning. She was a woman in her fifties with hair like fine-gauge wire wool, and the clear blue eyes and unlined, rosy skin of someone who has reached middle age without falling over too many of life's unkind obstacles. She appeared to have dressed herself in knitted porridge.

'Kate. Oh yes, very pleased,' said her husband approvingly as he looked her over. He too was scrubbed and pink, with little fat pouches under his eyes and soft, rounded hands with nails as perfect as a baby's. His head gleamed in the lamplight. This was the man her mother had been eyeing earlier. 'Roz here has just been telling us all about you.'

Kate's heart sank. Just what had her mother been saying, and how much of it was invented?

'Don't worry, it was all highly complimentary,' said the third stranger.

'Meet a lovely man,' said Roz shamelessly.

Thinning hair cut in the latest fashion, an earnest expression on the face and a professional smile, thought Kate as Roz said, 'Kate, this is the Reverend Timothy Widdows.'

'Call me Tim.' He had a flat Midlands accent, a gold earring and a blue T-shirt with a dog collar worn like a fashion accessory. At least he wasn't wearing a baseball cap. She wanted to say 'How do you do, Mr Widdows?' but settled for 'Hi, Tim,' as being more in keeping with his image. A widening of the smile and a slight closing of the eyes indicated that she had got it right.

'Mr Widdows is our vicar,' said Alison, who wasn't having any of this modern matey stuff.

'A recent arrival, like yourselves,' said Tim.

'But I expect you'll be staying longer than us,' said Kate.

Alison Fanning sighed. 'Our previous vicar, such a *spiritual* man, was with us for twenty-eight years,' she said.

'So perhaps it was time he retired,' put in her husband gently.

'Let's order another bottle of wine,' said Roz and immediately caught the waitress's eye.

'Your dessert,' said the other waitress, placing a bowl of ice cream in front of Kate.

'Am I the only one eating?' she asked.

'Apparently,' said Roz. 'You'll just have to listen to the rest of us making conversation while you make a pig of yourself.' She reached into her bag. 'Cigarette, anyone?'

Tim Widdows' eyes lit up for a moment, then he said, 'I've given up.'

'Permanently, or just for Lent?' asked Roz.

'Don't tempt me,' he answered. 'It's supposed to be for good.'

'And this isn't anywhere near Lent,' said Ken.

'Ken and I have never smoked,' said Alison, waving her hand in front of her face as Roz drew in a deep breath and then blew out a thin stream of smoke.

'Thank goodness a pub is still the one place where one can happily smoke in public without fear of disapproval,' said Roz, ignoring the gesture.

Kate concentrated on a spoonful of ice cream and chocolate fudge sauce while this exchange was going on, but caught an expression of amusement on Tim Widdows' face that he wiped off a second later. Perhaps he wasn't such a nerd after all.

'Now, what Kate and I want to do,' said Roz brightly, blowing her smoke away from Alison Fanning this time, 'is to join in all the activities in the village. We want to meet people, don't we, Kate?'

'Mmf,' said Kate, shovelling in fudge sauce and eyeing the rapidly emptying bottle of wine. Tim Widdows thoughtfully poured the last of it into her glass. She smiled at him. The man was definitely a member of the human race even if he did wear a dog collar.

'Yes,' continued Roz, 'when there's something happening in the village, you can count us in.'

'Well, that's good to hear,' said Ken Fanning, and Kate thought for a moment that she felt the pressure of a male thigh against her own. 'We must make sure Roz and Kate are included in all our social activities, mustn't we, Alison? Alison knows absolutely *everybody*.'

'Who lives in the lovely house at the bottom of the hill?' asked Roz.

'The Queen Anne one? It's called Gatt's House. Oh, that belongs to the Hope-Stanhopes.' There was a coolness in Alison's tone.

'They're the local big-wigs, are they?'

'Her family were the Hopes, who have lived at Gatt's Hill for generations – oh, since Henry the something, I believe – but they had no sons in the last generation, so it all came to Emma. Such a bright, lively girl, always riding one of her horses, or dashing round the lanes in her MG, but then she married an accountant.' Alison obviously didn't think much of accountants. 'His name was Stanhope, so they hyphenated it. A bit of a mouthful, don't you think?'

46

Kate sipped wine and managed not to give an opinion. Roz looked vague and waved a hand around in a foreign, uncomprehending way. 'Such funny English habits,' she said. She's going to get herself on the Hope-Stanhope visiting list, thought Kate.

'But then, everything seems to be about money these days,' said Alison.

'Not *everything*,' put in the Rev Tim, spotting a window of opportunity. 'Some of us like to think that there are other, *inclusive*, values in society that—'

'Yes, of course,' said Roz, interrupting, 'but go on telling me about the local inhabitants. So fascinating. You tell such a good story.' And she beamed encouragingly at Alison and Ken.

'Well, there are several farming families, of course. The Philbees and the Samsons, and the Robinsons. They've all been here since the Romans.'

'Who does the big farm down the hill belong to?'

'Just above the Hope-Stanhopes? That's Gatts Farm.'

'No apostrophe,' said Ken.

'I'm sorry?'

'They dropped the apostrophe when they bought the place. Emma Hope-Stanhope says they're too vulgar to know where it should go, but we think that's just sour grapes.'

'The Fullers seem to have made a lot of money in a very short time,' said Alison, as though that explained the Hope-Stanhope grievance.

'And of course they don't farm,' said Ken. 'The land has been sold off since the Fullers bought it.'

'And what do they do to make all this money?' prompted Roz.

'They buy and sell antiques,' said Ken Fanning. 'And

47

very successful at it they are, too, by the look of them.'

'Flashy,' said Alison.

'Rich,' corrected her husband.

'Gatts Farm Antiques are very generous investors in my projects,' said the Rev Tim.

'And of course their son is an Oxford professor,' said Alison, 'so they must be all right, don't you think?'

'I think you'll find he just has a junior fellowship,' said Ken. 'And in some funny subject. I forget what.'

'Is he married?' asked Roz.

'*Mother!*' growled Kate.

'Oh, no. He's much too busy for anything like that,' said Alison.

'I look forward to meeting them all,' said Roz with finality. 'Now, Alison, tell us what *you* do.'

'I'm the local Secretary of the Countrywomen's Guild,' said Alison grandly.

'Now what made me think you were going to say that?' mused Kate.

'What, dear? We have meetings every month in the village hall, and of course both of you are very welcome to join us. You'll meet *real* villagers at our little gatherings.'

'No Fullers? No Hope-Stanhopes?' asked Kate.

'Emma Hope-Stanhope is Chairwoman of the Guild, but she doesn't attend every meeting, I'm afraid.'

'Country*women*'s Guild?' queried Roz.

'Of course.'

'Well, actually . . .' said Roz.

'And then there's your local church,' said Tim. 'Services every Sunday, and men and women are equally welcome, I assure you.'

'Roz is an excellent hymn-singer,' said Kate, straight-faced. 'Just tell us when to turn up, and I'll make sure she's there.'

'Actually, you might enjoy some of our other activities,' said Tim. 'I try to involve the young people as much as possible in our Christian projects, but there are plenty of things for the older parishioners as well.'

'Pensioners' tea parties, perhaps? Roz would enjoy those, wouldn't you, Mother?'

'If you browse through your newsletter, I'm sure you'll find lots to interest you,' said Tim.

'The Countrywomen's Guild,' said Alison firmly, in her best Secretary's voice. 'We love to see new faces. We're a jolly bunch, and, who knows, you might make some new friends. This month's talk is on crocheting knick-knacks as gifts and for the home.'

'And if you don't like the talk, then the tea and cakes afterwards are worth waiting for,' said Ken, while his wife looked pained.

'I don't suppose either of you is an expert on something?' queried Alison. 'We're always in need of new speakers.'

Roz opened her mouth to say something, and Kate knew that she was about to be volunteered as an expert on writing historical novels. She cut in quickly. 'Roz, you could talk about your travels, couldn't you?'

'Have you got slides?' asked Alison eagerly. 'Mrs Hope-Stanhope would lend us her projector, I'm sure.'

'I'm afraid not,' said Roz. 'And other people's travels aren't nearly as interesting as one's own, don't you find?'

'Where is it you've been?' asked Tim Widdows.

Kate waited for the answer with great interest. 'Oh, all over the place,' said Roz vaguely. 'Wherever the fancy took me.'

'You must have enough fascinating material for a dozen talks,' said Tim. Was he winding Roz up? wondered Kate. Did vicars do such things?

'But I have such a bad memory! I'd be quite hopeless as a speaker.'

Kate could see that Roz was not going to be drawn on the subject of her travels. 'Gardening,' she said firmly. 'My mother is also an expert on gardening.'

'It's always the most successful topic,' said Alison. ' "New ideas for your hanging baskets". "Build your own water features". "Design a herbaceous border". Your friend Aphra Callan gave us a fascinating illustrated talk on the gardens of Italy, so we shall look forward to hearing your contribution, Roz.'

Kate had forgotten that Callie's first name was Aphra. No wonder she allowed none of her friends to call her by it.

'And then, if you really want to see what makes the village tick, you should come to a Parish Council meeting,' said Ken.

'Ken's a parish councillor,' said Alison predictably.

'Village life, red in tooth and claw,' said Tim.

'The meeting is open to all the villagers for the first half-hour,' said Ken. 'We find that all sorts of subjects are raised. At the moment we're discussing how to improve our Village Watch scheme.'

'It could provide a whole network of care and concern for the most vulnerable in our village community,' said Tim.

'It's supposed to stop us being burgled and murdered in our beds,' said Alison.

'And we want to reduce the car thefts and vandalism,' said Ken. 'I blame that crowd who live in Broombanks, and their thieving friends from Blackbird Leys.'

'I don't know why we have to have a council estate in the village,' said Alison. 'Hardly any of them are what you'd call locals. They're just the riff-raff from the wrong end of Oxford, not proper country people at all.'

'Not a green wellie among them?' asked Roz.

'We shouldn't be prejudiced against people who live in council estates,' said Tim, but no one took any notice of him.

'Have you seen the disgusting behaviour of the teen-agers on the rec. on summer evenings?' asked Alison.

'Not yet. But I shall make a point of looking out for it,' said Roz.

'You've been very quiet, Kate,' said Tim Widdows.

'I'm overwhelmed by the thought of all this social life in Gatt's Hill,' she replied.

Alison Fanning was rising to her feet. 'It really is time that Ken and I went home. We're early risers in the country, you'll find, Roz. But the two of you must attend the next Guild meeting.' She sounded genuinely welcoming. 'And I'll make sure you're invited to all our little social gatherings. Come along, Ken.'

And the two of them said their goodbyes and left the pub.

'We have an exciting morning in prospect, too, haven't we, Kate?'

'Have we?'

'We're going into Oxford, Tim. Kate's getting something done about her hair and I shall do a tiny bit of shopping. It will be the first time Kate's been back to the city since the tragedy happened.'

Tim's eyes opened wide. Here was a chance to show his caring and feminine side. But before he could enquire

51

about the nature of the tragedy and offer his own counsel-
ling services to dear, dear Kate, Roz had drained the last
of her wine, swirled her colourful wrap around her
shoulders and propelled her daughter out of the pub.

'Goodbye, Tim. We'll see you again soon!' she called as
they made their way into the starlit village street.

'Why did you say that?' fumed Kate. 'My past is none of
his business. I don't want him nosing into my private life.'

'I told him nothing,' protested Roz. 'I just thought I
should arouse a little interest in you. You were sitting
there like a lemon all evening. I had to do something to
make you look as though you were worth cultivating.'

'Thank you very much!'

They walked slowly back to the cottage under the
black, starry sky. A frosty-looking moon sailed over the
elegant roof of Gatt's House and lit the scene with its cold
light.

'I can't get used to how quiet this place is,' said Roz.

'Wonderfully quiet,' said Kate, looking out at the grey
landscape with its occasional clusters of lights and the
gold necklace of headlights that was the M40, swinging
down the slope of the Chilterns from Stokenchurch.

The only sound audible was the noise of their footsteps
on the road, and the humming that came from Roz.

'What's that tune you're humming?'

'I thought I'd better practise a few hymns in preparation for our attendance at the church of St Uncumber.'

'St Michael and All Saints,' corrected Kate. 'Why do we
have to go there?'

'Dear Tim Widdows would tell us that it was all part of
the healing process, I'm sure.'

'I think I'll limit myself to a meditation on the starlight,
the moon and the peace of the countryside.'

'But just think what interesting people you'd meet.'

But before she had to answer, Kate found they were at the gate of Crossways Cottage and she could plead tiredness and a headache and retire to her own room.

6

Earlier that same evening Donna had met the man she called Raven at their usual place. Raven had parked his car a few yards along a track running by the side of woodland, well out of sight of the road. Donna was waiting for him when he arrived, sitting on a low stone wall with a thicket of beech trees at her back.

'Which way did you come?' he asked, with no other greeting.

'Along the footpath, like always,' she said. 'No one saw me. You don't have to worry.'

'Good.'

'Is that all you've got to say? I don't know why I bothered walking all this way.' She sounded sulky.

'It's not that far. Only a few hundred yards.' He looked her over. 'Though I suppose it seemed further to you in those shoes.'

'I thought you'd like them.'

'I do. Very nice indeed. You're looking good. I particularly like you in that dress.'

'You told me to wear black, so I have.'

Raven himself was dressed in a dark suit, as usual, with a very dark green shirt and a cobalt blue tie. If the tie had been paler he would have looked like a Chicago gangster, Donna thought with approval. Although dusk was settling in to the fields, and the woods behind them were already dark and impenetrable, Raven wore Ray-Bans so that she couldn't see his expression. The skin around his mouth was drawn taut, though, which she knew meant that he was either annoyed with her or else was already thinking about the excitement ahead. Raven found his thrills on the edges of experience, at the point where inventiveness met danger. Donna shivered in the short black dress.

'Are you warm enough?' he asked. 'Didn't you bring a coat?'

'I'll be all right. I don't need a coat when we're in the car.'

'You are wearing stockings, aren't you?' he said.

'Bloody uncomfortable they are, too,' said Donna. 'The suspenders is digging into my thighs when I sit down. What I do for you!'

'Don't worry, you'll find I'm grateful later. Now, are you hungry?'

'Yeah!'

'We'll get something to eat, and then we'll discuss what we're going to do afterwards. I have an idea or two, but I'd like to see what you think.'

'All right.'

'Come on, let's get in the car.' He still hadn't touched her. He was like that. She swayed her flat hips as she walked round to the passenger's seat and looked over her shoulder at him, dipping her eyelids.

Raven sighed. He could read the signals. A blind man could read Donna's signals. He followed her round to the passenger door and gave her the sort of kiss that left her out of breath. He opened the door for her and watched the thin legs as she scooped them inside.

'I'll have to do my lipstick again,' she said, taking it out of her small purse and pulling the rear-view mirror round so that she could see herself.

'I've told you not to do that,' said Raven, but he waited while she painted on a coat of scarlet before twisting the mirror back again.

Then he reversed at speed to the road and drove some miles to a small, unpretentious Italian restaurant where they were the first customers, and no one took any notice of them at all.

'What we going to do later?' asked Donna, when she was no longer hungry for food, and impatient to find out what he had in mind.

'A bit of breaking and entering.'

'I didn't know you went thieving.'

'We might take something, just as a souvenir. But I was thinking of borrowing their ... facilities ... for our amusement.'

'What do you mean?'

'Don't you fancy making love in a stranger's bed?'

She laughed. 'Suppose they come back while we're at it.'

'That's what gives it an edge, don't you think?'

'You're mad, you are!' But Donna was laughing even louder, and her cheeks were glowing pink with the excitement of it.

'I like to think of those dull, boring people sitting downstairs watching some serious documentary on the telly while we're upstairs doing naughty things in their double bed.'

'Where we going? How do we get in?'

'I've planned it all quite carefully. And we don't want to go too far from home, do we? The risk of getting caught by someone who would recognize us makes it even more interesting, don't you think?'

They drove down dark, twisting lanes, through villages where windows were thickly curtained and no one walked the streets. Only the occasional pub showed lights and bursts of noisy conversation as a door opened briefly on to the night.

Donna had drunk most of a bottle of wine: Raven was very particular about not drinking more than one glass when he was driving. So now she sprawled back in her seat, only vaguely aware of where they were.

Eventually the car slowed, and Raven cut the headlights, sliding the vehicle into the narrow gap between a hedge and an anonymous building. The night was very dark and quiet except for the distant barking of a fox.

'Where are we then?' hissed Donna.

'Don't you bother your little head about that,' said Raven. 'You just keep quiet and wait for me back here.'

'Here, I know this place, don't I?' said Donna. Her voice was slurred.

'Maybe you do,' said Raven. 'But don't worry about it. It'll be fun.'

'What are you going to do?' whispered Donna.

'I'm going to check the back door. I bet they haven't locked it yet. We can probably just walk straight in.'

Donna giggled. The wine and the tension made the sound into a snuffle.

Raven was right. The door was open. The kitchen was in darkness and he could hear the television in a room at the front of the house. He left the door ajar and went back to the car to fetch Donna. His shoes had rubber soles and made no sound on the path.

'I'd better take my shoes off when we get inside,' said Donna, following him as quietly as she could.

'Don't do that,' said Raven. 'It makes it more of a gamble if you're wearing shoes.'

Some time later Donna raised her head and said, 'What's that?'

'Nothing.'

'I heard something. I know I did. Someone's come upstairs.'

'Just remember they'll be more scared of you than you are of them if they come in and find us.' But even Raven paused for a moment in what he was doing and they both listened.

Whoever had come upstairs was trying to be as silent as they were. They could hear the slight creak of a floorboard, then the soft footfall of someone tiptoeing along a carpet. The footsteps stopped outside their door and they saw the sliver of half-light as the door was gingerly pushed open.

'Who is there? What you want?' came a voice.

'Who the hell is that?' replied Raven.

Then a door opened downstairs, there were more voices and the approach of feet that were making no attempt whatsoever to be silent.

7

Next morning Kate found she had to force herself to leave the cottage and climb into Roz's car. Crossways had become her place of safety, a kind of sanctuary. Who knows what might happen to her if she left it. Meanwhile Roz was talking non-stop, as though she knew how she was feeling and didn't want to give her a chance to chicken out of the trip to Oxford.

'Why did they call it Crossways?' she asked. 'There's just the one street running through this village, and a T-junction down past Gatts Farm.'

They waited for a yellow van to pass so that they could get to the car.

'There was probably a drover's road or something that went past our gate,' said Kate vaguely. 'Are you sure you want to drive all the way to Oxford?'

'Seven miles? I think I can manage it,' said Roz. 'Now, come along, Kate. I know you don't want to leave your security blanket, but you've made an appointment to have your hair done, remember?'

She probably does know how I'm feeling, too, thought Kate. This must be rather like the first time she took me to school and left me for the whole day. I was terrified then, and I suppose she was nervous, too.

But once they got to Oxford and put the car in a monstrously expensive car park, Kate was so caught up in the round of activities her mother had planned that she had no time to feel nervous. No sooner was she out of the hairdresser's than her mother had whisked her into a coffee shop.

'I can bear to be seen in public with you now you've had your hair done.'

'I shall need a large sticky bun if you're going to be unkind to me like that.'

'Warm almond croissants,' decided Roz, and they sat munching contentedly as the world went past the window.

'What a lot of people,' said Kate. 'I haven't seen this many in the three weeks I've been in Gatt's Hill.'

'It will do you good. Perk you up a bit,' said Roz bracingly.

'You're right,' said Kate. 'I am feeling a bit more like myself. Would you like another almond croissant, or shall we try that thing with the apricots on top?'

'What a good idea. We need all the energy we can get for the next phase of our morning.' And when they had eaten, Roz swept her through the crowds and in and out of shops, so that Kate didn't have a chance to mope or notice places she had visited once with Andrew, and never would again.

'I'd forgotten how I hated the smell of diesel fumes,' said Roz, charging through a crowd of tourists and dodging two beggars, and she dragged Kate into another shop. Ten minutes later they emerged with a blue plastic bag containing a scarlet shirt.

'It's not my colour,' protested Kate.

'Neither is black,' said Roz, and marched briskly across the pelican crossing and into the Covered Market. 'No diesel fumes in here, anyway,' she said, and chose an emerald and turquoise patterned pullover for her daughter.

'Too bright,' muttered Kate.

'And we'll have those earrings, too,' said Roz. 'No, the biggest ones. Yes, those are the ones.

'You need earrings with that short haircut,' she said to Kate. 'And you must get something done to the colour next time you visit your hairdresser.'

'Yes, Mummy,' said Kate.

'*Don't* call me that. My name is Roz.'

'Your name is Rosemary.'

'And yours is Katharine. Shall we call a truce?'

'I think we'd better.'

'Good. Now, where's that lovely expensive shoe shop?'

It was, in fact, a little after lunchtime when they arrived back at Crossways Cottage, but they were both still full of French pastries and Italian coffee.

'Just scramble some eggs or something,' said Roz as they dropped their bags on the floor. 'Have you got fruit? Soup, perhaps?'

'You sit down,' said Kate superfluously. 'I'll make something for our lunch.'

And for the first time since she'd left her house in Oxford she opened the fridge and found the makings of a simple meal. She chopped and sautéed and blended with cream. She grilled and chopped some more.

'Here we are,' she said eventually, as they sat down at Callie's kitchen table and tucked into fresh soup and slices of warm ciabatta.

'I think I've turned the corner,' she told her mother as they sat with their coffee.

'I'm definitely feeling better,' she said, as she hung her new shirt in the wardrobe, folded her new pullover away in a drawer, and tried on her new earrings. She teetered downstairs in her new, impractical shoes and said, 'That little outing was exactly what I needed. Thank you, Roz.'

In the Vicarage flat, Tim Widdows was making himself a pot of strong tea, no teabags, the real thing, with dark leaves and a six-minute stew. He warmed his hands round the mug and tried to forget what he had seen that morning.

People imagined that professionals like him – police, doctors, vicars – had seen it all and could cope with anything. On the surface he could, of course, but afterwards, when he was alone, he was the same as any other human being who had just been asked to identify a dead body.

He should be in the church, saying a quiet prayer. Later, he promised himself. When he had finished the tea and calmed down a bit he would walk across to the solid old Norman building and pray for comfort for himself and the others affected by this death.

Gatt's Hill appeared to be such an ordinary English village on the surface, but there must be things going on underneath, out of view, that were as ugly as anything on the streets of the inner city. Worse, probably, he thought. Here they were hidden from the light, and so they festered and multiplied until they came bubbling up to the surface.

Tim Widdows sucked in another mouthful of tea and resisted the temptation to add a large slug of whisky to his mug. It wasn't a belief in the wickedness of alcohol that stopped him, but the knowledge that Emma Hope-Stanhope would smell it on his breath, and disapprove, when he met her and the other churchwardens later that evening.

8

The telephone had rung in the Vicarage flat soon after nine-thirty that morning, and Tim Widdows had answered it with no presentiment of tragedy.

'It's Hazel Fuller here, from Gatts Farm.'

He noticed immediately that she seemed upset. 'What's up?' he asked. 'What can I do to help?' For once his response was natural and immediate.

'Please come as soon as possible,' she said. 'It's dreadful, dreadful. I've rung for the ambulance and for the police, and Dr Bates is on his way.'

Tim felt like saying that the place would be a little overcrowded, but it seemed inappropriate in the face of her obvious distress. 'What's happened?' he asked.

'I don't know. I just don't know how it could have happened here,' she replied. He heard the struggle to regain her composure. It was difficult to imagine the immaculately groomed Hazel Fuller giving way to emotion.

'What is it you want me to do?' he asked. He had never thought of Hazel as the devout type.

'Please, just come, will you.' And she replaced her receiver.

So Tim Widdows picked up his black anorak and padded in his well-worn Reeboks across the village and down the hill to Gatts Farm Antiques.

Already outside the house there were black cars

parked, and a white ambulance, its blue light flashing. As he approached, someone switched the blue light off, as though speed of response was no longer important, and it was then that he first thought of death. Had something happened to Hazel's husband, Derek? Or to their son, Anthony? And why had they called the police?

There was an oval of grass in front of the farm gate, like a miniature village green, and small groups of people had gathered there, heads together, gossip buzzing from one to another.

'Do you know what's up, Vicar?' someone asked him.

'I'm afraid not,' he said, not even pausing to add, 'Call me Tim.' The villagers, perhaps a dozen or so of them, blocked his way, slowing him down as he approached the gateway.

'Someone's murdered him, I shouldn't wonder,' said another of his parishioners with relish.

'Probably the Mafia or summat,' said another.

'I always said he was mixed up in summat dodgy,' said a third.

'Please, you tell me what happen,' came a voice from just behind his shoulder. It must be one of the foreign waiters from the pub.

'I know nothing yet,' said Tim Widdows, trying to look serious yet caring, and hoping that he didn't have the avid, vulture-like expression that he saw on all the faces around him. 'If you'll just let me through, I'll try to find out for you.'

'They say you could hear her screaming from up by the church, Vicar,' said a woman in a red woolly hat.

'That's not so,' he said firmly, trying to traverse the final few yards of grass. 'I would have heard it, and I heard nothing until I received Mrs Fuller's phone call.' He wondered which 'she' was being referred to.

'I still say the bugger was asking for it,' said another regular churchgoer.

'They was probably after his money,' added another. 'He's been making enough of it to bring every burglar in the country.'

'Or else they wanted a turn at that tarty missus of his,' replied the first. There was a gust of laughter at this.

Tim reached the gate, and, to the great interest of the crowd, explained to a young policeman that he had been summoned, and was expected. He was allowed through.

The gate led into what had once, presumably, been the farmyard. Now it was gentrified with carefully reclaimed and well-scrubbed flagstones and edged with huge terracotta pots of expensive-looking plants. On the right stood the original farmhouse, also scrubbed clean, tidied-up and newly painted. It was built of weathered stone that glowed gold in the morning sunlight. The tiled roof was steeply pitched and uneven with age. The skeleton of a venerable wisteria surrounded the front door and a standard box tree, clipped into a perfect globe, stood like a sentry to one side of it. The curtains were half-closed, as though someone had wished for privacy, then changed their mind. There was no sign of life on this side of the courtyard and Tim hesitated to knock, not wanting to disturb the silence and whatever lay behind it. Eventually he tapped hesitantly with the brass dolphin knocker and waited for a moment or two. No reply.

On the other two sides of the yard were what had once been barns and cowsheds, which now housed the considerable stock of Gatts Farm Antiques. From here came the sound of voices, and Tim crossed the yard and approached the big double doors. He had never been inside the antiques part of the farm. If he was honest, it intimidated him, since he had never learnt to distinguish between art nouveau and art deco, and as far as he was concerned, the baroque was just a kind of music with a lot of stringed instruments sawing away for all they were worth. At a deeper level of self-knowledge he was aware that he was dreading what he might have to confront. It was bad enough when the Vicarage cat brought in a dead vole and left it, disembowelled, on his kitchen floor, but with the concentration of emergency service vehicles outside, he had an idea that this might be a lot worse.

He took a deep breath, reminded himself of his calling, and rapped on a small side door. It was opened by another policeman who looked him over, took in the dog collar and queried, 'Yes, Vicar? What was it you wanted?'

'Mrs Fuller telephoned me. She asked me to call.' It sounded inadequate, but was apparently enough to gain him admission.

'You'll find her through there,' the policeman said, pointing at another door. 'Don't touch anything,' he added. 'It probably doesn't matter, but better be safe than sorry, I always say. Keep your hands in your pockets, that's the best idea.'

Tim followed instructions, though he wondered how he would greet Hazel Fuller with his hands in his pockets, a posture which he felt lacked dignity for a man of the cloth.

The Fullers' barns and outhouses had been transformed into a series of rooms which were arranged to show off the furniture and *objets* they had for sale. It gave the customers the impression that they were invited into a private house – a house belonging to someone of taste and substance – and only the discreet price tags hinted that this might be a superior kind of shop. In the next room – late Victorian, with a few Edwardian additions, if Tim had been able to recognize them – he found Hazel Fuller, sitting unnaturally upright on an uncomfortable-looking sofa.

'Thank goodness you've come!' she said. 'Derek's away on a buying trip, and I'm all alone here.'

'Alone' was a slight understatement, Tim noticed, for there were a couple of policemen, muttering into mobile phones and taking no notice of either of them.

'What's happened?' asked Tim.

'She's in there,' said Hazel Fuller, indicating the door into the next room.

Tim walked across to look. The door was ajar, and he hadn't taken his hands out of his pockets, mindful of the policeman's instruction. 'Who is it?' he asked. 'What's happened to her?' He didn't venture into the room, and could see little except the end of a red brocade Knole sofa.

'I haven't the slightest idea who she is. I'd never seen her before I walked in and found her first thing this morning.'

One of the policemen approached Tim. 'I'm Inspector Price, sir. I gather you're the local vicar. Reverend Widdows, is it?'

'Call me Tim,' he replied without thinking.

'It's good of you to come so quickly, sir,' said the policeman, ignoring the invitation to informality. He was a tall, heavy man, who had removed from his expression and appearance anything that might be labelled 'personality'. His hair was light brown and receding, his features unremarkable, his eyes a light hazel. He wore a grey suit and a white shirt with a blue tie. Tim unconsciously removed a hand from his pocket and touched his own dog collar as though to reassure himself of his identity. 'We were hoping you could identify her for us, sir, assuming she's local.'

'If I can, of course I will,' said Tim, his voice squeaking a little with nerves. This was going to be worse than he had thought. Hazel had said nothing about identifying a dead body. 'She is dead then?' he asked.

'Oh yes, sir. There's no doubt about that. The doctor has already seen her, but he's not from the village, so he didn't know who she was.'

'What happened to her?'

'Let's take one step at a time, sir,' said Inspector Price, pushing the door wider and gently ushering Tim into the next room.

At first it looked to him like a stage set: some period drama, something by Jane Austen or one of the Brontës. The sort of thing they did so well on the BBC. There was an open book on a table, tasselled cushions on the chairs, brocade curtains at the windows.

And there, in the corner, was a life-sized doll leaning back in one of the chairs, looking like a player on the stage.

Only he knew, of course, that it wasn't a doll, but a young woman.

She was dressed in black, her skirt pushed up her thighs to show the tops of her stockings and black suspenders. *Stockings?* He thought young women always wore tights these days. Maybe he was out-of-date. Her thick, curly dark hair was spread over the red cushion behind her head; her right arm drooped over the arm of the chair, the sleeve pushed up above the elbow, the fingers nearly brushing the floor. Her eyes stared at a point on the opposite wall, as though studying the dark oil painting there. Her mouth was a wide gash of scarlet with ... he drew nearer. Yes, with dried foam at the corners, like a yellowish crust. Her skin was a ghastly colour, but then in death that was only natural, after all.

'What happened to her?' he asked.

'Do you know who she is?' asked Inspector Price.

'Yes. Her name is Donna,' said Tim.

'Surname?' asked Price, writing in his notebook.

'Paige.' He spelt it for him.

'Do you know her address?'

'She lives in the small block of flats at the far end of Broombanks. I'm not sure of the number, but I think it's on the second floor.'

'We'll find it. I thought they built those flats for old people?'

'They did, but then they found that pensioners couldn't afford to run cars, and since the village no longer has a bus, very few pensioners wanted to live there when they had no transport.'

'I know I'd want somewhere with a bit more life to it when I retire,' said the inspector.

'Yes,' said Tim. The inspector's remark seemed all too appropriate.

'Is there anything else you know about her that might be useful to us?'

'She worked as a gardener to various houses in the village. I didn't think she had anything to do with the Fullers: I believe they use a big Oxford firm to keep their garden in order.'

'Did you know she used drugs?'

'I'd be very surprised if she did.'

'Look on the table there.'

He'd seen the syringe, but somehow hadn't associated it with Donna. She belonged in the fresh air, in a garden, not in a smoky cellar with drug addicts. But then again, he was probably out-of-date on that, too. 'I suppose you're right, but I'm still surprised.'

'All these kids try it out at some time or another. It's a way of life with them, Vicar, not like when we were young. This one made a mistake, that's all. It's sad, but I'm afraid we've seen it before. And one of us will have to go and tell her parents. Do you know where they live?'

'I'm afraid not. I've never heard her mention them.'

'We'll try her flat. There may be some indication there of where she came from.'

Tim said, 'But why did it happen here? What was she doing in this room?'

'We don't know, but the door wasn't locked. Maybe she just wandered in to take a look.'

'All dressed up for a night out,' said Tim, forcing himself to look at Donna again. The sparrow's legs in their black stockings ended in awkward-looking platform-soled shoes with high, stacked heels. 'She can't have walked far in those,' he said. 'How did she get here?'

'We've called in the forensic team to check it out,' said Price soothingly. 'They'll soon let us know if there's anything dodgy here. But I think we'll find it was just an unfortunate experiment by an ignorant girl.'

'Where did she get the drugs? What was it – heroin? We really don't have pushers here in the village yet, Inspector.'

'We're only a few miles from Oxford. You have car thieves out here, and vandals, and burglars, all the other dregs of modern life. What makes you think you're immune from the drug pushers?'

'I don't like to think you're right, but I have to admit you could be,' said Tim stiffly.

'That's right, sir. Now, why don't you go and talk to Mrs Fuller. We've taken her statement, for what it's worth, and I think she might need some of your professional attention.'

'Yes. All right.'

Tim turned away from Donna and walked back towards the door. 'She can't have been alone,' he said. 'Have you tried to find out who else was with her when she died?'

The inspector didn't answer.

Hazel had left the outer room and returned to the main house. When Tim went there to look for her, he found her in her elegant sitting room (lacking only the price tags, he thought, to resemble one of the showrooms), pouring herself an inch of whisky into a tumbler. She was dressed in a cream cashmere sweater, short grey flannel skirt, kid pumps and a lot of heavy gold chains. Her hair was tinted a creamy beige to tone with her sweater, and her skin and lips were heavily made-up. She looked as though she had no intention of doing anything more demanding than reading a glossy magazine all day. Tim had to admit there was something oddly attractive about her indolence.

'Don't go telling me it's too early to drink,' she said defensively after he had been looking at her for a little too long. 'I need this. How about you?'

Tim was tempted, but thought of making his way back through the crowd of villagers. They would certainly notice, and comment on, the alcohol on his breath. 'I'd better not,' he said regretfully.

Hazel lit a cigarette and pushed the packet across to him. He noticed that even in the middle of this tragedy, and first thing in the morning at that, her nails were long and varnished a bright scarlet, without a chip. Unlike poor Donna's, he remembered. She always painted hers in ridiculous colours, and then chipped the enamel when she worked on someone's garden.

'I've given up,' he said regretfully. Then he took the packet, removed a cigarette and lit it from the silver lighter on the table. 'Just one can't hurt me,' he said. 'I'll stop again when I've smoked this one.'

'Do what you like,' said Hazel. 'Why don't you keep the rest of the pack?' Her attention was scarcely on what she was saying. She blew out a stream of smoke. 'Well? Do you know who she was? And how did the little bitch get into our showroom?' She sounded surprised and offended, as though the death had occurred with the express purpose of inconveniencing her.

'Don't call her that,' said Tim.

'She had no business there,' said Hazel.

'Probably not, but the girl is dead,' said Tim. 'And yes, I did know her. Her name was Donna Paige. She had a flat down at Broombanks. She lived on her own as far as I know, and made some sort of living by looking after people's gardens.'

'That crowd down at the Banks is nothing but trouble,' said Hazel resentfully. 'They should never have built the place. This used to be an exclusive neighbourhood. There was no need to encourage people like that to come and live here.'

'I doubt whether any village was ever very exclusive,' said Tim. Hazel's attractions were wearing thin already. Under the smooth exterior lived a sharp and vulgar woman. 'Surely it always consisted of a mixture of all sorts of people, farm labourers and landowners, schoolteachers and shopkeepers.'

'Those days are long gone,' said Hazel dismissively. 'It's them and us now, Vicar, whatever you may think. And it was too much for me to bear, going in this morning and finding her like that. And what was that stuff coming out of her mouth?'

'Had you ever seen her before?' asked Tim, ignoring the question.

'Me? No! Why should I have? I have nothing to do with people like that.'

'So she didn't look after your garden?'

'Derek wouldn't use a scruffy kid like that. We have a contract firm come in from Oxford every week. They do everything, I don't have to lift a finger.'

'I thought you might have seen her around the village.'

'They all look the same to me,' said Hazel loftily, and she drained her whisky.

'I suppose I'd better be getting back to the Vicarage flat,' said Tim into the short silence. 'Was there anything else you wanted me to do?' He would have liked to suggest they pray together, silently perhaps, but he lacked the courage.

'You can tell all those nosy parkers out there that it was nothing to do with us,' said Hazel. 'She was just some drug-crazed kid who wandered into our showroom and topped herself. It was just our bad luck it happened here.'

'Don't you usually keep the place locked?' asked Tim.

'Yes. And when I find out who left the door open, I'll see they regret it.'

'Will you be on your own for long?' asked Tim, remembering his manners. 'When will Derek be back? And Tony?'

'I've rung Derek on the mobile. He should be back by this evening. And Tony doesn't always live here, you know. He can afford his own place in Oxford.'

'I'm sure he can,' said Tim swiftly.

'But he said he'll be back as soon as he can. Round about four, he said. So you needn't worry about me. I'll only be on my own for the next few hours.'

'Good,' said Tim, ignoring the self-pity. 'And you have other people working for you, don't you?'

'There's the blokes in the workshops behind the show-rooms. They're busy on repairs and upholstery, but they'll be there all day, I suppose, if I need company.'

'I'll be off, then,' and he rose from his chair.

'Fine.'

'I'll see myself out,' said Tim.

Hazel was already pouring herself another inch of whisky.

'Why did the silly cow have to die *here*?' she complained.

Tim found the question unanswerable.

Outside the farm gates, he once more had to run the gauntlet of the village ghouls.

'Was it a bird?'

'Who was she, Vicar?'

'Did you see her?'

'How did she die?'

The same voices and faces that he saw each Sunday morning in the church of St Michael and All Saints. He felt that his sermons, so long pondered and worked over, had made no impression on these people at all.

'Did she top herself?' This was a young man with a profile like an ancient Egyptian and black hair swept back into a pony tail. His clothes were all black, too. It seemed the only colour the young people these days ever wore.

'It's Donna Paige,' he said. No one had told him to keep her name a secret, after all. 'She's had some sort of accident, I'm afraid, and she's dead.'

His words, cutting through the rumour and speculation that hummed around the grass oval, silenced them for a minute.

'Skirt halfway up her bum last time I seen her, it's no wonder she come to a bad end,' said an old man with a sour face and a scabby dog at his heels.

'You shouldn't talk like that now she's dead,' said someone else. 'It ain't respectful.'

'There will be communal prayers in the church at four o'clock this afternoon for all those who would like to remember their friend Donna,' said Tim impulsively before a full-scale argument could develop.

At the mention of church, the crowd shuffled and looked embarrassed. Church was for Sunday mornings. It smacked of enthusiasm to bring it into their weekday lives.

'I'll see you all at the church then,' said Tim Widdows, and walked away up the hill, leaving the villagers to disperse.

9

During the evening the wind rose, and all night it howled round the chimneys and rattled the window panes in their ancient frames. The rain lashed down and the flower pots rocked dangerously on their ledge, threatening to leave the hilltop and wing their way towards London.

'We can't go out in this,' said Roz next morning, looking out at the sodden fields, the lowering skies and the grey curtains of rain. 'What on earth does one do in the country in weather like this?'

'Read a book? Do our knitting? Prepare an interesting talk for a future Countrywomen's Guild meeting?'

'There must be something better!'

'Emigrate to a warmer climate?'

But Roz failed to react to this last suggestion. What had happened to her, Kate wondered, to bring her back to England and into her daughter's life?

'Have we got a radio?' Roz was asking. 'We need other human voices, for goodness' sake, if we're going to be cast away on this forsaken rural hillside. You make the coffee and I'll pop down to the village shop for a newspaper. There must be something happening out there in the real world that we know nothing about.'

Kate busied herself with cafetière and cereal bowls and cups while her mother was gone. Roz was away for longer than Kate expected. When at last she came through the front door, there was a hesitancy in her step that made Kate turn and look at her.

'What's wrong?' she asked. Her mother's expression was unusually grave. She even looked uncertain what to say.

'Bad news, I'm afraid,' she began hesitantly.

'In the newspaper?' She hated it when her mother sounded unsure of herself.

'No, I don't think so. I haven't looked.'

'Where, then? Please tell me.'

'They were talking about it in the village shop. Apparently we missed all the ambulances and police cars while we were in Oxford yesterday morning.'

'*What?*' shouted Kate. 'Stop faffing about and just tell me what's happened!'

'And it was on the local television news while we were watching that detective series on the other side. They found a body, down at Gatts Farm.'

'Oh, do they know who it was? Was it a tramp or someone like that?' *Please, please let it be someone nameless and unimportant. Someone I can feel sorry for and then forget in a matter of hours. Don't let it be someone I've met, or spoken to, or cared about.*

'No. No, it wasn't a tramp. It was a young woman.'

Kate stood very still. She knew what her mother was going to say next.

'It was Donna,' said Roz. 'I'm so very sorry.'

'How did she die? Was it an accident?' This was a village. Life was frequently boring, surely, but never nasty in a village.

'There were a lot of lurid stories and lively theories being tossed around in the shop, but I don't suppose anyone knows anything for certain yet. The local paper comes out this afternoon. We'll see what they say about it.'

'You can never trust newspapers to get things right! Isn't there someone we can phone? What about Alison Fanning. Or Tim Widdows?' Kate was walking rapidly up and down the room, her voice rising towards hysteria.

'Surely they won't know any more than we do.'

'I can't just stay here and do nothing. Why don't we go down to Gatts Farm and ask there. I have to know what happened.'

'I'll pour the coffee. Sit down and drink it. You haven't had breakfast yet. Eat something. I doubt whether we'd be welcome – we don't even know the people at Gatts Farm.'

'But I have to do *something*. Anything.'

'We'll make a plan – but calm down. Getting in a state like that won't do any good to anyone.'

'What could have happened to her? She was so strong and healthy. She wasn't old enough for a heart attack.'

'I've seen cars driving too fast on these lanes. Maybe it was a traffic accident.'

'A hit and run?'

'And then, the country is full of large and dangerous machinery. Maybe it was that sort of accident.'

'I can't believe it.'

'Drink your coffee. It's also true that there are all the same unpleasantnesses here as in the city. We're only a few miles away, remember. If you climbed to the top of the hill at the back of the garden, you could see it lying before you: bypass and factories, shops and colleges, and drugs, drunkenness and crime.'

'I thought I'd escaped from all that.'

'No one can escape from it. Let me pour you a bowl of muesli.'

'Thanks.' She was at least growing a little calmer, and food was always a help in a crisis. After a while she said, 'You said we should make plans.'

'They're not very exciting ones, I'm afraid. We can't go rushing out to kill dragons.' Roz collected the breakfast things and put them in the washing-up bowl.

'Let me do that,' said Kate.

'I'll dry,' said her mother.

They worked in silence, each busy with her own thoughts.

'It isn't your friend Andrew,' said Roz. 'Not this time.'

'I know. But it feels the same. All the same dreadful thoughts and emotions from his death have been dredged up and come flooding back. It's all too much, too soon.'

'Is that the last of the washing-up?'

'Yes.'

'Well, we'll start thinking what to do, if that will help. Any sort of action has to be better than just standing here, wondering.'

'I'll fetch paper and pencils,' said Kate. 'It's always helpful to make lists, I've found.'

'Well, at least there's one thing you inherited from me,' said her mother. 'I was beginning to think there was nothing at all.'

'Now,' said Kate when they each had a notebook and pencil, 'let's start with the simple part.'

'We want to know what happened,' said Roz. 'How can we find out?'

'Local newspaper. Gossip in shop. Gossip at pub.'

'Hmm. What about the police?'

'They never give anything away to people like us.'

'It's a pity we haven't picked up a tame policeman rather than a vicar,' Roz commented.

There was a momentary silence from Kate, as though she was considering her answer. 'Yes, isn't it,' she said at last.

'The hospital, then. She must have been taken to a casualty department,' said Roz.

'We could try telephoning. We'll have to say we're related.'

'On the other hand, if she was already dead, they probably took her to the mortuary.'

'Then there's the coroner. Surely there will have to be an inquest.'

'That won't be for a few weeks. Meanwhile we could ask Tim Widdows, and Alison or Ken Fanning.'

'I know this sounds like overkill.' Kate paused at her unfortunate choice of phrase. 'You're humouring me, hoping I'll forget about her, aren't you? I'd only just met her, after all. But we did spend quite a time over tea and chocolate biscuits discussing the purpose of life. And I did *like* Donna. She had an original view on life, I thought. She liked growing things, instead of destroying them. And she knew how to prune Callie's shrubs, too.'

'Very well,' said Roz. 'Maybe I was going along with you just to stop you from getting upset. But we both want to know what happened. I met Donna too, don't forget. So to begin with, why don't we go to the pub at lunchtime and listen to what people are saying, and then buy the local paper this afternoon? Then we'll know as much as anyone.'

'Sounds very sensible. Do you want to brave the Saloon Bar with the silent yokels?'

'I think we'll settle for The Butty again, don't you?'

'A good idea.'

'We are alike,' said Roz later. 'We can talk about anything except our real feelings. I have a black hole inside me where I crouch down and hide whenever any difficult feelings start to make their presence known. And I think it's the same for you.'

'I close the doors and shutters behind me and shoot the bolts,' said Kate.

'It's become such a habit that we hardly notice we're doing it,' said Roz.

'It must make things difficult for people who want to get close to us.'

'They try to get inside our walls of defence, and all they find is silence and another irrelevant list. The irony of it is, that I'm supposed to be so good at talking, and you earn your living by being good with words.'

'We're both good at silences,' said Kate.

'I suppose that if we weren't, I'd have been a proper mother to you in the years since your father died.'

'And I'd be married to someone in middle management, with a semi-detached house in the suburbs and a room full of babies.'

'Do you regret it?'

'Only sometimes.'

'Me too. Let's go to the pub.'

In the Saloon Bar they were still talking agribusiness. Conversation stopped when Roz and Kate entered, but resumed after only five seconds or so.

'We're starting to be accepted as locals,' said Roz.

'I doubt it,' replied Kate as they went through into The Butty.

The Butty was full, and they only just managed to grab

the last two seats at a table in the corner.

'Everyone's had the same idea as us,' said Roz. 'They've come here to find out what's happened. It must be a basic human instinct to huddle together in times of disaster. I expect the phone lines were buzzing all morning as people exchanged unlikely theories.'

Kate edged her chair nearer to the table as a waiter pushed past with a plate of steaming food. 'The good thing about this crowd is that whether we like it or not we can hear what people are saying at the tables around us.'

'Of course we like it! It's what we came for. And they all look like locals,' said Roz approvingly. 'Shall I try to order us some food and drink?'

'Go easy on the alcohol, we want to keep our wits about us.'

'Trust me,' said Roz, and returned with half-pints of lager for them. 'This doesn't count as alcohol,' she said as she placed them on the table. 'Now, what have you managed to earwig while I was gone?'

'A certain amount of "isn't it awful!" and "we're not safe in our beds!", but nothing more than we know already.'

'Do you mind if we join you?' called a voice from behind Kate. 'It's so crowded in here I didn't know where we were going to find a place to sit.'

'Alison,' said Roz. 'How nice to see you here. And Ken. Yes, move round a bit, Kate. I'm sure there's room for the two of you. Oh, so sorry! Was that your bowl of chips? I do apologize.'

And somehow they found a space, and were eventually all installed with their plates of food and glasses of mildly alcoholic drinks.

'Isn't it awful!' said Alison. Today she was encased in beige and green argyll checks.

'Just awful,' agreed Roz.

'We're not safe in our beds any more,' said Alison.

'How true,' sympathized Roz.

Kate sighed.

'I suppose you're thinking about our poor Donna,' said Roz.

'And have you heard about the latest burglary?' asked Alison.

'I haven't heard about any of them,' said Kate.

'I thought this was a Neighbourhood Watch area,' said Roz.

'And a lot of good that's done us!'

'I'm afraid there has been a spate of break-ins over the past few months and one or two major burglaries as well,' said Ken. His pullover was yellow, with a v-neck, his shirt a pale green, his trousers sky-blue. 'I think the break-ins, mostly in the daytime, are done by kids. It's what they call opportunist crime. They pick up video recorders and cameras, stuff that's easy to dispose of. But the big houses have been done over by professionals who know what they're looking for.'

'I'm sure it's all due to those dreadful people at the Banks,' said Alison.

'Donna lived at the Banks,' said Kate.

'That just proves it,' said Alison. 'She must have got mixed up in all sorts of things there. You know what these young girls from the council estates are like.'

'No,' said Kate. 'I don't think I do. Please tell me.' She felt a kick on her shin, but ignored her mother.

'They're brought up with no sense of morality at all. Truthfulness, honesty, let alone chastity, they don't understand any of them. They have no principles to live by.'

'How different from the home life of our own dear Queen,' murmured Kate.

'What?'

'Nothing.'

'And just think of poor Hazel. What a shock it was for her to find the girl like that. And it can't have been pleasant for Derek and Tony when they came home, either. It won't do the business much good, will it?'

'Oh, I don't know,' said Kate. 'It seemed to be drawing the crowds when I went past earlier. Perhaps they could quickly bring out a line in souvenirs.'

'I don't think so, not at such short notice,' said Ken seriously.

'And then there are the drugs,' went on Alison.

'That's what killed Donna, they say,' said Ken. 'She took an overdose.'

'On purpose, do you think?' asked Roz.

'I expect she was experimenting,' said Alison. 'That's what these young people do, you know. They take a whole cocktail of pills and capsules. No wonder they can't hold down a job.'

'I thought Donna was a very competent gardener,' said Kate.

'You seem to know her better than the rest of us,' said Alison. 'Is that why you're standing up for her?'

'No, not really. As a matter of fact I only met her once.'

'Well, there you are then,' said Alison.

'Shall I get us all another drink?' asked Roz desperately.

'Whisky for me,' said Ken.

'Gin and tonic, please,' said Alison.

'I'll have an orange juice,' said Kate. 'Let me help you

87

carry them.' And she squeezed out from her place and followed Roz.

'There must be other people in this village we can talk to,' said Kate as they elbowed their way to the bar.

'Look around you. They're all out of the same mould,' said Roz, and caught the eye of the barman ahead of all the other customers. 'Two large glasses of orange juice, a very small whisky and an even smaller gin and tonic, please,' she said.

The barman looked startled, but then shrugged and poured the drinks, handing them over on a tray. Before they could start to edge their way back to their table, a small, dumpy woman tapped Kate hesitantly on the arm and said, 'Excuse me, but are you the young lady who's living in Miss Callan's cottage?'

'That's right,' said Kate.

'Then you must be the famous novelist,' said the woman. 'Aphra told us to expect you.'

'Well . . .' began Kate modestly.

'What did you say your name was?' asked the tall, smart-looking woman at her side. Is that suit real silk, wondered Kate. It certainly looked like it. And that was no Oxford haircut, either: somewhere near Bond Street, more likely.

'Kate Ivory,' said Kate.

'Really? Do you write under your own name?'

'Kate, this is Emma Hope-Stanhope,' said the dumpy one. She made it sound as though Kate should be grateful to be insulted by such an exalted creature. 'And I'm Jenny Philbee. I expect Aphra told you about me.'

'Aphra? Oh yes, Callie. Ah . . . Yes, yes, I'm sure she did. How lovely to meet you at last.'

Emma Hope-Stanhope meanwhile was sweeping Kate

from head to toe with a look that priced every piece of clothing she was wearing. *Well under a hundred, including her underwear,* the look said, then paused at the feet. *Italian. Joan and David?*

'Kate is one of our best-selling historical novelists,' said Roz, exaggerating wildly. 'And I'm Roz Ivory, her mother.'

'Really?' said Emma Hope-Stanhope, and pursed her lips at the pink top that Kate had bought in last year's sale at Debenhams.

'Such a popular pub you have here in Gatt's Hill,' went on Roz. 'There's hardly a place left to sit down. Why don't you join us at the table over there?'

'I'll leave you,' said Jenny. 'My husband's in the next room with the Samsons.'

'I don't come here very often,' said Emma. 'It isn't really my sort of place.'

'Of course it isn't,' said Roz, leading the way back to their table and appropriating another chair as she went. 'But it's a marvellous place for picking up the gossip, don't you find?'

Emma choked with embarrassment and had to be handed Alison's gin and tonic to recover. Ken chivalrously offered to replace her drink and order for Emma while he was at the bar.

Roz turned to Emma. 'Did you know Donna?' she asked.

'There's nothing like being subtle about these things,' murmured Kate.

'Donna? Do you mean the unfortunate girl who broke into the Fullers' shop and then died?'

'We don't know that she broke in,' said Kate.

'If she didn't break in, then what was she doing there?' said Emma. 'I can't imagine that a girl like that was interested in antiques for their aesthetic appeal.' She gave a ladylike, tinkling laugh.

Kate opened her mouth to put Emma right on that, but received such a sharp kick on the ankle from her mother that she thought better of it.

'What are they saying about Donna?' asked Roz. 'Have you heard?'

'Well, half the village appears to think that she deserved everything she got, that she was no better than she should be.'

'And what about the other half?' asked Kate.

'They seem to think that she was a drug addict who took an overdose and died after breaking into the Fullers' showroom.'

'So they haven't been inhibited by good taste or charitable feelings towards the recently dead,' said Kate.

'What? Did you know the girl?' asked Emma imperiously. 'What had you heard about her?'

'I only met her once. What should I have heard?'

'I just wondered whether people were talking about, you know, the men in her life.'

'No one seems to know who she was seeing. It's odd that, don't you think?' said Alison Fanning, who had been silent so far in the presence of her social superior. 'Usually these girls are chatting about their boyfriends all the time.'

'She told me his name was Raven,' said Kate.

'Raven! No, there's no one of that name in the village,' said Emma. 'So he must have been an outsider.' She sounded relieved.

'I imagine you know everyone in the village,' said Roz. 'I doubt there's much here that you don't know about.'

'My family likes to think it has a responsibility towards

the villagers, certainly,' said Emma. 'We have lived at the big house for four hundred years, you know.'

'Really!' said Roz admiringly. 'I had noticed what a beautiful place it was. Queen Anne, isn't it?'

'Yes, the main part is Queen Anne, but there is an older part at the back, and the remains of the pre-Reformation chapel.'

'I've always been interested in old family chapels,' said Roz.

'Then you must come and see ours.'

'I'd be fascinated to visit it. You are so lucky to have one of your very own.'

'Ruined, of course, but that makes it still more beautiful, don't you think.'

'So picturesque.'

'Why don't you and your daughter come for drinks this evening? At six o'clock?'

'We'd love to.'

'In fact, if you have no other plans, why don't you stay for dinner? We were meant to be entertaining the Langleys, but they've had to rush off to see a pregnant daughter or something equally boring. But anyway, it's a shame to waste the meal, isn't it?'

'I hate to waste good food,' agreed Roz.

At which point Emma's meal was served and they sipped their orange juice and talked of other things while she ate.

'What was all that about?' asked Kate when they had left the pub and were walking back to Crossways Cottage.

'I wanted to see inside their house, so I buttered the old bag up until she invited us over.'

'I thought she was a frightful, condescending woman.'

'She made a change from Alison and Ken. I thought you were getting a little short with the Fannings.'

'Bloody people!' fumed Kate. 'As soon as she dies, they use her to hang their prejudices on. She lives in a council flat so she must be a drug addict. She's poor, so she must be a thief. She wears short skirts, so she must be a slut. Whatever happened to her, it must be because she deserved it.'

'They do it because it's more comfortable for them to think that way. If they admitted it was a random killing then it might happen to them next time. It's easier to distance themselves by saying "It could never happen to people like us." Then it can only happen to someone like *her*.'

'They say it because they're a crowd of bigots.'

Somewhere a bird was making a noise like a blunt knife being drawn down a dinner plate. 'They're frightened,' said Roz. 'Who knows what might turn up if the police, or her relations, start digging around in her life. It's safer to let it lie.'

'Bloody people!' reiterated Kate.

'So what are you going to do about it?'

'What do you suggest?'

'I think you should find out what really happened.'

10

As they reached Crossways Cottage, Kate said, 'Wait a moment.'

'What?'

In the sudden silence they heard the soft thudding of Reeboks on the road behind them, and the heavy breathing of someone unused to anything more than moderate exercise.

'Who's that?' asked Kate.

'I've caught you!' gasped their pursuer.

'Tim Widdows,' said Roz. 'What are you doing here, chasing after us?'

'I wanted to talk to you about Donna.'

'And what's *your* theory about her death?' enquired Kate coldly. 'Drugs? Alcohol? Sex?'

'No. That's the point. I know you disagreed with what they were saying in The Butty, and I wanted to tell you that I do too.'

'I didn't see you there,' said Kate.

'I was trying to melt into the background. One doesn't like to be seen too obviously drinking in a pub.'

'You'd better come in,' said Roz, opening the door and leading the way. 'I don't suppose one likes to be seen too obviously chatting up two unattached women in the village street, either. Kate, why don't you stop looking as if you're going to hit someone, and make us all some coffee instead.'

'Bossyboots,' said Kate, opening cupboard doors and putting on the kettle. She thumped mugs on to a tray and found the milk and sugar. The conversation in the next room was growing animated and she didn't wish to be excluded for any longer than necessary.

'It can't be that difficult, can it?' Tim Widdows was saying.

'What can't?' asked Kate, coming in with the tray of coffee.

'We've seen it on the television, we know what to do,' said Tim.

'Do you believe everything you see on the screen?' asked Roz.

'Of course, don't you?'

'No, not everything.'

'I believe in all the fiction, anyway. I'm not so sure about the documentaries. But anyway, I think we should do it,' said Tim.

'What's that?' asked Kate. 'I don't like the direction this conversation's taking.'

'I think we should find out what happened to Donna,' Tim told her.

'And I agree with him,' said Roz, handing him a mug of coffee, taking one for herself and sitting down next to him on the sofa.

'And how do we go about it?' asked Kate, sipping at her own mug, then stopping because the coffee was far too hot to drink.

'We go round asking questions.'

'And then?' asked Kate.

'We find the truth,' said Tim.

'It sounds like something out of Enid Blyton – *The Silent Three Go Adventuring Together*,' said Kate.

'I liked Enid Blyton when I was a kid,' said Tim. 'I read nearly everything she wrote.'

'I can tell,' said Kate unkindly.

'I'd hardly describe us as silent,' Roz objected. 'And Tim has a point. Why don't you stop snapping at everyone, Kate, and listen to what he has to say.'

'Very well. I'm sorry, Tim. I'll behave, I promise. Why not begin by telling us what you know?'

'You can be a bit sharp, Kate. It's something you should watch if you want to have meaningful relationships with people.' Having delivered himself of this reproof Tim leant back and pushed his hands through his hair so that it stood up in tufts above his ears. 'It started with the telephone call from Hazel Fuller. I went down to Gatts Farm because she sounded distressed and insisted that she wanted me to be there.'

'What about her husband?' asked Kate, sharp as ever, in spite of the criticism. 'Why wasn't he doing the consoling? Why did she need you?'

'Derek was away on a buying trip, apparently. And her son works in Oxford, so he wasn't there either.'

'Do let him go on with the story,' said Roz.

'She *was* upset when I got there,' continued Tim, 'but I noticed something else as well. It was as though she wanted an audience. Yes, that's it.'

'An audience for what?' asked Kate, ignoring her mother's scowl.

'Get us some more coffee,' said Roz. 'Tim will never reach the end of his story unless you leave him alone.'

'It's your turn to get the coffee,' said Kate. 'Go on, Tim. I am listening, really I am.'

'Well, who wouldn't be upset if they'd found the body of an unknown dead girl when they came to open up the shop. But I noticed, too, that she was angry. No, I can't put it as high as anger. She was annoyed, *irritated*, because it had happened to *her*. If Donna had to die, why should she do it at Gatts Farm?'

'Hardly a rhetorical question,' said Roz, forgetting her own advice.

'Quite. Well, to continue with the story. There were a couple of policemen there, and they seemed to think that I had come to identify the body.'

'So Hazel didn't recognize Donna?' It was Kate who interrupted again.

'So she said.'

'Didn't you believe her?' This from Roz.

'I think so. But I can't believe that Donna was a complete stranger to her. I don't suppose Hazel knew her name, or where she lived, but she must have known her by sight. After all, how many people live in this village? Two hundred? Three hundred at the most. If you see a stranger, it's usually because they come from somewhere outside the village.'

'I'm too recent a resident to know,' said Kate. 'But the Fullers have been here a few years, haven't they?'

'Longer than me, certainly,' said Tim. 'Though I believe they're newcomers by village standards.'

'And they made too much money, too fast, to judge by village reaction to them,' said Roz.

'You've sussed out the village animosities pretty rapidly,' said Tim.

'I just listen to the gossip in the pub,' said Roz modestly.

'I hadn't been expecting to have to identify a dead body,' said Tim. 'I suppose that in my job I should get used to death as well as birth. It comes with the territory, you could say. But it still isn't easy when the death is of a young woman of what, twenty – twenty-two? And there, in that showroom. Everything was so perfect: not a speck of dust, not a grubby footprint. Every detail was just so: every picture and vase. And the Oriental rugs on the floor, all laid out like a stage set. That's what I thought at first: this isn't real. They're making a film, or putting on a play. The figure lying back in the chair, with her hand trailing on the floor and her feet stuck out in front of her wearing those ridiculous shoes, she must be another prop.'

'Could you tell how she had died?' asked Roz.

'There was no knife, or gun, and no blood that I could see. She was horribly pale, and she had something crusted round her mouth, like dried froth.'

They were all silent for a moment, thinking about the scene in the barn.

'That sounds as though she might have been poisoned,' said Roz eventually.

'Yes,' said Kate. 'But that's weirder than ever. It seems such an unlikely thing to do to someone in those circumstances. I mean, you might take someone to a barn and then shoot them, or stab them, or even strangle them. But *poison*? It seems so premeditated.'

'And just as odd if it was suicide,' said Tim. 'She didn't look as though she had set out to kill herself that evening. She was wearing that short black dress, as though she was going out for a night's clubbing. What was she doing there? Hazel got that part right. She should have been out with her boyfriend, not sitting in a button-backed Victorian chair at Gatts Farm.'

'Raven,' said Kate.

'Sorry?'

'She said her boyfriend's name was Raven. Do you know who he was?'

'I don't know anyone called that. Do you know his surname, or anything else about him?'

'She said he was a "businessman", though what she meant by it I can't imagine. It could cover a multitude of possibilities.'

'Raven,' repeated Tim, thinking about it.

'Black hair in a pony tail, profile like an Assyrian, skin tanned by the sun,' said Kate suddenly. 'It's got to be him. He's the only exotic, fanciable man I've seen in the village.'

'And he was in the crowd outside Gatts Farm, if we're thinking of the same person,' said Tim, smoothing his hair down and wishing he had a more exotic profile.

'Could there be two?'

'Probably not. He looked to me like one of the single homeless who were put into the old people's flats.'

'Run that one past me again,' said Roz. 'I didn't quite understand it. You weren't describing some geriatric just now, were you?'

'The Council built a small block of flats for pensioners, in Broombanks. Then they found that the old people didn't want to live there because the village no longer has a bus, and the pensioners couldn't afford their own cars.'

'Wouldn't the other residents have given them a lift when they needed it?' asked Kate.

'Who wants to be that dependent on other people? Anyway, there were half a dozen flats sitting empty. They weren't big enough for families, so they moved in a few of the single homeless people who had been living in hostels in Oxford. The young man you described looks like one of those. And, incidentally, Donna lived in the same block of flats.'

'How do you suppose he earns his living?' asked Roz.

'I've no idea. But "in business" could describe anything from drug dealing to selling hand-made jewellery in the Friday market.'

'We need to find out more about him,' said Kate.

'Why don't you go visiting?' asked Roz.

'Me? Why me?'

'Because you're the right age and gender,' said Roz practically. 'And think how good you'd be at it.'

'I'll think about it,' said Kate, and drank her coffee.

'You haven't told us how you came to know Donna,' said Roz. 'She didn't look much like a churchgoer to me, though I suppose I shouldn't generalize.'

'You're right, I'm afraid,' said Tim. 'I'm having difficulty getting through to the young ones like Donna and her Raven. I haven't quite hit on the right approach yet.'

'I'm sure it will come to you,' said Roz. 'So how did you get to know her?'

'Through her gardening,' he said. 'The Vicarage has been sold, I expect you know, except for a small flat on the top floor where the vicar – me, that is – now lives. I have my own front door, at the top of an iron staircase on the outside of the house. I don't really have any rights to the garden but the family who bought the main house are very kind and let me use it when I want to.'

'And Donna was their gardener?'

'Yes. I was sitting on the bench under the apple tree and she was cutting the grass. We got talking.' Tim looked embarrassed, Kate noted with interest. 'I offered her a coffee when she took her break, and it sort of became a habit with us.' Tim's face was pink, he shuffled his feet, and blinked behind his rimless glasses. Aha, thought Kate. Our vicar was smitten by the pretty young gardener. Did she know about his feelings towards her?

'Did you by any chance give her a blue glass pendant?' asked Kate casually.

'The perfume bottle she wore round her neck?'

'That's the one.'

'No, I didn't. I don't know who did, either. I thought she might have bought it herself at one of those antiques fairs she was always going to.'

'Maybe she did,' said Kate. It had been an outside chance. She couldn't imagine that anyone would call Tim Widdows, with his thinning hair and soft, small-featured face, 'Raven'.

'She wasn't wearing it,' said Tim.

'What?'

'That pendant. She always wore it, didn't she? She took it off when she was working, but then she always put it back on when she'd finished.'

'Are you sure she wasn't wearing it when you identified the body? You'd be forgiven for missing it in the circumstances.'

'I remember thinking how she was dressed all in black. She was wearing stockings, which seemed unusual to me.'

'Some men like their women to wear them,' said Kate knowledgeably.

'Really? I didn't realize that.'

'Go on describing what she was wearing, and ignore my daughter,' said Roz.

100

'Her dress had a round, scooped neck, and her throat was bare. I'd have seen if she was wearing the pendant.'

'So the pendant was missing,' said Kate slowly. 'And there was something else odd about the description, other than the stockings, that struck me when you were telling us what you saw.'

'What was that?'

'It's gone again. But don't worry, it'll come back to me.'

'I'll have to go now,' said Tim. 'I have work to do. When shall we get together again?'

'We're going to dinner with the Hope-Stanhopes this evening,' said Roz. 'You know,' she added airily, 'the people in the big house at the bottom of the hill.'

'Oh, I know it all right. The Gatt's Hill Playhouse,' said Tim.

Roz looked puzzled. 'I'm sorry?'

'I'm sure you'll understand after an evening in their company,' said Tim. 'They specialize in melodrama, you'll find.'

'Amateur theatricals, do you mean?' asked Roz. 'Or games of charades after dinner? How dreadful.'

'I'm sure that between us we'll manage to subvert either of those,' said Kate.

'What I've been puzzling over is why on earth Emma Hope-Stanhope was at the pub today,' said Roz.

'Why shouldn't she be?' asked Kate.

'Your mother's right,' said Tim. 'I was surprised she was there, too. She didn't look at home among the plebs.'

'She was with Jenny Philbee,' said Kate.

'I wouldn't have thought those two were natural friends and allies,' said Tim. 'But a sudden death like that might make people behave uncharacteristically. She was probably just curious to find out what was happening.'

'Maybe you're right,' said Roz. But she didn't sound convinced. 'Why didn't she just ring up Hazel Fuller or some other crony of hers?'

'I don't think she'd ring Hazel. The two don't get on.'

'I thought people in villages all stuck together,' said Kate. 'That's the theory, isn't it? Living in their isolated community they help each other out in times of need. They can't afford to fall out over minor disagreements.'

'I think your ideas are out-of-date,' said Roz.

Tim said, 'And now I really must be going. Shall we meet tomorrow?'

'Make it the afternoon,' said Roz. 'Why don't you come to tea? Kate will be out questioning Raven in the morning.'

'Did I agree to that?' asked Kate.

'Of course you did, dear,' said Roz.

'Let me see you out, Tim,' said Kate. 'And do come to tea tomorrow afternoon. I'll try to make sure we have some chocolate biscuits in the tin.'

When she returned to the sitting room, Roz said, 'I think you've made a conquest there.'

'A bloody vicar! Just what I need.'

'Be grateful. He's the first man who's been interested in you for weeks.'

'But does he count as a man?'

'I told you you're getting too sharp for your own good, Kate.'

'Anyway, he was obviously keen on young Donna.'

'But it can't have been serious, can it? No, I think he's definitely attracted to *you*.'

'I'm quite sure you're wrong.'

'Enough of this. We need to look through our wardrobes and find something that will stun the Hope-Stanhopes.'

'Try to keep it ladylike,' said Kate reprovingly.

11

'Very nice,' said Roz, looking Kate over when she eventually came downstairs.

'You look all right yourself,' said Kate with relief. She had been afraid that her mother would wear one of her more outlandish outfits, but Roz was looking elegant in a plain dress in deep red, with dark brown tights and shoes.

'You're in pretty good nick for your age. Is that dress silk?' asked Kate.

'Silk twill. Of course.'

'And the shoes look Italian.'

'They are.'

'Shall we walk or take the car?'

'I think for the Hope-Stanhopes one should arrive on wheels, don't you?'

'A good idea.'

They took Kate's car which, although old and battered in places, was still newer and more respectable-looking than her mother's VW. They drove down the hill, past the now-deserted green in front of Gatts Farm, and turned the corner past the high stone wall that surrounded Gatt's House.

'Which way do we go in?' asked Kate, slowing down and looking up at the square grey frontage with its large, symmetrically placed lighted windows.

'Aim for the servants' entrance,' said Roz. 'That's where

they keep their cars, I expect.' Kate drove on round the gravel path.

Roz was right. Kate drove through an imposing archway and parked next to a Range Rover, a Volvo estate, and a Nissan Micra, and beneath a venerable chestnut tree. 'And I don't suppose the village kids have dared to throw sticks at *these* conkers,' she said. 'Now, how do we get into the house?'

'I should think the Hope-Stanhopes are so posh that they can ignore their front door and use this back entrance,' said Roz, leading the way to an oak door set in a deeply recessed porch. Doves cooed in the trees behind them, and in the porch, green wellies stood drying, and ancient, muddy tennis shoes, a badminton racket and a walking stick were stacked against the side wall. No one had scrubbed the tiled floor of the porch for years by the look of it.

Roz rang the bell, which pealed somewhere deep within the house. High heels eventually clacked across flagged floors and the door opened.

'So glad you could come,' said Emma Hope-Stanhope. 'And how clever of you to avoid the front door. It's so well locked and barred these days that it takes us an age to unfasten it all.'

'Is Gatt's Hill so dangerous a place?' asked Roz. 'I hadn't realized.'

'It's the insurance company that insists, apparently. Such dreary people. Now do come in and meet the others.'

They made their way down dark and dingy stone corridors to the front of the house, where the floors were of polished boards, and followed Emma Hope-Stanhope into an elegant drawing room.

'Jon, darling, come and meet the two lovely new people I told you about.'

Jon Hope-Stanhope was very much what they had expected: tall, thin and tweedy with regular features, well-brushed, greying hair and beautifully polished brown shoes. His nose was designed for looking down. He could have sat for his portrait to be painted by John Singer Sargent as 'An English Gentleman', *circa* 1900. He was probably somewhere in his forties, and when he shook Kate's hand he held on to it for just a little too long.

'Oh, jolly good, jolly good,' he said, smiling with well-shaped lips and staring at Kate's chest through patrician blue eyes. 'So glad you could make it. Have you come far? Jolly good, jolly good. And what can I get you to drink? Will G and T do you?'

'Perfectly,' said Roz.

'I hate gin,' muttered Kate when at last he dropped her hand and moved away to pour their drinks.

'It's what you drink in houses like this,' said her mother severely. 'I hope you're going to behave properly, Kate, and not shame your mother.'

Kate stifled the rude comment she wanted to make and walked over to join the other guests.

'Jenny Philbee,' said Emma. 'And her husband, Sam. Have you met Kate Ivory?'

'We met in The Narrow Boat,' said Kate, recognizing the small dumpy woman with straight grey hair cut in a bob and a pleasant face innocent of make-up. This evening she was wearing a slime-green knitted suit and the sort of complicated sandals that gave you blisters just to look at them. Her husband was taller and broader with a ruddy complexion and sparse fair hair. He was wearing

107

well-pressed tweeds, a flannel shirt and a woollen tie, and looked as though he would rather be chatting to his pigs than standing here in this fancy room with a glass of gin and tonic in his hand. He made the usual village 'mnerf' noises when he was introduced. Kate watched him take a mouthful of his drink and then wrinkle his snub nose. She had to agree with him about gin.

Small talk was humming all around her and people seemed to be getting on well enough without any contribution from her apart from smiles and nods and 'yes, how terrible,' and 'no, of course not,' occasionally, so she spent her time studying her surroundings.

It was an elegant room, as one might have expected from one belonging to Emma and Jon Hope-Stanhope, scattered rather sparsely with the sort of antique furniture that looked as though it had been in the family for generations. On the floor were one or two Oriental rugs that were well-worn and had an overlay of dog hairs. There was a lot of bare polished floor in between, and Emma's smart shoes snapped like pistol shots as she walked from one of her guests to another. There were portraits of her ancestors in wigs, in hunting pink, in satin and velvet, all framed in gold against the dull red walls. The sofa where Jenny Philbee was sitting, by contrast, was modern and comfortable, as were the two or three armchairs grouped around the fireplace.

Kate's inventory was interrupted by the arrival of two more guests. 'Hilary and Aubrey Massen,' said Emma, and Kate saw another county-looking couple entering the room.

'Hilary and I were at school together,' said Emma. Hilary looked as though she would be more at home on a horse than in front of a book, and she and Emma were exchanging the kind of kisses that didn't quite touch the cheek. Aubrey was well-scrubbed, well-dressed and conspicuously well-off.

Conversation for the next ten minutes was so bland that Kate found herself wishing for anything, even parlour games, to break the monotony. Why on earth had her mother angled for an invitation from these dreary people? If she was hoping to find out more about Donna's death, she had failed so far. And if she wanted to cheer Kate up by introducing her to some sparkling company she was even less successful. At that moment there was one of those pauses that sometimes happens in a group of people when everyone stops speaking, as though at some unseen signal.

'Do tell me about the lovely family at Gatts Farm,' said Roz into this silence.

Kate saw expressions ranging from horror to distaste pass across all their faces. Perhaps having an unscheduled death on your premises was a major faux pas in this social circle.

'Oh!' said Roz, with what Kate knew was deep insincerity. 'Have I said something foolish? I imagined that the owners of such a lovely old farmhouse and so many beautiful antiques would be great friends of yours.'

'Not quite our type,' said Emma frostily.

'They're no farmers,' rumbled Sam Philbee. 'They sold off the land soon as they bought the place.'

'Who bought it?' asked Roz.

'Man over Hensford way. I'd have liked to buy it, but it was too pricey for the likes of me, I can tell you.' And Sam glowered at the remains of his gin for the rest of the conversation.

'And those frightfully vulgar yellow vans of theirs,

driving up and down the lane at all hours of the day and night,' said Jon. 'It makes it fiendishly difficult to get your horsebox past them on the bends. Awful people!'

'I suppose the vans are for the furniture, since that's what they deal in,' said Roz reasonably.

'And how often do *you* drive the horsebox?' asked Emma, whose pink-tipped nose indicated that she had been on the gin for longer than the rest of them and was reaching the belligerent stage. 'You're always leaving that chore to *me*, Jon.'

'They are your horses, old girl, after all,' drawled Jon. 'Useless bloody animals, I call them, eating their heads off at my expense.'

'And I suppose you're going to begrudge me my one interest in life, are you?' said Emma, sounding tearful.

'You can hardly call it your sole interest when you spend so much time with your gin bottle.'

'What a disgusting thing to say! And in front of our friends, too!'

The volume rose inexorably. It was like listening to two orchestras playing two different symphonies, thought Kate, with two huge egos conducting. She let the sound play over her without attempting to listen to what they were saying, and let her thoughts wander, interrupted occasionally by particularly loud clashing of conversational timpani or flourishing of verbal brass.

The Massens, the Philbees, and Roz all pretended nothing untoward was happening and tried to make polite conversation about the weather. The argument between their hosts finally faltered and came to a halt and conversation could become general again.

'You have to feel sorry for Hazel Fuller, though,

don't you?' said Roz, who seemed unable to keep away from the subject of Gatts Farm.

'Why's that?' asked Aubrey Massen. 'I never saw her as an object of pity.'

'Finding that poor girl dead in her showroom. It must have been a dreadful shock for her.'

There was a short silence as everyone contemplated Roz's bad taste in introducing the subject of death into the drawing room. Apparently having a stand-up row with your spouse could be overlooked, but not the mention of a corpse.

'Hazel Fuller has never struck me as the sensitive type,' said Jon. 'I'm sure she could take it in her stride.'

'And you'd know Hazel Fuller much better than the rest of us,' said Emma nastily.

'And did you know Donna Paige?' put in Kate, before the Hope-Stanhopes could get into one of their noisy rows again.

'Who?' asked Emma with exaggerated nonchalance.

'The young woman who died,' explained Kate, just in case they thought they could get her off the subject.

'Good Lord, no!' Emma was surely going to cross Kate and Roz off her list of acquaintances after this.

'It might make more sense to ask Jon whether he knew her,' murmured Aubrey, who had taken the seat on the other side of Kate. He smelled pleasantly of after-shave, and there was a whiff of dark cigarettes, as though he had taken one final drag before throwing down the butt and coming into this smoke-free house.

'He's certainly a good-looking man,' said Roz, who had overheard.

'Who is?' asked Kate, who had lost the thread.

'Jon.'

'A good-looking man who likes his good-looking totty,' said Aubrey.

'But surely not on his own doorstep,' said Roz. They were speaking in an undertone while the Philbees chatted to Jon and Emma Hope-Stanhope on the other side of the room.

Aubrey laughed. 'If not, it would be the only place he'd failed to boff one of his lady-friends.'

Roz and Kate laughed, too, and looked across at Jon. He did look like a smooth operator, certainly, now that it was pointed out to them. As they watched, he leant over Jenny Philbee and offered her more gin in a way that made his wife look at him sharply.

'I can't believe he's really interested in Jenny Philbee,' said Hilary.

'He likes to keep in practice, I believe,' said Aubrey.

'I can't think why she married him!' said Hilary.

'He's an accountant,' said Aubrey. 'Everyone needs a good accountant.'

'What's that you're saying?' asked Emma suspiciously when she heard their voices rising with amusement. 'What are you gossiping about now, Aubrey? You mustn't believe a word he says, you know. He's a very wicked man.'

'We were just admiring your lovely furniture,' said Roz with a bland smile.

'It's been in the family for generations,' said Jon. 'We've never had to buy a thing from a shop, have we, Emma?'

Kate was wondering about the obviously twentieth-century sofas and chairs, but Emma was saying, 'This lot? Oh, these are nothing. You should—'

'Why don't you go and see how the meal's getting on, old girl?' interrupted Jon. 'Our guests must be getting quite hungry by now.'

'Oh, very well,' said Emma. 'But I don't know why you have to leave it all to me.'

'Would you like me to give you a hand?' asked Kate.

'Oh no, I can't let you do that. You're a guest,' said Emma.

'What happened to your wonderful Mrs Chapman?' asked Hilary. 'Don't tell me she's given you the elbow!'

'One gets so tired of servants in the house all the time,' said Emma. 'I decided to replace her by a woman from the village who comes in to clean a couple of times a week.'

'Really! I thought she was such a treasure,' said Hilary.

'The food, Emma,' prompted Jon.

'Oh, very well,' said Emma again, and repaired to the echoing depths of the house. She took her latest gin and tonic with her, and Kate hoped that she was still sober enough to know what she was doing with the food for eight people.

When she had gone, Hilary turned to Jon and asked, 'So tell us, Jon dear, what naughty things have you been up to since we last spoke?'

'I can't think what you're talking about,' said Jon, but he was smiling like a man who enjoys his louche reputation.

'Did you know this girl who expired in the Fullers' barn?' asked Aubrey. 'Was she one of your little friends?'

'Come on, Jon, give us the low-down!' added Hilary.

From the direction of the kitchen came a crash as of breaking plates. Everyone pretended nothing had happened.

'I don't think it is very nice in the circumstances,' said Jenny Philbee, whose eyebrows were disappearing into her hairline. She put down her glass of untouched gin.

'We oughtn't to be speaking about her like this.'

'Quite right,' agreed Sam Philbee. 'The girl's only been dead a couple of days.'

'Rubbish,' said Aubrey. 'All that *de mortuis* stuff is out of fashion. And it's not going to bring the girl back, is it?'

'Well, Jon. Tell us what you know,' urged Hilary.

But at this moment there was a wail from the direction of the kitchens and Emma Hope-Stanhope appeared at the drawing-room door and called, 'Jon! You must come and give me a hand. You know I'm hopeless at carving. I can't do this all on my own!'

And Jon made his escape from the eager questions.

In the car going home Kate asked, 'And what was all that about? Why did we have to endure that dreadful evening?'

'But it did brighten up a bit after the Massens arrived, don't you think?'

'The food was awful. And cold when it should have been hot. And warm when it should have been chilled.'

'I don't think dear Emma's quite got the hang of cooking yet. Perhaps she should practise a little more before inviting another six people to dinner.'

'I bet the Langleys knew what they were in for and invented an excuse not to turn up.'

'You could well be right. I think if Emma drank less during the preparation stage she might be more successful with her food.'

'So why did you make *us* go?' asked Kate.

'Emma Hope-Stanhope was so obviously out of place at the pub today that I wanted to find out what she was doing there.'

'Wasn't she there out of simple curiosity, like the rest of us?'

'I don't think so. The woman is too self-centred to be really interested in what's happening to anyone else. Her curiosity had to be connected to her husband or to herself.'

'And which was it?'

'From what her dear friends the Massens said, I'd guess that she was afraid that Jon was having an affair with Donna, and she wanted to find out whether the rest of the village knew about it.'

'Very good, Dr Watson.'

'What do you mean, *Dr Watson*? I was under the impression that *I* was the Sherlock Holmes here, not you.'

'Is this a competition?'

'Very likely.'

'Then I'm going to start making some new lists when we get home,' said Kate.

'What sort of lists?'

'Of things that don't fit.'

'Such as?'

'What happened to the Hope-Stanhopes' furniture?'

'You can start your lists when you've finished writing your thank-you note.'

'What about yours?'

'I am already composing something charmingly light-hearted in my head. We will dazzle them with our beautiful manners.'

'I think it's a bit late for that,' said Kate.

12

Next morning Roz reminded Kate that she had promised to look for Raven in the Broombanks flats.

'Are you sure I promised? I don't remember doing that.'

'I'm quite sure. And Tim Widdows heard you.'

'But I don't even know the man's name. I can't go enquiring after Raven, they'll think I'm a loony.'

'I'm sure you'll put your excellent brain to work and come up with some way of discovering his real name. And Tim's coming round this afternoon to drink our tea and check on how much you've discovered.'

'Do stop going on about Tim!'

'It's just my maternal concern for your emotional well-being.'

Kate made a noise that had something of the village 'mnerf' in it, and which was wholly uncomplimentary towards Roz *qua* mother.

But if Kate was honest, she was quite keen to get searching for the truth about Donna's death. And finding Raven and asking him what he knew seemed a good starting point. After all, if Donna had met him that evening after leaving Crossways Cottage, he might well be the last person to see her alive. He might know what she was doing in the Fullers' barn. Whether he would tell her all these things when she asked him about them was a separate problem.

Added to all of which, she didn't want Tim Widdows

to turn up that afternoon to find that she had achieved nothing. Not, of course, that she wished to fall in with her mother's plans in that direction. Oh, no. She thought about the problem for a moment, then made up her mind.

She went to the front door and looked out over the recreation field. There were a couple of young mothers, accompanied by children too young to go to school, sitting on the merry-go-round and talking and smoking in the sunlight. Kate wandered across the road and through the gate into the field.

'Good morning!' she called.

The two women looked up enquiringly. 'Yeah?' said one of them.

'Lovely day, isn't it,' said Kate, coming up to them. One of them was dark-haired and hugely overweight, the other was slimmer, with dyed blonde hair and black roots. 'I'm new here. My name's Kate,' and she smiled in a friendly and ingenuous manner.

'Yeah, all right,' said the overweight one.

'You just stop that, Ryan, or I'll land you one, you little bugger!' shouted the blonde. She managed the whole sequence with hardly a consonant, just a succession of glottal stops.

'Do you live nearby?' asked Kate.

'Down the Banks,' said the fat one unwillingly. 'Why? What is it to you?'

'That's at the other end of the village, isn't it?'

' 'S righ',' said the blonde. Both young women stared at Kate as though she came from another planet. As a matter of fact, she felt as though she did.

'I don't suppose you know a young man who lives somewhere in the Banks. He's got very dark hair pulled into a pony tail, and always wears black clothes,' she said as charmingly as she could.

The two women looked at each other and then stared at Kate. 'Why do you want to know for?'

'He knows a friend of mine,' she said. She was finding this conversation rather heavy going.

'Fancy him, do you?' asked the overweight one, and laughed.

'He'll do you a favour if you ask him nice enough,' said the other.

'It wasn't quite what I had in mind,' said Kate frostily. 'Do you know the man I mean?'

'Yeah. That'd be Russell, I reckon, don't you, Michelle?'

'I suppose.'

'And he lives in the block of flats in the Banks, doesn't he?'

'If he's a friend of this friend of yours, how come you don't know his name, or where he lives?'

'It's a very long story,' said Kate. 'I'm sure you don't want to hear it.'

'Reckon you just fancies him,' said the overweight one. 'Lots do. You're not the only one, you know. You'll just have to join the queue outside his door.' And they both laughed.

'Here, Melissa, stop doing that, will you, you little cow!' suddenly called the fat one.

An angelic-looking child hung upside-down on the climbing frame, showing her knickers and screaming at top volume. At the sound of her mother's voice she dropped to her feet and started to tear the head off a tough-looking small boy, presumably the Ryan who had been in trouble earlier. Ryan screamed.

'I'll be off now then,' said Kate. She felt that she had

once again failed to make two new friends, but at least she now knew the name of Donna's friend Raven – if the two women could be trusted, of course, which was far from certain.

She could feel their eyes boring into her back as she walked away from them and up the village street. Doubtless they would spend the next ten minutes talking about her and her unnatural attraction to Raven. No, Russell. She must start to think of him as Russell, or she would give herself away before she was ready.

She turned into Broombanks and stopped to get her bearings. Identical square semi-detached boxes were ranged on either side of the street. All along the kerb were parked rusting cars, once large and expensive, now come down in the world. She looked for someone to ask directions from. A couple of children were teasing a third just ahead of her, but she didn't like to interrupt them. They probably wouldn't understand her accent, anyway. Then an angry-looking old man with a black-and-white dog skulking at his heels came out of the gate to her right and turned towards her.

'Excuse me,' she said politely.

'What you want?' he replied.

'I was looking for . . .' What could she call him? 'Friend' seemed a bit of an over-statement. 'I was looking for someone called Russell,' she said.

'And what do you want with him?' responded the old man. The dog was now peeing against the front nearside tyre of a red Fiesta. His master did nothing to stop him.

'That's my business,' said Kate, who was starting to learn the local language. Keep on the offensive seemed to be the rule here.

'I believe he lives in the flats,' she added, with as much

aggression as she could manage, unprovoked.

'Well, there's the flats,' said the old man, pointing towards the far end of the street. 'You see them? I don't know which one's his, but you could try ringing a few doorbells, I suppose, see what happens.' And he laughed nastily, called his dog to heel and walked away without a word of goodbye.

Kate carried on past the children, past another house where the occupants appeared to be having a major row, complete with breaking furniture, past houses where the gardens grew nothing but motorbikes and rusty old baths, another house where a German shepherd dog snarled and strained towards her at the end of its chain, and finally confronted the grey, unattractive block of flats at the end of the street. What now?

The entry and hall smelled vaguely of mould and fungus, but luckily of nothing worse. Inside the lobby was another door, of reinforced glass, and this was locked. She was confronted by a row of six bells. It was obvious that she should ring one, announce herself, and she would then be buzzed in. None of the bells sported the name 'Russell', though if it was his first name, she wouldn't expect it to. She pushed at the door, but it didn't budge. The metal holder by the fifth bell held a card with a pencilled 'Paige'. So that was Donna's. Not much point in ringing that bell, then. She tried the sixth bell. No reply. The fourth. Still no reply. She tried the third.

The speaker grille by her left eye spluttered and a voice snapped, 'Yeah?'

'Russell?'

'Yeah.'

'Let me in!'

To her surprise, he buzzed her in. She took a quick look at the name next to his bell. It was Stevenson. All she had to do now was to talk herself into his flat, though if she had understood Michelle and her friend correctly, the fact that she was young and female would probably get her past his front door quite easily.

She walked up to the first floor. There were two flats on each floor, and she saw that one of the doors was open, and a young man was waiting for her in the doorway. He was about six feet tall, his skin was bronzed by the sun, his hair was black and held back in a pony tail, and his profile was that of a classical statue.

'Russell Stevenson?' she queried.

'Russell yes. Stevenson no,' he said. 'Stevenson's me mate. He rents this flat and I share it with him.'

She hadn't expected anyone this forthcoming in the village of Gatt's Hill. She smiled at him in a warm and friendly but asexual way. Or so she hoped. And she walked up to his door.

Close to, he was still good-looking, but his skin was pitted with the ancient craters of adolescent acne and he smelled of engine oil, stale cigarette smoke and raw onions.

'I'm looking for someone called Russell,' she said. 'I don't know his surname.'

'Who's looking?' he asked. His voice was a little higher than she was expecting, too.

'My name's Kate Ivory. I was a friend of Donna's.'

'Yeah?' He smiled, but not pleasantly, showing white, uneven teeth. 'I didn't know she had posh friends like you. Not women, anyway.'

'Can I come in? I'd like to talk.'

He snorted through his nose. 'It's all at your own risk,'

he said, and stood back to allow her to pass through the door.

She had been expecting a mess, she realized: tandoori takeaway cartons and squashed empty beer cans littering the floor. But Russell's flat was clean and tidy, and the only signs of occupation were the television flickering in the corner with the sound turned down and an ashtray on the low table with a couple of stubs in it. The carpet, patterned in ugly red and blue, had been recently vacuumed, and there were no dirty mugs lying around.

'Sit where you like,' said Russell.

Kate took a seat.

'Shall I get you a tea or something?' he asked awkwardly, as though drilled in this politeness long ago by his mother.

'No thanks.'

'Well, what you want? You a social worker or something?'

'No, nothing like that. I'm a writer, actually, and I'm staying in Aphra Callan's cottage at the other end of the village.'

'What sort of name is that!' Russell had taken a chair next to hers but at right angles to it, and he leant back with his long legs stretched across the carpet. His clothes were all black, and there was something disturbing about the physicality of the man. I can see the animal nature hidden inside the human male, thought Kate in what was for her an uncharacteristically flowery way.

'Aphra's a daft name,' agreed Kate. 'I always call her Callie. Anyway, like I said, I'm staying in Crossways Cottage, and a couple of days ago Donna Paige turned up to do the gardening.'

'Yeah? So?' Russell began to roll himself a cigarette.

'You want one of these?' he asked. Kate shook her head. She was mesmerised by his nicotine-stained fingers as they delicately packed the tobacco into the thin paper. He looked at her sharply, then licked the edge to close the tube of tobacco. He had a long, very red tongue, and it caressed the paper for what seemed too long a time.

'Donna said she was meeting her boyfriend later that evening.' Kate was ashamed to notice that her voice was not entirely steady. 'She didn't tell me his name, but she said she called him Raven. Is that you?' There seemed no point in beating about the bush. Either Russell would tell her or he wouldn't. Any more pussyfooting around wasn't going to help, she knew. Not that Russell really looked like a raven. She would have chosen a more dangerous bird to name him by. An eagle, or some kind of hawk.

'Why do you want to know? What's it got to do with you? I don't understand why you come round here asking me these questions. You sure you're not from the social?'

'Quite sure.'

'Or the police, maybe?'

'Certainly not. Do I look like the police?'

'You look like a posh bird who's lost her way and wandered into a council estate,' said Russell.

'And that's rather what I feel like.'

'So go on. Tell me why you're asking all these questions about my mate Donna.'

'I feel sort of responsible.'

'Don't be daft! She just come to do the garden. She wasn't anything to do with you.'

'But I'm interested. And I don't like what they're saying in the village.'

'What's that, then?'

She was sure he knew already. 'They say she died of an accidental drug overdose.'

'And why don't you think she did, then?'

'She just wasn't the type.'

He laughed at her. 'You can tell the type after an hour or two over a cup of tea, can you?'

'Do you think she was taking drugs?' She went on the offensive, the way she was learning to do in Gatt's Hill.

'Nah, I don't believe she'd do a thing like that. Though with the company she was keeping, I can't be sure.'

'And are you her boyfriend? Did she call you Raven?'

'Nah! Not me. We was mates. We'd have a laugh, and maybe share a roll-up, but there wasn't anything more to it than that. And don't go calling me Raven. That's not what she called me. I was Russell to her. She wasn't interested in me. She had her sights set on something much higher.'

'What do you mean?'

'I don't know who the man was, but she would talk about him sometimes. About his posh car and his suits and his money and that.'

'And you think he was the one she called Raven?'

'I know he was. That's what she always called him when she talked about him.'

'Did he have anything to do with the antiques fairs she went to?'

'Maybe. I don't know about that. She only talked about going to fancy restaurants and that when she was with him.'

'But she was interested in the fairs.'

'Yeah. She reckoned to make money at them. Buying and selling stuff and that.'

'Where can I find out more about her?' Kate was really

just talking to herself. She didn't expect an answer.

'She looked after quite a few gardens in the village. And then there was one of them blokes down at Gatts Farm. He was the one who knew about old furniture and stuff.'

'Derek Fuller?' She was surprised.

'Nah. Not him, nor his poncey son. No, it was one of the workmen, carpenters and that, they had working for them out the back. I don't know which one, but I suppose you could ask around. You found me, so I suppose you can find him.'

'They were saying in the pub that Donna would go with anyone. Do you think she was like that?'

'Who was saying that?'

'It was the general opinion, I think.'

'Tell me his name and I'll smash his face in for him.'

'I don't know any names, I'm afraid.'

'You don't believe it, do you?' he asked belligerently, taking a final drag on his roll-up before stubbing it out in the ashtray.

'Like you said, I only knew her for an hour or two, but I wouldn't believe it of Donna, no.'

'Good.'

'And you're sure you didn't see Donna that evening?'

'Oh yes. I saw her all right. She was going out in a skinny little black dress and a stupid pair of shoes, teetering along with her bum stuck out. She didn't see me but I saw her.'

'Where did she go? Did someone come to pick her up in a car?'

'No. She was on her own. She went off down Broombanks, but I didn't see which way she went after that. And that bloke of hers, that Raven, he never come to the flats. He always made her go to where he was.'

'I wonder why,' said Kate.

'Maybe she was ashamed of where she lived. You never know what's going to happen out there. You can get your big shiny car scratched and dented, and the wheel trim will be ripped off before you can turn round.'

'But you never saw her with this man?'

'I see her with different blokes over the last year or so, but I don't think none of them meant nothing to her. There was no one she would call Raven.'

'Just one more thing,' said Kate. 'Did you happen to notice whether she was wearing that blue pendant thing of hers?'

'The little glass bottle? She always wore it. I don't remember seeing her without it.'

'But was she wearing it that evening?'

'I don't remember particularly. But I'd have noticed if she didn't. She must have had it on.'

'Thanks for the information,' said Kate. 'I'll buy you a pint next time I see you at the pub.'

'No need for that. And you best be going now,' said Russell. 'I got to go out and meet me mates. They'll wonder where I got to. And your mates will wonder what you've been getting up to in here.'

'Thanks for your help,' said Kate.

'See you around,' said Russell, and opened the front door for her to leave.

'Goodbye, darlin'!' he called after her on the stairs. 'Come back any time. I won't throw you out.'

But Kate had the impression that these remarks were for the benefit of any mates of his that might be listening, rather than for herself.

13

'You're looking very pleased with yourself,' said Roz when Kate returned to Crossways Cottage.

'I am. And I deserve to be,' said Kate, hanging up her jacket and throwing herself down on to a chair. 'What's for lunch?'

'You don't fancy the pub again?'

'No, I do not. And I suppose that means you want me to cook.'

'That would be a very nice idea. Thank you, sweetie.'

While Kate looked for vegetables and peered into the freezer to see if anything could be put straight into a hot oven, Roz said crossly, 'Are you going to tell me what happened? I can't bear that smug expression on your face any longer.'

'I thought I'd wait for Tim Widdows to turn up. What time did you expect him?'

'Not until four o'clock. I can't wait till then!'

'You'll just have to. I'm not going through it all twice.'

And when Kate had set the lunch to cook, she went upstairs and made detailed notes on her conversation with Russell. If they were going to play at *Three Go Adventuring*, then she'd better get serious about it.

'Truce,' said Roz when she went downstairs again. 'I've opened a bottle of New Zealand sauvignon blanc and poured you a glass.'

Kate looked at her suspiciously. 'Does this mean you're

not going to nag me about my findings until Tim gets here?'

'I shall be discretion her very self.'

'Hmm. I'll believe that when I see it.'

Tim arrived at five minutes past four. He had a newspaper in his hand and the three of them gravitated naturally towards the kitchen, where they sat at the table with the newspaper spread out in front of them.

'It's the local rag,' said Tim. 'It had just come into the shop and I thought I'd pick up a copy to see what they've said about Donna.'

'It looks as though someone's been doing a fair bit of homework,' said Kate. 'This gives us quite a bit of background on her.'

'Share out the pages,' said Roz. So they pulled the paper to pieces and each took a page to read. After a minute or two, Kate went to fetch her notebook and pen so that she could make notes. She caught the look that passed between Roz and Tim.

'No, this is not therapy for me,' she said. 'But I think that if we're going to try to find out what happened, we'd better approach the problem methodically.'

'How did I ever give birth to a daughter like this?' asked Roz.

'I can't imagine,' said Tim. And then they all read in silence for a while.

'Swap you,' said Roz eventually, and they exchanged pages.

Kate looked at her notes. *Donna Paige*, she had written.

1. Background.

Age: 22. Born in village of Middle Hensford to Annette Paige, then aged 28 and unmarried. Father generally supposed to be a local farm labourer who did not marry Annette when she found she was pregnant, and who moved away from the district before Donna was born. He disappeared from view and was never seen again. Annette Paige worked at various cleaning jobs and got by on a combination of her wages and social security. Donna went to local schools where she was lively but uninterested in any academic subjects. She left school at sixteen, as soon as she was able. She had three GCSEs, grades unspecified. When she was 17, her mother met and married a younger man, who didn't like the idea of having Donna to live with them. Annette and her new husband went to live in Australia (they said) the following year. No one seems to have an address for them and they have not been seen since they moved away. Donna was then left on her own. Her only other relation was her mother's Uncle Len, Annette's mother's eldest brother, who is now in his late eighties and in residential care in East Oxford. Staff at the home did not think that it would be helpful to question him about Donna as his memory was not very good and he would get upset if they insisted. They did not feel that he had any information to give about Donna's life in the past couple of years.

2. *Recent history.*

After Donna's mother left, she joined several squats, living on social security and by begging for a time in the streets of Oxford. Then, about three years ago, she was offered a flat in Broombanks, which she accepted, and she started to remember her love of and skill at gardening. By the time of her death she was working for about twenty-five hours a week in various gardens in and around the village of Gatt's Hill. All her employers spoke of her reliability and dedication to the job.

3. *Comments by those who knew her.*

A schoolfriend: 'She was just ordinary, really. She had big ideas about what she was going to do, but it was just the usual stuff about marrying a rich rock star or someone like that and living in a big house.'

Her head teacher: 'I think she was just a normal girl, looking for the normal things in life. I believe that she wanted an ordinary home with a mother and father, and when she couldn't have them, she was looking to settle down with a boyfriend and start her own family. I can't believe that this has happened to her. And I don't believe all the uncharitable things that people are saying about her. That certainly isn't the Donna I knew when she was here.'

'Shall I make the tea now?' asked Roz.

'What?'

'You look as though you're set to write a complete novel there. I thought Tim and I could do with some sustenance, even if you're above all that sort of thing.'

'Oh, thanks. Yes, what a good idea.' And Kate returned to her notes while Roz and Tim boiled kettles and rummaged around for biscuits and the end of a fruit cake.

A neighbour in Broombanks: 'Donna was a weird one, really. She was always bragging about what she was going to do and how much money she was going to have. She used to talk about this posh boyfriend

of hers, with the big flash car, who used to take her
out to restaurants and that, but none of us ever saw
him and I don't believe he existed really. Yes, I
suppose she had quite a few boyfriends. She wasn't
bad-looking, really, and if you're not too particular, I
suppose you can be popular with blokes.'

Another neighbour: 'She was just a little tart, like
all them young girls nowadays, walking around
showing their legs up to the crotch. Well, it's not
right, that sort of thing. It's asking for trouble, isn't
it? What else can they expect? You can't blame the
men for taking them up on an invitation like that.
And playing that music all day and night so that a
person can't get any peace. It isn't right.'

'Give it a rest for a while, Kate,' said Roz. 'Come and join
us in the other room.'

Kate found that her mother had not only made tea,
but had put together a green salad and a boiled egg with
fingers of brown bread and butter which Tim was
tucking into. She raised her eyebrows at her mother in
enquiry.

'I'm sure dear Tim never gets any proper food in the
Vicarage flat,' she said. 'I thought he could do with
building up.'

'Is this one of your rare attacks of maternal feeling?'
asked Kate.

'That's not fair of you,' said Tim. 'Your mother is being
very kind to me, and I really appreciate it.'

'Take no notice of my daughter. She has been turned
into a sour old spinster by her unfortunate experiences
of life.'

'Roz!' protested Kate.

'I suppose I shall get used to the way you two talk to each other, eventually,' said Tim in a puzzled tone.

'Don't you worry about us. You just eat up your nice egg like a good boy,' said Kate.

'That's the sort of thing I mean,' sighed Tim.

Kate drank her tea and watched the two of them. Tim ate in a pernickety, precise way, chewing his food a couple of dozen times, like a well-behaved child in the nursery. He had doubtless had two conventional, loving parents who had brought him up to be a responsible member of society; one day, he would make some lucky woman a very good and reliable husband. Roz, on the other hand, was slurping her tea with gusto, and had managed to transfer some of the chocolate from her biscuit on to her chin. At that moment she realized what she had done and wiped it off, then licked the chocolate off her finger. Oh dear, no wonder there's no hope for me in the polite world, thought Kate. Neither of us will make any man a very good wife, I'm afraid.

'Now, I've been amazingly patient,' said Roz. 'But I think you can stop writing up your research notes, Kate, and tell us both what happened when you went to see Raven.'

'Give me a chance to drink my tea,' said Kate, knowing that she was teasing her mother.

'Sod the tea! You've always been able to eat and drink while talking,' said her mother. 'Sorry, Tim. I'll try to watch my language while you're here, but it's very difficult when my daughter's behaving like this.'

'I think you'd better get on with your story, Kate,' said Tim.

'Very well. I found out where the man with the classical

profile and the pony tail lives. His name is Russell, by the way, and he lives in the same block of flats as Donna.'

'Brilliant!' said Roz.

'But I don't think he's Raven. In fact, I'm sure he isn't. He knew about Raven, but he'd never seen him. He reckoned that Donna kept him hidden from all her Gatt's Hill mates.'

'Did he know whether she went out with Raven, or someone else, the night she died?' asked Tim.

'He saw her going off, and he assumed, as we did, that she was meeting a boyfriend. She was all tarted up, apparently, and he saw her walking down Broombanks, but he didn't see which way she went when she got to the end of the road.'

'Pity,' said Roz.

'Yes. One thing does occur to me, though. Russell mentioned her impractical shoes, and I imagine they're the same as the ones she was wearing when Tim identified the body.'

'I expect so,' said Tim.

'But it doesn't sound as though she'd go walking far in shoes like that. We know she owned shoes for tramping around these lanes, so she must have been going a few hundred yards at the most in those heels.'

'Good thinking,' said Tim.

'And there's one more thing. Russell thought she must have been wearing her blue pendant. He said he'd have noticed if she wasn't.'

'Do you think that means much?' asked Tim.

'I think so. After all, I'd not really notice if you were wearing your dog collar. But I would if you weren't, if you see what I mean.'

'Yes, I think so.'

'It's not exactly a one hundred per cent certainty,' said Roz. 'But it must be an eighty per cent chance that she was wearing it, don't you think?'

'I'd go along with that,' said Kate.

'What do we do now?' asked Tim.

'I'm going back to my note-making,' said Kate. 'Then we can see what we know and what we need to find out.'

'Have you got to the part in the report where it talks about how she died?' asked Roz.

'Not yet. I was just going to start on that section.'

'Well, don't get too upset. I'm sure they've got it all wrong. You know what these newspapers are.'

4. Death.

The police say that the post mortem shows that she died of heroin poisoning. An empty syringe and a packet with traces of the drug were found near the body. Other equipment usual with drug-takers was also present. There was no evidence that Donna had taken the drug before, and at the moment it is being assumed that she was experimenting with it for the first time, with fatal consequences. They did not know whether anyone else was involved, or present at the time, but they appealed for anyone with information to come forward.

5. General comments.

The general impression given was of a girl who lived in a fantasy world and who dreamed of escaping to an exciting lifestyle. She had a number of boyfriends, and one of them doubtless introduced her to this new thrill, with fatal consequences.

'Bastards,' said Kate. 'Oh, sorry, Vicar. But they aren't

exactly full of goodwill towards their fellow men, are they? They all seem to have put the worst possible interpretation on to everything that happened.'

'It makes it easier for them,' said Roz. 'If they can make Donna fit a stereotype they can explain away her death in the usual way.'

'Well, I don't believe them,' said Kate.

'And neither do I,' said Tim bravely.

'There are too many loose ends,' said Kate.

'Like what?' asked Roz.

'There's the boyfriend, Raven, for one. Just because Russell turned out not to be him, it doesn't mean he doesn't exist. Who is he? And what was he doing the night she died? And is Emma Hope-Stanhope right? Was her husband having a fling with Donna? I can't see it myself, but it's a possibility. There's even a remote chance that Jon could be Raven. I suppose she could have been attracted by his money and background. Then there's the pendant. If Donna was wearing it when she went out – and I think we can assume that she was – then what happened to it? Who has it now? And there's a third thing. Her shoes.'

'You mean she couldn't have walked as far as Gatts Farm in them,' said Tim.

'That's true. But from your description of the show-room, and how immaculate it was, I can't believe that she wouldn't have taken them off. She always took her shoes off, didn't she?'

'She certainly took them off before she came into the Vicarage flat,' said Tim. 'I remember she always wore brightly coloured socks to pad around in.' He stopped suddenly, took off his spectacles and rubbed at his eyes. 'I'm sorry about that,' he said. 'It's just that I suddenly saw her the way she used to be, so alive, so bright, so pretty.'

'Yes,' said Roz. 'We remember her that way, too, Tim. Which is why the three of us are going to find out what really happened.'

'There's another thing,' said Kate, leafing through her notes. 'When I was talking to Russell, he told me that she knew one of the men down at Gatts Farm. Do they have many people working there?'

'Quite a few of them,' said Tim. 'The yellow vans you see driving through the village are theirs. Derek goes on buying trips and the vans collect the goods he buys and bring them to the farm. Then the furniture is mended and done up, and generally made to look expensive and desirable. There are quite extensive workrooms beyond the showrooms, and there must be a couple of dozen people working there, as well as the drivers.'

'I never imagined that the business was that big,' said Kate.

'They keep it looking like a modest, intimate place, but it's more like a small factory,' said Tim.

'It is the first real link we've found between Donna and the place where she died,' said Roz. 'Can we find an excuse to go and nose around?'

'I imagine the ghouls have mostly left by now. I could go and visit Hazel Fuller again, to make sure she's recovered from her ordeal,' said Tim.

'But you couldn't really take us tagging along with you, could you?' said Kate. 'I'm sure it's against vicars' regulations.'

'No, we can't follow Tim in to comfort Hazel,' said Roz. 'But we could take a small, desirable piece of furniture down to sell, couldn't we? Preferably one that needs some work doing to it.'

'But we haven't got any furniture to sell,' said Kate, hoping that her mother was not about to suggest that they help themselves to some of Callie's.

'I'm sure your friend Callie wouldn't mind if we borrowed a small piece of hers,' said Roz.

'I'm not at all sure about that,' said Kate.

'I can help you here,' said Tim before they could get going on one of their vigorous arguments. 'There's a rather pretty little bureau that my grandmother left me, and it's in the Vicarage flat. If we could fit it into the boot of Kate's car, we could take it down to Gatts Farm and ask their opinion of it.'

'What an excellent idea,' said Roz. 'Do you really want to sell it?'

'No. I'm rather fond of it, actually. But they could take a look at it, and give me a quote for the repairs I'm sure it needs.'

'Excellent man,' said Roz. 'When shall we go?'

'How about tomorrow morning?' said Kate.

'I'll try to get it down the iron stairs ready for you,' said Tim valiantly.

'I'm a big, strong woman. I wouldn't like to think that you'd do your back in, or even worse, damage the bureau. I'll come up and give you a hand,' said Kate. 'Would ten o'clock suit you?'

14

Luckily the bureau was both small and compact. Kate had arrived in the Vicarage flat and she and Tim were considering how to get it down the stairs.

'I've taken everything out of it,' said Tim.

'So I see,' said Kate, looking around her with interest.

Heaps of papers, books and pamphlets lay around the small room. A scattering of paperclips and biro caps filled in some of the empty spaces.

'It's a bit untidy in here,' said Tim, as though he had only just noticed.

'Funny, I had you down for an impeccably neat person,' said Kate.

'Most people take me for an anal retentive,' sighed Tim. 'But I do make an effort to fight against it.'

'And I'm sure you've succeeded,' said Kate, picking up a sock from the middle of the desk and reuniting it with its pair on the arm of the sofa. She was starting to like the vicar, after all.

'Would you like a coffee before we begin?' he asked.

'I think we'd better get on with moving the bureau. We could reward ourselves with a coffee at Crossways Cottage later. What's supposed to be wrong with the bureau, by the way? It looks perfect to me. You'll find yourself selling it to the Fullers if you're not careful.'

'It is pretty, isn't it? But there's damage to one of the drawers. I'd like them to make a new back for it.'

'Are they any good, do you reckon? They look pricey to me.'

'I expect they are. But it would be bad PR for them to overcharge the local vicar, don't you think?'

'I do hope you're right.' She looked at her watch. 'We'd better get on. How do you suggest we get it downstairs?'

'I think it will go through the door sideways,' said Tim, starting to turn the bureau. 'Which side of it do you want to go?'

'I'll take this side. You can manage the walking backwards down a flight of stairs part,' said Kate.

Luckily the stairs were broad, the treads shallow and the flight straight. With a certain amount of minor swearing (from Kate) and huffing (from Tim) they reached the bottom with the bureau still intact. Kate had already folded down the back seats of the car and they slid the bureau into the space with no trouble.

'Is Roz not with you?' asked Tim.

'She decided to leave it to us. And anyway, she didn't fancy being squashed in with the bureau.'

'I'm glad we're on our own,' said Tim.

'She can be a bit overpowering, certainly,' said Kate, wilfully misunderstanding him. She put the car into reverse and executed one of her seven-point turns.

'Should we have warned them we're on our way?' wondered Kate as she drove out of the Vicarage and aimed for Gatts Farm.

'I think we should keep the advantage of surprise,' said Tim.

When they reached the gate to Gatts Farm Antiques they found it standing open and Kate drove through into the courtyard and parked at the end by the side of one of the barns.

Showrooms Open said a wooden sign and helpfully pointed them in the right direction.

'Have we got a plan?' asked Tim belatedly.

'We look at everything we can, talk to everyone we can meet, and talk about the bureau only when challenged.'

'Why don't we just walk in and say I've brought it to be repaired?'

'Because we'd be in and out again within five minutes.'

'Oh, I see.'

'I'd have thought your job would have made you more devious,' said Kate. 'We want to find the man who was Donna's friend, and possibly the one she called Raven.'

'I'm starting to lose faith in the existence of Raven.'

'Don't do that. Think of all the other things you have to believe in, in your line of work. Raven's a doddle after them.'

'I'd feel more comfortable if you stopped attacking my beliefs.'

'Sorry. Take no notice of me.'

'What else should we do, do you think?' asked Tim in a forgiving tone.

'We can just nose around, see if there's anything the police have missed that will mean something to us.'

'I don't think the police were very interested in looking for clues. They'd made their mind up as soon as they saw her. You don't think there's a possibility they're right?'

'Of course not. Come on. Follow me.'

They went into the first showroom, which was much as Tim remembered it from his last visit. Perhaps one or two items had been sold and replaced with others, but he was too ignorant of what he was looking at to be sure.

'Do you know anything about antiques?' he asked.

'Hardly anything. How about you?'

'Even less.'

'So we'd better not pretend. We'd be found out far too quickly. Only lie if you're sure you can get away with it.'

They wandered round the room, which was deserted except for the two of them.

'I can't see anything unusual here,' said Kate. 'Let's try the next room. Is this the one where—'

'Yes.'

Again, the room looked unchanged from his last visit, except that someone had removed the chair where Donna had been sitting, and there were no syringes on the small table.

Kate was examining the carpets. 'This is a lovely rug,' she said. 'At least as good as the ones Callie has in her cottage. I can't believe that Donna wouldn't take off her shoes.'

'I'm sure you're right.' Tim was bent double, searching the floor for something, peering under chests, sliding his hands down the sides of chair cushions.

'What are you looking for?'

'The pendant. I agree with you that she wouldn't go out without it, and I know she wasn't wearing it when I saw her next morning. I wondered if she dropped it in here somewhere.'

They were both busy in their search, Kate shifting a bookcase in order to look behind it, Tim lifting up a tasselled cushion and shaking it, when someone entered the room.

'Do you need any help?' he said.

'Oh. Ah,' said Tim unhelpfully.

'I seem to have dropped one of my earrings,' said Kate with what she thought was great presence of mind.

'You're wearing two of them at the moment,' said the

man. 'Did you have many more when you arrived?'

'I am? Goodness! How silly of me!' And she gave him the benefit of her most outrageous smile. 'How do you do? I'm Kate Ivory and I'm staying in Aphra Callan's cottage for a while. And this is the Reverend Widdows, vicar of St Michael and All Saints' Church, Gatt's Hill.'

'Call me Tim,' said Tim.

The man was looking amused at this performance. 'How do you do?' he said very politely. 'And I am Dr Anthony Fuller, of Leicester College, Oxford, temporary furniture salesman. Why don't you call me Tony?'

Tony Fuller was average height, average build, and a very average-looking man. He had a lot of light brown curly hair and the blue eyes and fair skin that often go with it. He wore a faded red sweatshirt and baggy corduroy trousers, suitable for both an antiques salesman and for an Oxford don, thought Kate. His accent, too, was unplaceable and classless, equally suitable for don and salesman.

'Did you say Leicester?' asked Tim.

'Yes. Do you know it?'

'I was an undergraduate there.'

'Really? We must get together over a pint some time.'

Kate remained silent on the subject of her own Leicester connection.

'So you're Hazel's son,' said Tim, working it out.

'Correct. Though she's away for the present, recovering from the shock of recent events.'

'Of course. I am so very sorry about what happened.' Tim had gone into professional mode again.

'I'm sure you were very helpful to my mother,' said Tony briskly. 'Now, is there anything in particular you were looking for, or do you just want to browse?'

'We're just browsing,' said Kate.

And, 'I've brought my bureau to be repaired,' said Tim simultaneously.

'We've heard you have workshops here,' said Kate. 'Do you think we could have a look? I keep telling Tim that he shouldn't take everything on trust.'

'You want to check out our workmanship before you commit yourself,' said Tony Fuller. 'How very sensible of you. I can take you through to the workshops if you like, and you can browse away as we go, Kate.' He turned to Tim. 'What sort of bureau is it? What do you think needs repairing?'

'I don't know exactly what it is, but I do know it's old,' said Tim. 'It came to me from my grandmother and one of the drawers is damaged.'

'Come on through,' said Tony.

They passed through several more showrooms, then out into another yard. This one was still clean, but less prettified than the entrance courtyard. There were no tubs of plants, but serviceable-looking buildings with wide doors. Sounds of sawing, planing and hammering came from within, with a background of Fox Radio middle-of-the-road pop music.

'Goodness! This place is much bigger than I expected!' gushed Kate. 'How many people do you employ?'

'I couldn't tell you exactly. I'm afraid I don't get all that involved with the business. But quite a few.'

'Of course, you have your own work, don't you?' Kate was twinkling up at him in a shameless way.

'Yes, although I've always been interested in the antiques my father deals in,' he said. 'It's only a question of work priorities that keeps me away. Now, let's go in here. I think we'll find items being repaired in this workshop.'

The first thing Kate noticed was the wonderful smell of wood, then the heady scent of glue and varnish. She reminded herself that she was supposed to be looking for Raven rather than getting high on solvents, and she looked round the workshop, trying to gauge how many people were employed here. Seven or eight at least, she calculated. Maybe even ten or a dozen. And this was only one of a number of workshops. How was she to find out which of the workmen was Donna's friend?

'Let's go and talk to Joe,' said Tony.

Joe was about fifty and wore a thick gold band on his left hand. He was square and weathered and had a flat tweed cap on wispy grey hair. Not Raven, decided Kate. Joe was working on a desk that was much bigger and clumsier than the one now lying in the back of her car, and while Tony introduced Tim to Joe and let the older man show him what he was doing, Kate wandered off on her own.

There were alleyways between the benches, lined with furniture and parts of furniture. Where on earth had it all come from? She hadn't the knowledge to place it as to date or even country of origin. But surely there wasn't still this much old furniture lying forgotten in grannies' attics? She turned a corner and came upon another workman, younger this time, who was doing something incomprehensible to a chair leg. Kate smiled at him.

'Hello,' she tried.

He put the chair leg down. He was rather nice-looking if you liked your men young and hunky, thought Kate.

'That looks fascinating,' she said.

'You interested in antique furniture, then?' he asked.

147

'A bit,' she ventured. 'But I don't really know anything about it. I suppose you must have learned a lot, working here.' She had found that this flattering approach worked with most men. By the way he was smiling at her she judged that she was winning this one over.

'I know some. It's wood I know about mostly,' he said. He looked Kate over approvingly as though she were a particularly well-matured oak plank. She practised her twinkling technique in return. He looked at his watch.

'I'm due for a break,' he said. 'Do you want to come outside?'

'What for?' asked Kate suspiciously. The twinkling was working a little too well.

'We're not allowed to smoke in here. The whole place would go up in a few seconds if someone dropped a lighted match.'

'I hadn't thought of that.' And she followed him outside.

Someone had placed – or constructed, more likely – a south-facing bench against the barn wall. A thick sprinkling of cigarette ends showed that this was where the company's smokers came to pass their breaks. They sat down. The sun was trying to shine through the layer of grey cloud and this spot was pleasantly warm.

'My name's Kate, by the way,' she said.

'I'm Carl,' he said. 'Here, have one of these.'

Kate shook her head. 'Sorry, I don't smoke.'

'Suit yourself.' He lit up.

She waited for him to draw in the first couple of lungfuls of smoke, then she said, 'It must have been terrible for you all.'

'The dead girl, do you mean?'

'Yes.' What else was there!

'Is that what you come here for? You from the press or summat?'

'No, no. I've come with a friend of mine who's finding out about getting an old desk mended. I read about the death in the paper yesterday, though. Makes you wonder, doesn't it?'

'Yeah. Funny old business.'

Kate was thinking that she hadn't chosen the chattiest of Fullers' employees. She tried again. 'Did you know her? Donna, that is.'

'I've seen her around, but I didn't know her. Not as such. You sound like you did.'

'Not very well, but she did the garden at the cottage where I'm staying in the village.'

'Miss Callan's,' said Carl.

'I suppose everybody knows everybody else's business here.'

'We knew she was off to the States and lent her cottage to some writer woman.'

'That's me,' said Kate modestly.

'I don't read books much,' said Carl, dismissing the subject.

'And I don't know about antiques,' said Kate, summing up their lack of common interests. 'Donna did, though, didn't she?'

'I don't know if she knew much about this furniture. She certainly didn't know much about wood, but she was into those knick-knack things.'

'Perfume bottles,' said Kate.

'Yeah. She and Graham were always off to those antiques fairs. They thought they were going to make their fortunes.'

'And were they?'

'Fat chance. You only make money in this game if you've got the capital to invest in the first place. It's the same as any other business.'

'Does Graham work here?'

'He used to. He's left now.'

'Did he leave recently?'

'What are all the questions for? Are you sure you're not from the press? I don't mind talking to reporters, but you got to pay me the going rate.'

And there was I thinking my grey eyes were currency enough, thought Kate. 'I'm still not a reporter,' she said. 'But I am interested in 1930s scent bottles and I wondered whether Graham could put me on the track of something interesting. Do you know where he lives?'

'Out Cowley or Rose Hill way, I think.'

'How am I going to find him?'

'You'll find him at an antiques fair,' said Carl unhelpfully.

'Any idea which one? I gather there are thousands of them.'

'There's one in Lower Hensford tomorrow. I know he usually tries to do that one.'

'Thanks, Carl. I owe you one.'

'Yeah, well—'

But at this moment they were interrupted by the appearance of Tim Widdows, who came round the corner of a barn into their sunny enclave.

'There you are!' he exclaimed.

'Morning, Vicar,' said Carl.

'Call me Tim,' said Tim predictably. 'Kate, we've been looking everywhere for you.'

'Now you've found me. What is it you want?'

'The keys to your car. I'm leaving the bureau here to be

repaired, but I can't get it out of the boot.'

'I'll come and open it for you.'

She waved goodbye to Carl and she and Tim Widdows made their way back to the front of the antiques show-room where Kate unlocked the car for them. Two strong men from the workshop manhandled the bureau out of the car and away to the back of the barn while Tony Fuller supervised the action.

'Thanks, Tony,' said Tim, shaking hands. 'I'm really impressed with what you're doing here.'

'Thank you, Tim,' said Tony. 'We'll try to live up to your expectations.' He turned to Kate. 'Did you manage to find everything you were looking for?' he asked.

'I wasn't looking for anything specific,' she said. 'But I had a very interesting tour, yes.'

'I'm so glad. You must come and see us again. If you need expert information, of course, you'll have to see my father. I'm sure you and he would get on well together.'

'Goodbye, Tony. Don't forget about that pint,' said Tim.

Tim and Kate got into the car and Kate turned it round and drove out of the gateway and up the hill to the main part of the village.

'Well?' demanded Tim.

'Well what?'

'What were you doing in that compromising situation with the woodworking Romeo?'

'You have got sweet old-fashioned notions, haven't you? Carl and I were just having an informative conversation.'

'It looked like a heavy flirtation when I turned up.'

'Rubbish. And Carl told me the name of Donna's friend at Gatts Farm Antiques.'

'Oh! Well done!'

'I thought you'd approve. His name is Graham.'

'Graham. Graham what? Where does he live?'

'I don't know. Carl was getting a bit narked at all the questions I was asking. I couldn't ask any more without making him too suspicious.'

'So how are we going to find him? Does he still work at Gatts Farm?'

'He used to, but he's left. We can find him at an antiques fair.'

'There are thousands!'

'But he's going to be at the one at Lower Hensford tomorrow. I can't believe there'll be too many Grahams to choose from.'

'Saturday,' said Tim, looking worried. 'It's a busy day for me. What time is the fair?'

'I don't know. But I imagine that the local paper you brought us yesterday will have the details. Come back to Crossways Cottage and I'll make you the coffee I promised you, and if you're very lucky, you can stay to lunch.'

15

'Here it is,' said Tim, turning to the back of the well-thumbed newspaper and scanning the advertisements for forthcoming events in the neighbourhood.

'Lower Hensford Antiques Fair. The New Parish Hall. From ten in the morning until four-thirty,' said Kate, reading. 'Well, that gives us plenty of chance to get there and suss out Graham. How are you fixed for free time tomorrow, Tim?'

'How about between twelve and two?' he asked. 'I know it's not the best of times, but it's the only window I have free.'

'Fine. We'll pick you up at twelve o'clock at the Vicarage.'

'Are you coming with us, Roz?' asked Tim.

'I thought you'd never ask,' said Roz. 'As long as I'm not playing gooseberry, that is.'

'Don't be ridiculous,' said Kate briskly. 'You know you'll be very welcome to come with us. Now, what would people like for lunch?'

After lunch, when Tim had departed to do whatever vicars do in the afternoon, Kate wandered round the cottage, feeling unsettled. She had made some progress that morning, after all. She had seen the place where Donna had died, even if it had been well tidied up by now. She had chatted to Carl and found out about Graham. She might even be on the track of Raven when she and Tim went to the antiques fair and found his stand. And she had met Tony Fuller. She would prefer to meet Hazel and Derek, who seemed to be central players in the affair, but meeting their son was a start, certainly.

'There was something wrong about this morning, wasn't there?' said Roz, appearing to read her mind. 'What was it?'

'It was something to do with Tony Fuller.'

'Was he tall and dashing, with black hair and flashing eyes?'

'I'm afraid he was pleasant, intelligent, and on the mousy side.'

'So what was wrong with him?'

'He said he was a Fellow of Leicester College.'

'That's in Oxford, isn't it? Part of the university.'

'Yes. I used to have a friend who was a Fellow there.'

'Ah.'

'What do you mean "Ah"?'

'I sense a story.'

'Well, I'll keep it short for you. I thought he and I were a couple, an item, and it turned out that he'd been two-timing me for months. He was just a lying bastard. End of story.'

'What was this snake's name?'

'Liam. Liam Ross.'

'You shouldn't let it turn you sour for the rest of your life.'

'Me, sour? Don't be ridiculous! He's in America now and I'd forgotten all about him until Tony Fuller mentioned his college.'

'If you say so.'

'I think I'll do some cleaning. The cottage is starting to look a mess.'

'That's right. Change the subject.'

'I'm changing the subject because there's no more to say on it. Shove over a bit. I want to hoover behind that chair.'

'You shouldn't be hoovering that rug,' said Roz. 'You'll ruin the fringes and your friend will be justifiably annoyed when she sees it.'

'How do you suggest I remove the crumbs and nail clippings?' asked Kate.

'With a dustpan and brush,' replied Roz seriously. 'A little gentle brushing, always in the direction of the pile, that's all it needs.'

'If you say so,' said Kate, opening the cupboard door and rootling around for the dustpan and brush. She knew Callie must have them somewhere. It was easier to go along with what Roz demanded than attempt to argue with her. It always had been. She wondered for a moment how she might have developed if she had argued with her mother more often. Too late to worry about that now. She swept the rug, gently, in the direction of the pile, avoiding the fringe. It was a surprisingly soothing thing to do.

When she had cleaned through the cottage, which didn't take long since it was in fact quite clean already, Roz tackled her again.

'I think you've punished yourself enough for one day,' she said.

'What do you mean? I have no need to punish myself. I don't know what you're talking about.'

'So why have you isolated yourself up here? If that isn't punishment for a gregarious person like you, I don't know what is.'

'I had to get away from that place. I told you about it. Andrew died there, remember?'

'I know. You told me that. But that isn't all you've done. It must have been terrible – oppressive – to be living in the house where your friend was killed, but I still don't understand why you've cut yourself off so completely from your life in Oxford. No one's phoned since I've been here. No one's called. You haven't telephoned anyone, or received a letter, or had anyone in to tea.'

'There was Donna,' said Kate.

'But she wasn't from your other life, was she?'

'No. I met her for the first time when you arrived that day.'

'That's what I mean. Well?'

'I feel as though I'm a bringer of bad luck. That my friends are safer without me.'

'That's ridiculous.'

'Ask Emma Dolby.'

'Who?'

'I took over her writing class while she was having a baby, and brought chaos into her life. It turned out that one of her class was a madman, a murderer, and the peaceful world of creative writing was never quite the same again. She's never forgiven me. I'm a menace.'

'What makes you think you're all-powerful?'

'I'm not, but disaster follows me like a dark shadow.'

'That's a good line. I should use it in your next book.'

'You're not taking me seriously.'

'I am. But you're dramatizing yourself and I can't be serious about that.'

'The other half of it is,' said Kate, carefully rearranging the small porcelain boxes on Callie's table, 'that I'm afraid of caring about people in case I lose them.'

'Now *that* I can understand.'

'Well, there you are then.'

'I didn't say I agreed with it.'

At that moment in the discussion, the telephone rang.

'Aren't you going to answer it?' asked Roz.

'No.'

Roz went to pick up the phone and came back a moment later with an amused expression on her face. 'It's for you,' she said.

'Who is it? I don't want to speak to them.'

'Stop sulking. It's a man. And he won't give his name.'

'But you think you know who it is.' Kate snapped out of her sulk and went to take the call.

'Hello?'

'Kate? It's Jon Hope-Stanhope here.'

Now this she had *not* been expecting. No wonder her mother looked amused.

'Hello, Jon. Thank you so much for such a lovely evening. My mother and I had a wonderful time.' How was that for good manners, then?

'Yes. Jolly good, jolly good. Emma received your letter. So kind of you.' There was a pause when it appeared that neither of them knew what to say next. 'Ah,' said Jon. 'I was wondering whether you could meet me for a drink, this evening, say?'

'In The Narrow Boat?' asked Kate with surprise. Surely that would get the village gossiping!

'No. Ah, I thought we could meet in that little place on the other side of Abingdon. Down by the river. Ah, The Old Ford, I believe it's called.'

'That's quite a distance away,' said Kate.

'Ah, yes. Is that all right? Could I meet you there at six-thirty?'

'Fine,' said Kate, mystified.

'Ah. See you then.'

'Yes. Goodbye.'

'What was all that about?' asked Roz, who had been shamelessly eavesdropping.

'Jon Hope-Stanhope wishes to meet me for a drink this evening in a pub so far from Gatt's Hill, without actually being on the other side of Birmingham, that no local person is likely to see us.'

'He's obviously well practised at deceiving his wife.'

'I can assure you that Emma need have no worries about me stealing her beastly husband.'

'Then why are you going?'

'Curiosity. I don't really believe he's overcome with lust at the thought of meeting me, so why?'

'A good question. I'll have your dinner ready for you when you return.'

The Old Ford might have been designed for illicit meetings. It consisted of a series of small rooms with comfortable chairs and soft lighting. From no single point could you see everyone who was drinking there that evening, and from each nook and cranny rose the hum of amorous dalliance – or so it appeared to Kate.

She found Jon Hope-Stanhope in a small bar with chintz curtains and hunting prints on the walls. They were the only occupants.

'Ah. So glad you could make it. What would you like to drink?'

Kate opted for a spritzer. She wanted to keep a clear head, but orange juice seemed a little austere. She saw that Jon was drinking a hefty whisky. She only hoped that he would be taking a taxi home.

'I suppose you're wondering why I asked to meet you,' said Jon when they were installed at a dinky little table decorated with a vase of fresh flowers and a pink-shaded lamp.

'I am, rather,' said Kate, sipping her spritzer very slowly. She had no intention of drinking more than one.

'Quite a jolly evening we had, don't you think?'

'Very jolly,' said Kate, who was still wondering when Jon was going to get to whatever was on his stunted mind.

'Of course, it's always a pleasure meeting such a lovely young lady,' he said, as though he couldn't let such an opportunity slip. Kate wanted to look behind her to see whether he meant someone else. Her – lovely? And she wasn't even young by some people's standards.

'This is a very pleasant place,' she said, for want of any more original idea. Not that Jon Hope-Stanhope looked as though he was capable of understanding anything approaching an original idea.

'But I was afraid you might have got the wrong idea from Hilary and Aubrey.' This was the longest and most coherent sentence she had had from him so far.

'Which idea was that?' she prompted.

'About that girl.'

'Donna?' She had been wondering whether he was leading up to Donna.

'Yes. They were joshing me about her, but you know what old friends are like.'

'Very jolly, I thought,' said Kate, trying for some of his own language.

'Now it is true that I appreciate the company of a young woman from time to time,' said Jon pompously.

'Naturally,' said Kate.

'All quite innocent, of course.'

'Of course.'

159

'And I must say that young Donna was a very pretty little thing.'

'So you did know her?'

'I'll just get myself another drink. How are you doing with yours? You've hardly started it yet. Drink up! You mustn't let me get too far ahead of you.'

Kate just smiled and placed the palm of her hand over the top of her glass. She waited for him to return with another large whisky. How many was that? At least three by her count. He looked just the same, though his eyes were going a bit pink.

'I can understand it,' said Kate. 'A lovely young thing like Donna, standing there in the spring sunshine, bending over a daffodil or tulip.'

'It was summer, actually,' said Jon. 'And I didn't actually do anything. You mustn't imagine that I did.'

'Of course you didn't.' *But you wanted to, didn't you?* 'But I can understand the temptation.'

'I only tried to kiss her.' Jon was starting to feel aggrieved. 'That's not much to ask, is it?'

'And what did she do?'

'She pushed me away. Quite roughly. And told me I was—'

A dirty old bugger, supplied Kate's imagination.

'Anyway. She made it clear she wanted none of it.'

'So there's no harm done, is there?'

'But I think she went off and told all her friends about it.'

'That was a bit naughty of her.'

'Yes, wasn't it? I got the impression that whenever I met anyone in the village they were – well, laughing at me over something.'

'How unfair!'

'Ah. Quite.'

'Not jolly at all.'

'What?'

'And you think that Emma might have heard about it?'

'I'm sure she did. But I managed to convince her there was nothing in it.'

'So what's the problem?'

'Ah. What?'

'What is the problem? Why have you invited me here to tell me this story?'

'Oh, yes. Jolly good. It's a bit awkward now that the girl's dead, don't you see?'

'You think people are still talking?'

'People are saying she was with someone that night and it might have been me.'

'So where were you?'

'Sorry?'

'If you weren't with Donna, where were you? Who were you with?'

'Ah. Bit awkward, you see.'

'You were with someone else, and it wasn't Emma.'

'You've got it exactly. I knew you were a bright little thing.'

'And what do you think I can do to help?' Goodness, this man was heavy going. He couldn't keep a single idea in his head for longer than a few seconds.

'I think I'd better get myself another drink.'

'Is that wise?'

'Drink yours up and I'll get you another, too.'

'Really, I'm fine. My glass is nearly full.'

Jon tottered across to the bar and returned with a double whisky for himself. Kate sipped at her original spritzer.

161

'Now, you were telling me what it was you wanted me to do to help,' she said when he seemed ready for more conversation.

'I was wondering whether you could say that I was with you and Roz.'

'But that would be a lie,' said Kate gently.

'Only a little one,' coaxed Jon. 'You could do it, Katie.'

'Kate,' she said firmly. 'I'll think about it on one condition.'

'What's that?'

'You'll have to tell me where you really were.'

'Ah.' Jon's bleary eyes crossed themselves with the effort of remembering.

'Come on. It's only a few days ago.'

'Ah. It might have been my friend Wendy, over at Brightman's Farm.'

'Yes? I need more details.'

'Hmph. Well, we met, here actually, at six-thirty.' Yes, that made sense. Jon wasn't a man to have more than one idea for a meeting-place. 'We had a drink or two, and Wendy said to come back to her place for something to eat. So we did. And one thing led to another, you know.'

'What time did you leave?'

'It was late.'

'How late?' Extraction of blood from stone had nothing on this.

'After midnight. I let myself in quietly and Emma didn't hear me. I spent the rest of the night in the spare room.'

'And who do you think is going to ask you questions about that evening?'

'The boys in blue.'

'The police? Why should they do that?'

'It's possible, isn't it? And I wouldn't want to drag

Wendy into it. It would upset Emma.'

'No, Jon. You cannot lie to the police like that. If they ask you, and I honestly don't think they will, *you must tell them the truth.*' Surely even Jon Hope-Stanhope could understand that.

'But you promised you'd help me!'

'No, I didn't. I said I'd think about it, and I've thought, and I've come to the conclusion that it would be a very bad idea to pretend that you were spending the evening, let alone the night, with me and Roz.' Had he understood? He was shaking his head in a puzzled way.

'I'm very disappointed in you, Kate.'

'And I'm sorry about that, but you'll thank me for it one day.'

'You haven't even finished your drink.'

'No, and I'll have to be going now. Roz is expecting me back for dinner.'

'What am I going to do?'

'Why don't you go and visit your nice friend Wendy? I'm sure she'll tell you the same as I have.'

'Do you think so?'

'Yes, I do. Thank you for the drink.'

'Goodbye.'

As she left, she saw that he was making his way to the bar for another whisky. She hoped that he would ring Wendy and that she would come to collect him. She didn't like to think of him loose on the country lanes in that condition. Mind you, she didn't think that Wendy would find much use for him if he went on drinking whisky like that.

When she arrived home, Roz sat her down at the table and presented her with a plate of healthy-looking food, then joined her with her own meal.

'I thought you needed your vitamins,' she said. Then she poured her a glass of white wine. 'But on the other hand, after an hour of Jon Hope-Stanhope's company, you probably need this, too.'

'Absolutely right,' said Kate, and tucked in. When they had both eaten something, and she had drunk half the glass of wine, she told her mother about their meeting.

'I think I believe him about his friend Wendy,' she said. 'The man hasn't got the brains to invent a story. Any story.'

'You think he's not in the frame for Donna's murder?'

'No. And I don't think he's her Raven, either. She sent him off with a flea in his ear, as far as I can tell. No man would make that up, would he?'

'Not unless he was rather more intelligent than dear Jon.'

'Well, having provisionally crossed Jon Hope-Stanhope off our list of suspects, we now prepare ourselves for the visit to the New Parish Hall, to find the whereabouts of Graham.'

'Before we do, there's just one more question I have about the Hope-Stanhopes.'

'Yes?'

'I still want to know what happened to their furniture.'

16

'It's time my car had an outing,' said Roz the next day. 'I'm sure its battery is going flat with all this sitting around doing nothing.'

'Very well,' said Kate. The VW seemed an appropriate vehicle to use to visit an antiques fair.

The engine started at the fifth attempt, and although it sounded more like a treadle sewing-machine than ever, they arrived at the Vicarage at five to twelve. Kate raced up the iron staircase to ring the bell. When Tim answered, it was obvious to her that he had given some thought to his appearance. Clerical leisurewear you could call it, she thought: pale beige cotton slacks, short-sleeved cream shirt with dog collar. But the dog collar was hardly noticeable against the other light colours. He was playing down his role as vicar today. He had waxed his hair into a fashionable wet-look spiked style, and the rimless glasses and gold earring underlined the fact that he was off-duty for the next couple of hours. He had thrown a black baseball jacket over his shoulder in a casual manner, in case he felt cold later.

'Cool,' said Kate, smiling.

'Yes, well. One likes to fit in with the crowd,' said Tim stiffly, following her down the stairs.

'Off we go!' cried Roz.

'Here we go adventuring,' murmured Kate.

'Are you all right in the back there, Tim?'

'Yes, really. If I can just shift some of this . . . er . . . stuff a bit, I'll be fine. Don't worry about me.'

They found Lower Hensford New Parish Hall quite easily. Already the car park – which was extensive – was full of cars and vans and they had to pull into a small space at the far end of the overflow park in a neighbouring field.

'Let's hope it doesn't rain, or we'll be stuck,' said Roz, getting out of the car and looking at the deep ruts in the muddy grass.

'This fair's certainly popular,' said Tim, following the stream of people making their way to the entrance. The hall was a low, red-brick building with steeply pitched roof, and gables, much in the style of an out-of-town supermarket.

They paid their entry fee, took a programme and entered the hall.

'Where do we start?' asked Roz, looking around.

The room was large, there was a second hall beyond the first, and both were covered in stalls and booths.

'This place is packed with goodies,' said Kate approvingly.

'I'm sure they're called *objets*,' said Roz. 'And I expect most of it is tat.'

'You sound as though you know what you're talking about,' said Kate, surprised.

'I have seen a few of these circuses before,' said Roz.

'Where shall we start?' asked Tim. 'I have to get back in a couple of hours, if you remember.'

'Don't worry. We'll take care you get home before you turn into a pumpkin,' said Roz soothingly. 'I suggest we start at this end and work our way down each aisle in

166

turn. When we see someone who might be Graham, we ask him his name.'

'That's got to be too simple,' said Kate. 'Nothing is ever that easy in my experience.'

If Tim grew impatient with Roz and Kate over the next twenty minutes, he managed not to show it. For, once the two of them started to look at the goods on offer, they moved into Shopping Mode.

'Look at this!' said Kate.

'What about those little pearl earrings?' said Roz.

'Have you seen the garnets?'

'Oh, look! 1950s sheet-music!' cried Roz.

'Can you believe how hideous these cups and saucers are?' cried Kate.

'Woolworths. *Circa* 1960,' said Roz.

'Graham,' murmured Tim.

'Who?'

'We're looking for Graham. Remember?'

'What? Oh yes, of course we are. But look at this little silver box, Kate.'

And so they went on, very slowly, down the first aisle. As it was now after half-past twelve, the stall-holders were delving into boxes and bags and coming up with vacuum flasks of coffee and packets of sandwiches, which they ate surreptitiously behind the stands.

'Did you bring a packed lunch for us?' asked Roz.

'No. Did you?' replied Kate.

'No, I didn't think of it.'

'We'll have to forget we're hungry. Maybe the pub will still be open when we've finished here,' said Tim, moving on to the next stall, which displayed what could only be described as knick-knacks in a glass-topped case. '*If* we ever finish here,' he added, as the two women stared avidly at the goods on display. 'Come on!' he urged, finally. 'We're hardly a tenth of the way round yet.'

'Wait!' said Kate.

'What is it?'

'Donna's pendant. I know that's Donna's pendant.'

The three of them leant over the glass case and stared at the blue perfume bottle.

'It could be a similar one. It needn't be hers,' said Roz sensibly.

'No, it is hers. There's a chip, there, on the neck,' said Kate. 'We talked about it. She showed me the chip. It's hers.'

'All right. Calm down,' said Tim. 'Where's the stall-holder?'

He or she must have gone looking for hot tea or sand-wiches, because the chair behind the stall was empty.

'Are you interested in something, love?' asked the woman at the next table. She was in her forties, with dyed blonde hair, and dressed in a way that Kate thought of as 'arty'.

'Is there no one on this stall?' asked Kate.

'He's just popped off for a moment. He'll be back. But I can help you with something if you want to buy.'

'This stall is Graham's, isn't it?' asked Kate.

'Graham? No, dear. I'm Cheryl, and this is Chaz's stall. I don't know a Graham.'

'I'd like to look at the blue perfume bottle,' said Kate.

'I'll get it out for you. Wait a tick while I find the key.'

The key was found, the case opened, and Cheryl handed the perfume bottle to Kate to examine. 'French, I think you'll find – 1920s. Very pretty,' she said. 'Do you want me to quote you a price, dear?'

'I just want to look at it for the moment,' said Kate. She

twisted the stopper and pulled out the glass dipper.

'Smell it,' she said to Tim and Roz. 'Essence of Twenties flapper. Isn't it marvellous? Eton crops, the Charleston, smoky nightclubs.'

'I can't smell anything,' said Tim.

'Cat's pee,' said Roz.

'You have no soul!' exclaimed Kate crossly.

'I don't think you can say that,' said Tim. 'Even if—'

'Oh, sorry! I'd forgotten about your day job.'

'Are you interested in it, dear?' asked Cheryl, who was getting tired of their squabbling.

'How much is it?' asked Roz. 'It is damaged here quite badly, of course, and the surface is scratched, which reduces the value quite considerably.'

'Is it? Let me see. Yes, I see what you mean. That's a pity. Well, I think I could let you have it for, say, ten pounds.'

'Five,' said Roz.

'Mother!'

'Leave this to me, Kate, and don't interfere.'

'I couldn't let it go for less than eight,' said Cheryl.

'Seven-fifty,' said Roz. 'Take it or leave it.'

'Done,' said Cheryl.

Roz paid with the correct money, in cash, while Cheryl wrapped the bottle in white tissue paper and put it in a brown paper bag.

'What about Graham? Or Chaz, even?' asked Kate, as they walked away from the stall.

'We'll keep going round the fair, and return later to that stall. Chaz will have to come back at some point, won't he?'

They walked on, picking up objects, looking at them, and putting them down again. Most of the stall-holders were middle-aged, many of them were in couples, and they all looked most respectable.

'The Crimplene and blue rinse brigade,' said Roz gloomily. 'I can't see anyone who looks like a raven, can you?'

'I can't see a man under fifty,' said Tim.

'No, and I'm getting hungry,' said Kate.

'Let's go back and see if Chaz's returned yet,' said Tim.

'All right. And if he hasn't, I'm going to find a chair to sit in and a cup of tea to drink,' said Roz. 'My feet are killing me.'

They made their way back to the first room. From the door they could see that there was now a young man sitting in the chair behind the glass case where they had found Donna's pendant.

'Maybe it's him! Maybe we've found him at last!' said Kate.

But when they reached the stall, they were disappointed. The man was young, certainly, but he was also overweight, with a round face, small features and large, sticking-out ears. He wore a baseball cap and a faded T-shirt with an advertisement for a rock concert which had taken place some three years previously. It was difficult to believe that this was Donna's crush.

'Chaz?' asked Tim.

'Yeah,' said the young man.

'We were looking for Graham,' said Roz.

'Why?' asked Chaz

'We want to talk to him,' said Kate. 'Just a little chat. Nothing heavy.'

'Don't know who he is,' said Chaz. 'Never heard of him.'

'I don't believe you,' said Kate.

'Who are you?' asked Chaz.

Kate opened her mouth to reply, but, 'I am the vicar of the church of St Michael and All Saints, Gatt's Hill,' said Tim.

'You can call him Tim if you like,' said Kate.

Chaz stared at them in disbelief.

'Check out his dog collar,' said Kate. 'It's not a fake. It's the real thing. It's stamped "Genuine C of E" on the inside.'

'You're all loonies,' said Chaz.

'And you'll only get rid of us by telling us where to find Graham,' said Roz, smiling sweetly.

Chaz sighed. 'He's in the other room. Bottom of Aisle 3. Silver and jewellery. You can't miss him.'

'Well, somehow we did miss him our first time round,' said Tim.

'Come on!' said Roz. 'The sooner we find Graham, the sooner we can repair to the pub for a pie and a pint.'

'I apologize for my mother,' said Kate to Tim.

'Don't do that. I really like her,' said Tim seriously. 'Don't you?'

'I suppose so.'

'There he is!' said Roz. 'I'm sure that's our man.'

'What shall we do? We can't question him here,' said Tim.

'Let's take a look at his stall first,' said Kate. 'I'm sure a plan will come to us.'

They sauntered as casually as they could to Graham's stall. It was simple to identify, being at the bottom of Aisle 3, and consisting of several glass-topped cases full of silver and jewellery, and being in the charge of a young, personable man. He was in his twenties, tall, skinny and dark-haired.

'Raven,' said Kate. 'He's the most likely candidate so far.'

'I have to agree with you,' said Tim.

They looked at the pieces he had for sale. Very nice too, thought Kate, gazing at the gold rings, the pearl earrings, the garnet and moonstone brooch.

'Do you want me to get something out for you?' he asked.

'No, thanks,' said Roz. 'We're just looking.'

There was a pause while all three of them tried to think of a way of broaching the subject of Donna.

'Have you managed to have any lunch yet?' asked Roz in her most motherly voice. 'It must be difficult for you having a stall on your own like this.'

'I'll just have to wait until after four,' said Graham, if indeed it was Graham.

'Oh, I don't think so,' said Roz. 'Now, what I suggest we do is this. My daughter Kate here will sit in for you for half an hour and our dear friend the Reverend Tim Widdows and I will take you over the road to the pub and buy you a pint of best bitter and something to eat.'

'What are you on about?' The man looked at them as though they were out of their minds.

'Is your name Graham?' asked Tim, thinking that perhaps they should find out this fact before committing themselves to anything.

'What if it is?'

'I think we can take that as a "yes",' said Kate.

'The fact is, Graham, we're very anxious to talk to you,' said Roz.

'You can trust us,' said Tim. 'We just want this little chat.'

'Don't you think we're sounding too much like the Mafia?' asked Kate.

'You can all piss off or I'm calling Security.' Graham was scowling at them.

'I shouldn't do that,' said Roz. 'Or I might ask them to check out the diamond and emerald ring in the front of the case. That would be rather inconvenient, wouldn't it? It might even give rise to unfortunate gossip about your stock.' Roz had stopped smiling in her motherly way and had injected a surprising amount of malice into her voice.

'Are you the police?'

'Certainly not. And we just want to talk to you about a friend of ours.'

'I can't leave the stall, I'd lose too much business. Twenty quid this pitch has cost me. I'd be out of pocket.'

'I told you, my daughter will cover the stall for you. She's much more sensible than she looks.'

Kate said, 'Why have I been volunteered to look after the stall? Why can't Tim do it?'

'He's wearing his dog collar. We don't want to draw attention to ourselves or to Graham's stall, do we?'

'I don't think I'd be much good at selling things. I'd rather do the talking. I think I'm quite good at that,' said Tim. 'Go on, Kate, you'll enjoy yourself.'

'Oh, all right,' said Kate.

'I'm not sure I've agreed to all this,' said Graham.

Roz produced a ten-pound note. 'You know you have, Graham dear. And this is a small token of our gratitude, in advance. All right?'

Graham looked at Kate. 'Do you know what you're on?'

'I'm a quick learner,' said Kate.

'Everything's priced,' said Graham. 'Trade gets thirty per cent discount.'

'I'm sure I'll manage,' said Kate. 'Bring me back a bacon sandwich, will you?'

* * *

The pub opposite was anonymous and crowded. They pushed their way through into the saloon bar, where food was being served, and Tim found them a table and three seats.

'I'll get the drinks,' he said.

'Better let me do it,' said Roz. 'I have a way with barmen.'

And she was back, with drinks and large quantities of high-fat, low-fibre food, in record time. They helped themselves and there was silence for a minute or two as they ate.

'What's this all about?' asked Graham, his mouth full of factory-produced steak and kidney pie.

'We're friends of Donna's,' said Roz.

'Who?' But he didn't sound convincing.

'Donna Paige. Your friend from Gatt's Hill,' said Roz. 'We're trying to find out how she died. You see, we don't believe the story in the paper, and the version the police are putting out.'

'Why would you think I know anything about it?'

'Because we think she was your girlfriend. She called you Raven, didn't she?' said Tim.

'No,' said Graham. And this time he did sound as though he was telling the truth.

'But you did know her. So tell us about it,' said Roz.

There was something very persuasive about Roz Ivory when she was determined to get information from someone, but Graham made them all wait for a while. He swallowed the remains of his pie and washed it down with the rest of his bitter.

'Same again?' asked Tim.

'Yeah. Better make it a half. Thanks.'

Tim disappeared into a clump of people and forced his way through towards the bar.

'Now. You can tell me all about it,' said Roz.

Graham looked shifty. 'You mean about Donna. Well, I've done nothing wrong. I wasn't there when she died.'

'But you did know her.'

'She used to be my girlfriend,' he said, 'but that all ended a few months back, when she met this bloke she called Raven. The thing about Donna was that she wanted to get out of Gatt's Hill. She wanted to make money.'

'So you went into business together?'

'In a way, yes. It was her idea to come and do the antique fairs. She thought we could make money at it.'

'And how did you get the capital to buy your first stock?'

Graham now looked even shiftier. 'We picked it up here and there,' he said. 'You know how it goes.' He looked over towards the bar where Tim was still trying to attract the barman's attention.

'Yes, I believe I do,' said Roz. 'Now, before the vicar comes back with your drink, and before we face my rather fierce daughter again, I suggest that you and I sort this out.'

'Sort what out?' Graham wasn't very good at looking innocent.

'That was a very interesting collection of goods you had in those glass cases of yours. Unfortunately for you, I recognized some of them.'

'You can't have done. You were bluffing about the emerald ring, weren't you?'

'Certainly not. Do you want me to be specific? There was a pretty brooch, set with peridots and pearls. Late Victorian. Gold safety chain.'

'Well?'

'I know where it came from, Graham. Now, we don't want anything official to happen, do we? Or at least you don't, I imagine. Well, nothing need go pear-shaped for you as long as you give me a little more detail about the business you were running with Donna.'

'If I tell you, you'll keep it to yourself?'

'I'll tell my daughter, but you can trust her. I'll see to that.'

'I'm not sure.'

'You'd better hurry. Even Tim will get served eventually, and it's more difficult to convince a vicar that he should do something illegal than it is me.'

Graham looked over at Tim, took in the gold earring and the spiky hair. 'Are you sure he's really a vicar?'

'Quite sure.'

'All right, I'll tell you. It's a well-known fact: no one bothers to fence nicked stuff any longer. You just hire a stall at one of these antiques fairs and sell it direct to the public. No bother.'

'That's what I thought. Yes, I had heard this was the way to dispose of stolen goods. And what about the police? If even I've heard about it, they must know about it, too.'

'There's too many of us for them to get round to everyone. There are thousands of these fairs every week, all over the country. Hundreds of stalls at some of them. Acres of ground. The police only ever pull in a tiny number of the thieves.'

'And who did the stealing? Was Donna involved?'

'No. She came out once or twice for the kicks. She acted as look-out. I think she liked a bit of excitement from time to time, but she soon got fed up of it. She was just interested in the selling. She put us on to a few likely houses, ones where she'd done the garden. But it was too risky to keep doing that. Someone would have made the connection in the end. And once we had enough to buy proper stock, she wanted to go legit.'

'But you didn't?'

'I didn't argue with her. But sometimes I added a few nicked items to the stock, yes. Now, that's it. I'm not telling you any more.'

He had finished his story just in time. 'Here,' said Tim. 'I managed to get served at last. Here's your half-pint, Graham. Does anyone want anything else to eat?'

'No thanks,' said Roz.

Graham drained his half in record time. 'I've got to get back to my stall. God knows what that chick's doing with my stock.'

'God probably does know,' said Tim seriously. 'You see, Graham—'

'Not now, Tim,' said Roz. 'Save it for the congregation. There's one final thing we need to know.'

'What's that?' asked Graham, looking hunted.

'Do you remember the blue pendant that Donna always wore?'

'The perfume bottle?'

'That's the one.'

'Well?'

'We just want to know how it ended up on Chaz's stall.'

'I don't know. It was nothing to do with me. I didn't even know he'd got it.'

'You must know,' insisted Roz, but she hadn't the heart to start threatening him again.

177

And Graham wasn't to be budged. They walked back across the road to the Parish Hall. Kate looked quite pleased with herself since she had sold three items while they were gone. Roz thought she'd better not tell her that they might well have been stolen goods.

'Thanks for your help, Graham,' said Roz. 'See you around some time.'

'Don't bother to get in touch again,' he said.

'Just one other thing,' said Tim. 'Have you any idea who Raven is?'

'Some rich bastard,' said Graham. 'A lot richer than me, anyway. I don't know what he offered her, but she was addicted to the man.'

'Did you ever see him?'

'I saw her with some man at one of the fairs. She was drooling over the stuff on some stall, and I think he was gonna buy something for her.'

'What did he look like?' asked Kate.

'I dunno. I didn't really notice. I was too busy trying to sell my own gear.'

'Try to describe him,' said Kate urgently. 'Was there anything at all you remember about him?'

Graham looked hard at Tim. 'It could have been you,' he said. 'Same build, same type.'

Tim went pink, Kate noticed with interest.

'No, of course it wasn't me!' he said when he saw that the two women were staring at him in their turn. 'Anyway, I've got very distinctive hair,' he added.

'Red,' said Roz.

'Carroty,' said Kate.

'Auburn,' said Tim. 'You'd have remembered it, wouldn't you, Graham?'

'I'd have called it ginger. But since this bloke was

wearing a baseball cap, I wouldn't know what colour his hair was,' said Graham.

'Didn't you follow them?' asked Roz. 'I would have done.'

'I tried to. But when I looked for them again, they'd left. And that's all I can tell you. Now, piss off and leave me to get on with my job, will you?'

As they were walking back to the car park, Roz said, 'Excuse me a minute, I've forgotten something. Take the keys, Kate, you can drive back to the entrance. I'll meet you there by the door in a couple of minutes.'

'What was all that about?' asked Tim as Kate made heavy weather of reversing the VW out of its parking space.

'I expect it's a woman thing,' said Kate, and revved the engine mercilessly until they were back on the tarmac.

On the way back to Gatt's Hill, Roz told Tim and Kate what she had learned from Graham in the pub.

'How did you persuade him to tell you all that?' asked Kate.

'I told him I knew most of his stock was nicked. In particular, I told him I recognized a pearl and peridot brooch.'

'That was a bit of luck, recognizing a piece like that,' said Tim.

'I didn't, but it was a pretty safe bet.'

'What if you'd been wrong?' asked Kate.

'You and Tim were short on ideas, so I had to use my initiative. What were the two of you proposing to do – beat the information out of him?'

'I could have managed Graham. I've dealt with rough characters in my time,' said Tim.

'Maybe. But you look like a caramel-flavoured marshmallow in that gear, and marshmallow doesn't scare
anyone.'

'I think that's rather unkind of you.'

'Not at all. It makes you quite endearing to the rest of
us,' said Roz cheerfully. 'Now, if I can find the accelerator,
I'll put my foot down. We want to get you home in time to
preach to the converted, don't we?'

17

'That's a pretty brooch,' said Kate. 'Pearls and peridots. Haven't I seen it before somewhere?'

'On Graham's stall,' said Roz breezily.

'I remember now. He was asking over a hundred for it. Did you pay for it? Or did you extort it from the poor man as the price of your silence?'

'Of course I paid for it. Though I must admit I did get quite a bargain. I reminded him that I had already given him ten pounds for his co-operation. Another ten, I suggested, and we'd be quits.'

'You're incorrigible!'

'I do hope so. I must teach you the basic skills of haggling. You'll find it useful.'

'If I were you I'd put the brooch away until you've left Gatt's Hill. Think of the embarrassment if someone recognized it as their property.'

'It's Saturday evening,' said Roz later. 'Haven't we got a party to go to?'

'I'm afraid not. Just for a change, we're having a quiet night in. I've been looking through my notes, though.'

'And what have you found?'

'A lot of interesting information, but still no real clue as to how Donna died and who Raven was.'

'What do you think of Graham's suggestion that it was Tim?'

'I put that down to spite.'

'He did blush rather prettily when it was suggested, though, don't you think?'

'Very well, I'll ask him about it next time we meet,' said Kate. 'But I don't really see him as a sleek, dark seducer, do you?'

'I never cease to be amazed at what turns young women on,' said Roz. 'One year it's Robert Redford, the next it's Chris Evans.'

'Tim doesn't look like either. But it would explain, of course, why he never wanted to be seen with her in the village. I suppose the vicar can't afford gossip about a love affair with a parishioner.'

'But does he have a flash car and lots of money?'

'Who knows what he has? How much do we really know about Tim Widdows?' wondered Kate.

'I think you should take the next opportunity to find out. Don't put the poor man off next time he says something pleasant. Be nice to him, Kate.'

'Mnerf,' said Kate.

'Perhaps we should widen the search,' mused Roz. 'It's possible Raven doesn't come from Gatt's Hill.'

'Then what about the impractical shoes? How did she get to where he lived? No one saw him pick her up in his car.'

'I had an idea about the shoes. I've been out looking around the village.'

'I wondered where you'd got to this afternoon.'

'I went for a walk. If you leave Broombanks, you're out of the village in a few yards. At this time of year, with most of the leaves still on the trees, there are a dozen places to park a car out of sight of the road. There are field gates and tracks, bridle paths and footpaths. They could arrange to meet in any one of them, and no one would notice.'

'That would explain why they were never seen together. After all, if he *was* from the village, surely *someone* would have seen them by now. We know what this village is like for gossip,' said Kate. 'The trouble is, that once we move out of Gatt's Hill, the possibilities are endless. Where do we start?'

'I wonder where she met him,' said Roz. 'The possibilities for that aren't endless, are they?'

'They are if you think of the antiques fairs she went to. They could have taken her anywhere in the country. I wish Graham could have remembered more about the man he saw. He didn't tell us anything, did he, apart from making us wonder whether it was Tim.'

'Which is odd when you think about it. If you'd just been ditched by someone, and then you saw them with their new partner, you'd be gutted, wouldn't you? You'd want to know what he had that you hadn't. What could she see in him? You'd leave your stall unattended and follow them round the hall until you were quite sure you'd recognize the bastard again.'

'That's what I'd do, certainly,' said Kate. 'And I'm sure everyone else is just like me.'

'So he was lying.'

'Or at least not telling all the truth. It's a pity we don't know his full name and where he lives.'

'Oh, but we do,' said Roz. 'I insisted on a receipt for my brooch. I'll get it and we'll take a look.'

While Roz was upstairs, finding the receipt, the telephone rang. Only sad people answered their phone on a Saturday evening, Kate knew, but she picked it up anyway.

'Hello, Kate? This is Tim.'

'Tim. What can I do for you?'

'It's a bit awkward, actually.'

'It takes quite a lot to make Roz and me blush, so fire away.'

'Right. Well. Tony Fuller rang just now and asked me down to Gatts Farm for the drink we'd talked about.'

'Yes. Fine. And?'

'And I said I was seeing you this evening.'

'A porkie! You told a porkie! What a shocking thing to do! Do you want me to give you absolution or something?'

'No, no. That isn't necessary. He suggested I should bring you with me.'

'I see. So if I don't turn up you'll be in the shit. What time are we due there?'

'Um. Ten minutes?'

'Walk down to Crossways Cottage and I'll be ready soon after you arrive. I'm sure Roz will look after you if you have to wait.'

'Oh, thanks, Kate.' He sounded immensely relieved. 'You're a wonderful person.' Kate rang off and remembered that she had told him only yesterday that you shouldn't tell lies unless you were quite sure you wouldn't be found out. Some vicars never learned.

She ran upstairs. 'I'm going out!' she called.

'What? Where?'

'Tim's taking me for a drink at the Fullers' place.'

'Well, keep your eyes open for clues at Gatts Farm. And see what you can find out about Tim.'

'And you'll be playing your violin and making up the five per cent solution while I'm out, I suppose.'

'Very funny, Dr Watson.'

* * *

184

It was a pleasant evening, one of the last mild evenings of the year, and so Tim and Kate walked down the hill to Gatts Farm instead of taking the car. They went in past the *Showrooms Closed* sign and rang the bell at the main house.

'Very smart,' said Kate, who hadn't been there before, looking round her.

Tony answered the door and took them into the sitting room where Tim had been before when he had been summoned by Hazel.

'My parents,' said Tony. 'Hazel and Derek. You know Tim Widdows, and this is Kate Ivory, who is a novelist staying in Aphra Callan's cottage while she's in America.'

Very good, thought Kate, very succinct, no factual mistakes. She shook hands, accepted a glass of wine and sat down in a deep, soft sofa, covered in some expensively pale fabric. I think I underestimated Tony Fuller before, but I suppose I should remember he teaches at an Oxford college. She studied the older Fullers while Tim and Tony started to reminisce about college days.

Hazel looked like a lottery winner in the 'after' picture. Her hair was streaked, tinted and waved, her face was toned, massaged and painted, her legs were waxed, her clothes were brand new. Kate had a nasty feeling that she and Hazel were going to have nothing at all in common.

'What sort of writing is it you do, Kate?' asked Derek. He was a big, beefy man, in a silver-grey suit and a light blue silk shirt. He had heavy gold cufflinks and a Rolex watch. There must be very good money in antiques.

'I write historical novels,' said Kate, knowing that the subject was bound to bore him.

'Really? I don't do much reading, myself. Not of fiction,

anyway. I must admit I haven't heard of you. Do you write under your own name?'

'I do indeed,' said Kate through teeth that she was trying hard not to grit. 'But a writer's life is hardly an interesting one. We spend most of our time sitting in front of a word processor, making up stories as we go along. Why don't you tell me about the world of antiques? I'm sure it's more exciting than mine. Do you specialize in anything in particular?'

'I'm a businessman,' said Derek. 'I'm not one of these Mayfair connoisseurs who only deal in the eighteenth century. I sell the sort of good solid stuff that the new country people want in their houses. I provide what they see as English country furniture, and they buy it, in large quantities.'

'So you cater for the sort of people who have a fantasy of country life, rather than for the ones actually working in the rain and mud with a muckspreader.'

'You've got it.'

'There was one thing that intrigued me, Derek, when Tim and I came to the workshop yesterday.'

'What was that? Tony mentioned that you'd been having a look around and I wondered what had taken your eye. I gather you had a long chat to Carl.'

'He was telling me all about wood,' said Kate.

'He must have liked you. He isn't usually very communicative. But what was it that struck you as curious about our operation?'

'I think I was surprised by the enormous quantity of furniture you had in the barns. Where on earth do you find it? I should have thought that a small country like England would be running short of old furniture by now.'

'You're an observant little lady, aren't you? The answer

is to be found in Eastern Europe,' said Derek, his cufflinks winking in the light as though to remind her that
there was gold to be made in his workshops. 'There are
thousands of farmers – well, peasants really – who are
only too happy to part with Granny's old kitchen dresser
for a fiver or two in hard currency.'

'So you take your van and go on the knocker? Isn't that
what they call it?'

Derek laughed, but there was no humour in the sound.
'I take my Range Rover through the muddy tracks of
Romania, looking into farmhouses and barns. Then I
drive on through Hungary and into the Ukraine, buying
anything I can do up and sell on. Local contractors take
the goods to a warehouse I own near the docks. You've
seen the showrooms and workshops here – well, they're
nothing to the place I have over there.'

'And then I suppose your yellow vans bring the goods
here for repair and refurbishment.'

'Are you two going to be talking bloody antiques all
night?' interrupted Hazel. 'It's all I hear all day, and then I
have to listen to it half the night as well.'

'Sorry, dear,' said Derek. 'It's just that Kate here was
interested in the business.'

It was amazing, thought Kate, that an intelligent, successful man like Derek could be brought to heel so easily
by a dumb babe like Hazel.

'Aren't you interested in antiques?' Kate asked her
politely.

'I like them all right. They can furnish a room quite
nicely, but I don't go potty over them like some people.'

'The Hope-Stanhopes,' prompted Kate, seeing an opening, or window of opportunity as Derek would doubtless
call it. *What had happened to the Hope-Stanhopes'*

furniture? 'Emma seemed very concerned about her family furniture.'

'Well, it was her own fault marrying that fool Jon in the first place,' said Hazel.

'Really?' prompted Kate. 'Do tell.' She made herself sound all-girls-together.

'You'll have to excuse me for a few minutes. I have a phone call to make,' said Derek and left the room, pausing only to pour himself another drink before he went.

'You'd think that Jon Hope-Stanhope being an accountant he'd have a brain in his head. I can understand her marrying someone good with money, since the Hopes had been squandering their fortune for decades, but he's just a tailor's dummy, that man,' said Hazel when Derek had left.

'He and Emma didn't seem to be hitting it off the night my mother and I were there,' said Kate primly.

'Hitting it off! You must be joking!'

'I gather he's a bit too keen on other women. He has what you might call a roving eye.'

'She must have known that when she married him. The other little faults were better hidden.'

'Really?'

'You shouldn't play poker if you can't afford to lose,' said Hazel.

'And he lost his furniture?' asked Kate.

'Came round here, begging Derek to take a look at some of that old tat of theirs and make him an offer. Derek did him a favour!'

'But Jon and Emma weren't grateful?'

'People have very silly ideas about what their old furniture's worth,' said Hazel knowledgeably.

Buy cheap, sell dear. That's the Fullers' motto and it

seems to have worked for them, thought Kate. 'Well, at least it paid off his gambling debts,' she said.

'For the moment. I don't give them more than a year before they have to start remortgaging the house.' Hazel's eyes snapped like a cash register and Kate could have sworn she saw pound signs illuminated in green.

'I wonder what those two men can have found to talk about,' said Kate, looking across to Tony and Tim, who appeared to be still deep in conversation. She was getting a bit tired of her girlish act and could have done with a change of topic.

'The odd thing is, Tim,' Tony was saying, 'that I never had you down for a God-person.'

'You didn't think I was vicar material?' Tim liked to believe he could take this sort of banter in his stride, and match it.

'It's not that so much, but your interests all lay elsewhere. What subject was it you read?'

'Law.'

'There you are. One doesn't often link law and religion, does one? It's almost as bad as banking, I should have thought. Mammon versus God, one might call it.'

'Oh, I don't know about that. There's a similar serious cast of mind, I suppose.'

'But that's what I mean,' said Tony. 'You may have been serious about your studies, I don't know anything about that, but when it came to outside interests, I seem to remember that yours were rather unusual. Weren't you the man who started the college bungee-jumping club?'

'It was a fashionable thing to do at the time. And I've always enjoyed a touch of danger in my hobbies.'

'There you go. "Fashionable" is hardly a word one

189

associates with vicardom, let alone "danger".'

'Are you winding me up?' asked Tim, adjusting his rimless glasses and checking that his earring was in place.

'Would I do a thing like that?' said Tony, smiling. 'Would you like another drink?'

'Thanks.'

They sat for a minute or two in companionable silence, communing with their respective whiskies.

'And then again, there was the cabaret for the college ball,' said Tony, as though his mind hadn't moved from its previous line of thought.

'I'd forgotten about that.'

'I doubt whether anyone who saw it would ever forget it.'

'I used to enjoy acting.'

'In drag?'

'It was just a light-hearted sort of thing. Amateurish, really. The usual stuff that students get up to.'

'And all that singing and dancing, too. And didn't you parachute into the Fellows' Garden during Rag Week?'

'You do remember all my youthful adventures, don't you?'

'You made quite an impression at the time, Tim. Not to mention a large dent in the lawn. Did they send you the bill for that?'

'The Rag Committee paid, luckily.'

'Well, I look forward to the church fête next year. I'm sure it will be . . . original. Not to say lively.'

'And you were a quiet, studious lad, weren't you?' Tim decided it was time to fight back. 'But then I suppose you had your sights set on the academic life even then.'

'I was very dull compared with you, certainly. But what interests me is this: what made you change? Was it a sudden revelation, the light on the road to Damascus, or had you always secretly hankered after incense and cassocks?'

'You're making me sound like some kind of weirdo, but I wasn't. I just wanted to practise decent law, do something for society. Is that such a bad idea?'

'An excellent idea. Don't mind me, Tim. I'm only teasing, you know. I admire what you're doing, really. Go on. You were telling me about the start of your career.'

Mollified, Tim said, 'After my articles, I went to work in a Legal Aid centre in an inner-city area. What I saw there made me think again about what I was doing with my life. It seemed to me that there were other ways of helping people.'

'How meritorious. So, no more bungee-jumping after that.'

'Just because I'm in holy orders doesn't mean that I don't know how to enjoy myself,' said Tim huffily.

'Oh, I'm sure you know how to do that,' said Tony.

'Come on, you two!' called Hazel. 'It's time you joined the ladies. What have you been gossiping about all this time?'

'Common acquaintances,' said Tony. 'And remembrance of times past.'

'We were only a year apart as undergraduates,' said Tim.

Boring, thought Kate.

'And Tim certainly made a mark in his time at college,' said Tony. 'Have you told Kate about your exploits, Tim? I'm sure she'd be fascinated to hear about the bungee-jumping, the parachuting, the—'

'It's all in the past,' said Tim.

'But is it really true?' asked Kate.

'It really is,' said Tony. 'He was the liveliest under-graduate of his year, they tell me.'

'I'll have to hear more about it,' said Kate thoughtfully. This was a new light on the vicar, certainly.

'I was wondering whether you and Tim would care to come as my guests to dinner at college,' said Tony. 'There's a guest night coming up next week, in fact.'

Kate looked enquiringly at Tim. Did they want to be considered a pair?

'That would be very nice,' said Tim. 'How about it, Kate?'

'Yes, I'd like that,' she said. And it was only afterwards that she realized that she had accepted an invitation to an Oxford college without being reminded of the tragedies of the past. Maybe the detective work she was involved in on the mystery of Donna's death was doing her good, after all. She only wished that she'd found out more at the Fullers'. The subject of Donna hadn't come up at all, and she didn't think that her recent lesson in buying and selling antiques would prove very useful in her own life.

'It's time we were going, don't you think, Kate?' said Tim.

They said their thanks and goodbyes and went outside. Tony came with them to the gate.

'Wonderful night,' he said. 'The air out here is so clear.'

'And dark,' said Kate. 'Did one of us remember to bring a torch, Tim?'

'We'll have to navigate by the stars,' he said. 'Goodbye, Tony. We'll see you next week at Leicester.'

As they started back up the hill in the velvet black night, they saw the headlights of a large vehicle coming towards them down the narrow, winding lane. They pressed themselves back against the hedge and watched

as it drove in through the open gateway of Gatts Farm.
The sides of the van shone yellow as it passed under the
security light. The gates swung closed with a clang, and
they could hear the sound of a key turning in the lock.

'Another load of furniture from the East,' said Kate.

'China?'

'Romania,' said Kate, 'or possibly the Ukraine, from
what I could understand.'

'I hadn't realized just how big those vans are. They're
shifting a huge amount of furniture, aren't they?'

'No wonder they're making so much money.'

They walked on in silence.

'Would you like a coffee?' asked Kate as they reached
Crossways Cottage.

'It's not very late, is it? Yes, thank you.'

'I forgot to tell you. Roz believes she has Graham's full
name and address written down. We can see where he
lives and make plans for our next move.'

18

'Yes, yes, I have it here, Kate. But let Tim sit down and drink his coffee, won't you?' Roz was waving a piece of paper in the air, out of the reach of Kate's grabbing hand. 'Stop being so impatient. You can't rush out and grill the man tonight, you know.'

'Why not?' demanded Kate. 'I want to know what he saw, and *who* he saw, before he disappears off into the night and we never catch up with him again.'

'I thought Roz had already extracted all his information,' said Tim. 'Why do you need to see him again?'

'We believe he went and took a good look at Donna's new boyfriend,' said Roz. 'I would have done; Kate would have done. We're sure Graham would have followed them round the hall until he'd seen him properly.'

'So he must know who Raven is. Or at least, he must have a good idea of what he looks like, and maybe *we* can recognize Raven from his description,' said Kate. 'Which is why we have to drive straight over there before he disappears again. It's our best chance of identifying the man.'

'It's too late for me. I have an early start tomorrow,' said Tim. 'And you're not to go there on your own. Goodness only knows what might happen to you with your aggressive style of questioning.'

'Oh, very well,' said Kate grudgingly. 'Let's have a look at the address, though.'

She and Tim pored over the badly written scrap of paper.

'Graham Peters,' she read. 'Do you think that's right? Was he telling the truth?'

'Can you read this address?' asked Tim.

'I think so. It's off the Cowley Road, isn't it? It would only take about a quarter of an hour to get there.'

'But not tonight,' said Roz firmly. 'Listen to your mother for once.'

'Tomorrow's Sunday,' said Kate. 'That's the day you have to work, isn't it, Tim?'

Tim sighed. 'We work *every* day,' he said.

'Yeah, yeah. I'll believe you.' Huh! Who was he kidding? Everyone knew about vicars and work!

'You're right, though. I haven't got much spare time tomorrow.' He turned the page in his diary. 'How about between three-thirty and five?'

'You've found a window for us? Oh good. I thought you might. Yes, I'll be there.'

'Me too,' said Roz.

'Don't worry, I'd counted you in already,' said Tim.

'Shall we pick you up?' asked Kate. Then, cunningly, she added, 'Or would you prefer to take your own car?'

'I thought the journey in the yellow VW was so unusual that I can't wait to repeat it at the earliest opportunity,' said Tim solemnly.

'Very well. We'll come to the Vicarage at three-thirty tomorrow,' said Roz. 'And, by the way, while you were out, I had a long chat on the phone to my dear friend Alison Fanning.'

'Knitted porridge clothes, home-styled hair,' said Kate. 'Just your type, Roz.'

'She is at the hub, the very centre of the village news-gathering service. And she was telling me, among many interesting facts, that the police are apparently quite content to let Donna's death go without any further investigation. They believe they know what happened, and are putting it down to an unfortunate accident. That is what the coroner will conclude when the inquest is resumed in a couple of weeks' time. They will doubtless give their usual warnings against the use of hard drugs, and then forget all about it.'

'So we really are the only ones still trying to find out the truth,' said Kate.

'Yes. And we mustn't give up until we've found some answers,' said Roz, getting up from her chair. 'And now I'm off upstairs for a relaxing bath. You sit and finish your coffee, Tim. And make Kate find the chocolate biscuits for you if you're a bit peckish.'

Tim rose politely to his feet as Roz went upstairs, closing the door behind her.

'I think she's being tactful,' said Kate. 'She hasn't had much practice at it, which is why she's rather heavy-handed.'

'Don't worry. I can't stay long,' said Tim. 'I really do have an early start tomorrow.'

'Would you like something a bit more exciting than coffee to drink? We have a bottle of single malt in the cupboard.'

'I'd certainly enjoy a wee dram,' said Tim.

So Kate poured two whiskies and they sat in companionable silence for a while, sipping their drinks and watching the logs burning in the stove. It was very restful, and Kate could almost ignore the problem of who had engineered Donna's death. Wasn't this how normal people spent their Saturday evenings? She had almost forgotten what normal felt like.

'Your mother hinted that you'd had some bad things happening in your life before you came to stay in Gatt's Hill,' said Tim.

'Did she? She talks too much.'

'Don't you want to tell me about it?'

'When I was first here – well, up until Donna's death really, it was on my mind all the time. But now it's fading into the past. It's still painful, but today is starting to take over again from yesterday, if you see what I mean.'

'You feel you can move forward in your life.'

'If you want to put it like that.'

'You can be very dismissive, you know,' said Tim. 'It's not easy to talk to you about anything personal.'

'I know. It's the way I am.'

'Perhaps I could help you to fight against it.'

'No thanks.'

They both sipped whisky and were silent again for a short while.

'Oh, all right,' said Kate eventually. 'The thing is that in the past two or three years I seem to have got involved in various unpleasant happenings. There was the woman in my running group who was killed. And then Liam, who I thought was . . . well, you know, I thought we were in a proper relationship . . . I found he'd been having this affair with another woman for years, and then *she* died. And then there was Andrew. He was an old friend of mine. He took me out for meals when I was hungry, to the wine bar when I wanted company, found me temporary work when I was broke, and was just generally *there* in the background of my life. And then, about four months ago, he died. He was killed in the hallway of my house in

Oxford. That's why I'm here. I just had to get away from it.'

'Thanks for telling me all that. It's the longest uninterrupted speech you've ever made in my hearing.'

'And, don't you see, Tim, I feel as though it's my fault. If it weren't for me, those people would all still be alive.'

'That's ridiculous. Did you kill any of them?'

'No, of course not.'

'Well then. Don't feel guilty for things you haven't done.'

'That's more or less what Roz said.'

'Your mother is a very sensible woman. You should listen to her more often.'

'I've never thought of her as sensible before this. Flighty, yes. Scatty, disorganized, irresponsible. All those. Perhaps it's only now that I'm starting to appreciate her.'

'As long as you do. We never know how much time we have left, do we?'

'And thank you for that cheering thought.'

'You know what I mean. I know I didn't get to appreciate my parents while they were alive. And now it's too late.'

'I'm sorry, Tim. I've been talking about myself all evening. I should have listened to you. We'll spend another evening together when you can tell me all about your childhood, your parents, and your exciting time at Leicester College, I promise.'

'Next time. I'll make sure there is a next time and hold you to it.'

'Of course.'

Tim left soon after this, kissing her swiftly on the cheek as she stood by the open door. She watched him walking up the village street towards the church. He wasn't such a bad bloke, after all. Probably the sort of man she needed in her life at the moment.

As soon as Kate closed the door, Roz came downstairs, wrapped in a red velvet robe and with her hair swathed in a pink towel.

'Pour us both some of that whisky, why don't you?' she said.

'I thought you'd gone to bed.'

'You thought wrong. I was just waiting for The Rev to leave.'

Kate poured the drinks, making her own a very small one.

'Now, I want to hear what happened at the Fullers'.'

'Nothing much. I was mostly quite bored – except by Derek, I suppose. He filled me in on the practicalities of the antiques business. I'd say he was more interested in the business side of it than the aesthetic.'

'And what about Hazel?'

'She didn't seem interested in any of it. All she wanted was the money to spend – on herself.'

'And what about the son – Tony, isn't it?'

'He was talking to Tim most of the time. All about their old college days, as far as I could make out. Oh, and then he invited Tim and me to dinner at his college next week.'

'Will you go?'

'Yes.'

'Well, there's an improvement, anyway. A few days ago I could hardly persuade you out through the front door, let alone into Oxford.'

'You're right. I am getting better. I've been thinking, though. Graham, Graham Peters. He was Donna's boy-friend before Raven came on the scene.'

'You mean he's the one with the motive to kill her.'

'Yes, that's just what I mean. We hadn't considered him before, we were too hung up over discovering the identity of Raven. And Graham's the one with the link to Gatts Farm. He might well still have a key to the showrooms. It's the sort of thing one does walk off with when leaving a job.'

'Do you think she met him there? And what about the heroin?'

'It does seem an odd way to kill someone, certainly. But perhaps Graham's an addict, and he happened to have the gear about his person.'

'I think we have a lot of questions to ask young Graham when we go to see him tomorrow,' said Roz.

'And I hate to say this, but I don't think Tim is out of the frame yet, either. Do you?'

'We can't eliminate him, no. But my gut feeling is that he's not the one.'

'I'd like to agree with you. But he did know Donna. And he did have a crush on her, that's obvious. Then there's the way Graham implied that it might have been Tim who was accompanying Donna to the antiques fair. Tim and Graham. They're the two hot favourites at the moment.'

'Certainly Tim went pink and sheepish when Graham suggested he might be Raven.'

'Though he might well do that if he was innocent.'

'True enough. I noticed that you were trying to find out whether he had a car, and what sort it was, but he wriggled out of that one, too.'

'Maybe he rides a bike,' said Kate. 'That would embarrass a man in front of two attractive women, wouldn't it?'

'Maybe it's a motorbike and he couldn't fit both of us on the back.'

They giggled.

'I don't know whether he was just winding Tim up, but Tony Fuller was telling us what a daredevil character Tim was as an undergraduate.'

'*Tim?*'

'Bungee-jumping, parachuting, tightrope-walking. Well, perhaps I exaggerate, but not much.'

'It's certainly a new light on a dull vicar.'

'And it puts him back as a prospective lover for Donna.'

'There's nothing more we can do about any of it tonight,' yawned Roz. 'We're just going round and round in circles. I'm going to finish my whisky and take myself to bed.'

'And tomorrow we'll go and confront Graham Peters.'

19

Next day was cold, grey and autumnal, with the threat of rain to come. Kate and Roz went for a healthy walk in the morning, then sat close to the glowing wood stove, reading the four Sunday papers they had bought between them.

'I suppose I ought to mow the grass and demolish a weed or two out there,' said Kate, looking through the kitchen window at the back garden which was now reverting to its wild state.

'You can't mow grass in the rain,' said Roz. 'We'll have another look at it tomorrow and do something then if we think it really needs it.'

Kate was only too willing to let the garden go to seed.

'Three-fifteen,' said Roz eventually. 'I'm going to comb my hair and put on a jacket. Then it will be time for us to collect your vicar.'

Kate muttered, 'He's not *my* vicar,' but it was only a formality. Her heart wasn't in it. In fact, she was starting to feel quite happy and optimistic about life for the first time since she had run away from Oxford.

'I shall put on my new scarlet shirt to cheer everyone up,' she said. And then she added lipstick and earrings to match.

'Kate can sit in the back this time,' said Roz when they had collected Tim from the Vicarage. 'I shall drive and you will navigate, Tim.'

'You should never rely on a vicar to know the right road. He's bound to lead you astray,' said Kate lugubriously. But Tim was getting used to her sharp tongue and didn't react. This afternoon, perhaps because it was a Sunday, he was dressed in clerical black. Kate wanted to tell him that it suited him better than his cool vicar gear, but didn't have the heart. At least he was still wearing his earring.

'Take the Hensford road to the bypass,' he said to Roz. 'Then aim for Rose Hill. I think that's the simplest way.'

They found Graham Peters' house eventually, after Tim had navigated Roz into a maze of back streets in East Oxford, and out again into the Cowley Road. The house was in the middle of a grey-brick terrace, built at the beginning of the century for poor but honest working men. Roz parked the car a few doors away, reversing into a space between an overflowing skip and a Y-registration Cortina.

The three of them squeezed through the narrow iron gate, up the weed-infested path and on to the uneven porch.

'There are three bells here,' said Roz.

'Goodness, it's only a tiny house,' said Kate. 'How do they fit them all in?'

'Houses like this were home to families with a dozen children in years gone by,' said Tim. 'We forget how lucky we are at this time, in this society of ours, to have a room, or even a whole flat if we're lucky, to ourselves.'

'Thank you, Vicar,' said Kate rudely, and rang the bell marked Peters.

Heavy steps on the stairs approached the front door. Then they heard him – for the steps sounded male – stop just inside the door as though wondering whether to open it or not.

Tim rapped on the glass panel. 'It's only us!' he called.

The figure behind the door still hesitated.

'Who is it?' he called out eventually. It sounded like Graham Peters, anyway.

'It's Kate Ivory and her friends,' replied Kate in her clear voice.

There was an indistinct sound behind the glass.

'What did he say?' asked Tim.

'I think it was "bloody hell",' said Roz. 'Or maybe the first word started with an f.'

The door opened a couple of inches. It was held on a solid-looking chain.

'What do you want?' The segment of Graham's face that was visible to them looked paler and gaunter than it had yesterday.

'Just to ask a supplementary question or two,' said Kate soothingly.

'I don't want to talk to you.'

'We gathered that. But my daughter is a very determined woman, and it's probably much easier and quicker to let us in. After we've asked our questions, and you've answered them, we'll go away and never bother you again.'

'Very clearly expressed, Roz,' said Tim approvingly.

'Is it just the three of you?'

'Yes.'

They heard the chain rattling as he released it, then the door opened wide enough to let them in. A smell of fungus and damp greeted them as they entered. Tim sneezed.

'Dry rot,' said Roz. 'And mould. They have a problem with damp.'

Kate looked hard at Graham. He wasn't looking at all well, and he hadn't shaved that day. He smelled of old sweat and takeaway Indian food. They followed him up the stairs and into the front room on the first floor. It wasn't very large, but it was quite neat, and was well-fitted with shelves and chests, presumably made by Graham himself. There were one or two interesting pieces of china and pottery standing around, doubtless picked up at the fairs he visited. The tidy room was strangely at odds with its unkempt owner. Roz and Kate sat on the neatly made bed. Graham and Tim took the two upright chairs.

'Well?' said Graham. 'What is it you want?' His voice was slurred. Was it drink or drugs? Kate sniffed. She couldn't catch the whiff of cannabis, so it was probably alcohol.

'What's wrong with your face?' asked Tim.

'It's none of your business.'

'It looks rather painful,' said Roz. 'Are you sure it has nothing to do with our last conversation?'

'Ask your questions and get out,' said Graham.

'You're a lot less friendly than last time we met,' said Kate. 'I wonder why that is.'

'You can't stay more than ten minutes max,' said Graham.

'Do you need our help?' asked Tim. 'Is there anything we can do to assist you?'

'You can fucking well leave me alone,' said Graham. 'You've caused me enough grief as it is. I only asked you in so's you wouldn't be stuck out there on the doorstep looking like the Marx Brothers.'

'I think there were four of them rather than three,' said Roz. 'Or was it five? I fancy myself as Harpo. Kate can be

Groucho. Which one do you want to be, Tim?'

'I think we should ask Graham our questions before he has an apoplectic fit,' said Kate kindly.

'We were thinking about what you said yesterday. You said you saw Donna with her new boyfriend,' said Roz.

'I told you everything I know about that. I hardly saw the bloke.'

'And that's the part we don't believe,' said Kate. 'We find it quite unlikely that you didn't follow them and take a good look at him. That's what I'd have done if I'd been you.'

Tim had got up from his chair meanwhile, aware that the unfortunate Graham was facing a three-pronged inquisition and wanting to reduce the size of the opposition. He wandered round the room, listening to what was going on.

'What's this?' he asked sharply. 'What happened here?'

'None of your business,' said Graham. 'It's nothing to do with you.'

'What is it?' asked Kate.

Tim had a dustpan and brush in his hand. Someone had swept broken shards of china into it.

'What was this when it was in one piece?' he asked. 'It looks as though it was rather pretty.'

'Bisque,' said Graham. 'Early nineteenth century. A partially draped figure of Persephone. I was very fond of it.'

'And what happened?' asked Roz. 'Have you had another visitor since yesterday?'

'I knocked it over. It broke. It was an accident.'

'And then you walked into a door and bruised your face,' said Kate. 'What an unfortunate evening you must have had. So unfortunate that you had to drink

207

solidly ever since to forget about it.'

'Who did it?' asked Tim. 'If you tell us, we'll go after him. You'll have no more trouble, we promise.'

'If I tell you, he'll kill me,' said Graham starkly. 'And who's to say it had anything to do with what we were talking about yesterday?'

'It's a bit of a coincidence, isn't it?' said Roz. 'You can't expect us to believe that the two aren't connected.'

'And there's another thing,' said Kate. 'If you were really upset about Donna leaving you, did you go after her to have a row? Did you follow her that night? Did you arrange to meet her at Gatts Farm?'

'You want to ask if I killed her,' said Graham flatly.

'Yes,' said Tim. 'Just that.'

'Well, I didn't. I thought you lot were looking for her new boyfriend. What did you call him? *Raven*, wasn't it? Well, why don't you go looking for *him* and leave me alone. I've got enough trouble of my own, I don't need any more. Just believe me, won't you. *I know nothing more about Donna and how she died.* And you can just piss off out of here now.'

'I think we'd better go,' said Roz.

'But we haven't had the answers to our questions,' said Kate stubbornly.

'You've had as much as you'll get,' said Graham. 'You should piss off out of here before you get involved in something you wouldn't like.'

'Come on, Kate. Your mother's right.'

'Very well. But I'll leave you my phone number,' Kate said, writing it on a leaf·torn out of the notebook she always carried. 'If you want to tell us anything at all, just ring.'

Graham snatched the paper from her and stuffed it into

the pocket of his jeans. 'Don't sit by the phone hoping,' he said.

They trooped out of the room and down the stairs, Kate unwillingly at the back of the group. Graham unbolted the door and let them out. They heard him putting back the bolt and chain as they walked down the path.

'This is a nice neighbourhood,' said Roz, looking at her car.

Someone had broken the side window and the front seat was covered in glass granules.

'Why on earth did they do that? There's nothing in here to steal.'

'They were after your radio,' said Tim.

'But I haven't got a radio.'

'That wouldn't stop them.'

They drove back to Gatt's Hill in a mood that was close to depression. They hadn't enjoyed their visit to Graham Peters, and the cool wind, laced with a smattering of rain, blew unimpeded through the broken window and whipped the women's hair round their faces.

'Do you think we've really put his life in danger?' asked Kate of the car in general.

'He's been warned off us, certainly,' said Tim.

'Or warned off something or somebody,' said Roz.

'Will they check that we went back to question him again?' asked Kate.

'But he didn't talk to us, did he? He didn't tell us anything new.'

'Let's hope that whoever attacked him believes that,' said Tim.

'The difficulty of this investigation is that the nearer we get to Raven, the greater the danger we put Graham in,' said Roz slowly. 'Graham is only safe if we fail.'

'But we're not going to fail,' said Kate.

'If I were Graham, I'd leg it,' said Tim.

'Maybe he already has,' said Roz.

They continued the journey in glum silence until they reached Gatt's Hill.

'Come and see us tomorrow afternoon for a case conference, Tim,' said Roz. 'I think we should review the situation. It's all getting rather heavy, don't you think?'

'It's your turn to visit me,' said Tim. 'Come to tea at four o'clock and I'll get in a new supply of chocolate biscuits.'

They dropped Tim off at the Vicarage, where he went to prepare himself for his Sunday-evening duties. Kate and Roz returned to Crossways Cottage, where they redistributed the Sunday papers over the sitting room. The cottage seemed warm and homely after their visit to Graham and they prepared a meal and ate in companionable silence in front of the wood stove. After the washing-up, they returned to their newspapers.

The phone rang. It was such an unusual thing to happen in this cottage that they both looked startled for a moment.

'I'll get it,' said Kate.

She came back a minute later. 'He or she hung up as soon as I answered. I dialled 1471 and they told me it was a payphone. I rang the number anyway, but no one picked it up.'

'Could you tell from the number whereabouts the payphone was?'

'It was an Oxford number. It could have been East Oxford, I suppose.'

'Graham, do you think?'

'If so, he changed his mind about talking to me.'

'Or someone interrupted at his end.'

'Or it could have been a wrong number,' said Kate, returning to her newspaper.

They were both silent for a while after that.

'I think we should consider the question of motive for the death,' said Kate, looking up from an article on white-water rafting.

'I think we should put the subject out of our minds until tomorrow afternoon,' said Roz. 'Pass me the section on "fun and profit for your retirement years", will you?'

Kate had taken a small packet out of her handbag and was inspecting it carefully. 'And how *did* Donna's pendant get on to Chaz's stall?'

20

Roz and Kate went out the following morning to get the VW's side window fixed. It was another breezy ride round the bypass and they were grateful when the car once more had its full complement of windows. From the windscreen repair centre they drove to the supermarket and stocked up the car boot with food. They idled an hour away in a coffee shop then dawdled back to Crossways Cottage and made some lunch.

'Time for a little lie-down and a read of an undemanding book before teatime,' said Roz, disappearing upstairs. 'Life has been rather tiring recently, don't you think?'

'Stimulating, certainly,' said Kate, who also had a book she was itching to read. She stretched out in her familiar place on the sofa, head at one end, feet (minus shoes) over the other, book in hand, and closed her eyes.

The weather was growing colder and the cottage was warm and cosy, so neither of them was tempted outside for a walk. It was two relaxed and cheerful women who turned up at the Vicarage flat that afternoon for tea.

Tim had tidied up, Kate noticed, and hoovered the carpet. He had moved some of the folders from the table and placed cups and plates ready for his guests. One of the plates was filled with chocolate biscuits. As soon as they arrived he put the kettle on.

'He'll make someone a lovely wife,' murmured Kate to her mother.

'Which is more than you'll ever do,' she retorted.

'Your tea,' said Tim, passing cups. 'You two must stop squabbling, you know. It's setting me a bad example.'

'Maybe we've been living together for too long,' said Roz.

'You haven't been here a week yet!' exclaimed Kate.

'Have a chocolate biscuit,' said Tim. 'And then we can start our case conference.'

'I've brought my notes with me,' said Kate. 'Shall I run through them briefly?'

'It might be a good idea to remind us all of the facts,' Tim nodded. 'Something new might strike us.'

So Kate read her notes out loud and the other two listened carefully.

'Well?' she said when she got to the end. 'Any new thoughts?'

'No,' said Roz. 'It all sounds too familiar.'

'Well, something did strike me,' said Kate. 'When I went through them yesterday evening, I started thinking about it. We've been wondering endlessly why Donna died at Gatts Farm.'

'And we still haven't found the answer,' said Roz.

'Maybe that's because we've been asking the wrong question. Maybe we should be asking ourselves *why did she die at all.*'

'What do you mean?' asked Tim.

'What was the motive for her death, or her murder if you prefer? We've made a rather cynical assumption that if we find her boyfriend, Raven, we'll have found her killer. The idea that people are murdered by their nearest and dearest has become a commonplace. But why? Even a husband or wife has to have a reason. Why should anyone want Donna dead? She was just a gardener who liked going to antiques fairs. She had a boyfriend or two and a small flat on a council estate. What's unusual about any of that? What motive is there for someone to want her dead? Unless we go along with the village view that all residents of the Banks are thieves and murderers, and all young women are sluts who deserve what they get, we're left with that basic question: *why?*'

'Jealousy,' said Roz. 'She dumped one man for another and the first was driven homicidally jealous.'

'Money,' suggested Tim. 'She had bought something at a fair that was worth a lot of money. Someone stole it and killed her to keep her quiet.'

'What did they steal? Her pendant? We bought it back for a fiver and change,' said Kate.

'There could have been something else. Something we don't know about. Something that she recognized as valuable and bought for a song. She was always talking about being rich one day. Maybe that's how she planned to achieve her ambition.'

'Maybe she knew too much,' said Roz. 'Like Graham. Only instead of beating her up, her attacker went too far, and he killed her.'

'Graham,' said Kate. 'I'm worried about him now. What have we dragged him into?'

'I agree. I'm worried about what we may have brought on him by our visit,' said Tim.

'I don't think he was any great innocent,' said Roz. 'I doubt this is the first time he's been in trouble. He probably knows how to look after himself.'

'But we marched into his life and threatened him with the police, without any thought of what might happen to him afterwards. If something *does* happen, we'll be responsible.'

'I hope Roz is right,' said Tim. 'I agree with Kate about him. Perhaps we—'

But at this moment the phone rang.

'Let's pray it's not an emergency,' said Tim, rising to answer it.

'Emergency *what*?' Kate whispered to her mother. 'Emergency *baptism*, do you think?'

But then they fell silent, for Tim's face had paled, and his tone was certainly one of urgency and dismay.

'Are you sure no one knows?' he was asking. Then: 'Yes, of course. If you think I can help, I'll come right over. I'll be with you in five minutes.'

He put the phone down. Kate and Roz looked at him expectantly.

'They've found another dead body,' he said.

'Graham!' said Kate.

'Is it Graham?' asked Roz.

'I don't know. It's a man, certainly, probably in his twenties. The body has been found in the lobby of the flats in the Banks. No one knows who he is and they're hoping that I can tell them since I was so helpful over identifying Donna.'

He was pulling on a jacket even as he spoke. 'I must go. I said I'd be right over. Do you want to wait here until I get back?'

'We'll clear up the tea things for you and then get back to Crossways,' said Roz. 'Come and see us, or telephone with any news, as soon as you can get away.'

Tim just lifted a hand to say thank you and goodbye. His mind was obviously on whatever he was going to have to look at when he got to the Banks. Roz and Kate cleared up in silence. Neither of them wanted to voice their fears about the identity of the dead man.

Is this death my fault, too? wondered Kate. *If it is Graham, then he probably died because we went to question him yesterday. What did we think we were playing at? This isn't a game. What have we done?*

'Could he really have killed Donna?' she asked eventually.

'Who, *Tim*?'

'No. I was still thinking about Graham.'

Roz considered the question. 'I don't think so. He seemed more concerned with our actual presence at his house than arguing about her death. If he'd been guilty he'd have tried to convince us that he couldn't have done it, that he'd been drinking at the pub with fifteen of his mates on the night in question. I think he's probably mixed up in something illegal but quite different.'

'Loan sharks,' suggested Kate. 'Or drugs, maybe. If it's drugs, I don't suppose we looked like typical customers, so people might wonder who the hell we were, and whether he was being investigated. Word might get back to his suppliers, and then they might want to find out whether he'd given us any names.'

'Whoever he's involved with has already been to see him. There were the marks on his face and the broken bisque figure.'

'A warning,' said Kate.

'Come on,' said Roz a few minutes later. 'We've finished here. We can get back to the cottage. I'm sure Tim will be in touch as soon as he has any news.' She sounded as worried as Kate felt.

'I can't go back and sit waiting for news like a Victorian heroine. I have to go and see for myself.'

And so when they reached the gate of the Vicarage, the two women turned left towards the edge of the village,

217

instead of right to Crossways, and strode along to Broombanks. At the end of the street they saw a couple of police cars and an ambulance. The area in front of the flats was taped off and a policeman was holding the sightseers back.

There was, as they might have expected, a small crowd gathering in front of the flats: some people with grey hair, a few young unemployed men, mothers with young children. Kate recognized Michelle and her friend, with their children at their side. The two youngsters seemed as interested as their mothers in the proceedings at the flats.

'Do you know what's happened?' Kate asked one of the women.

'There's been another murder,' she said with relish. 'They found his body in the lobby at the flats.'

'It was pushed round the back with the dustbins,' said the other. 'It could of been there for days.'

'All stiff and livid,' said the first. 'And it smelled horrible.'

'I'd have thought someone would find it pretty quickly if it was by the dustbins,' said Kate hardily. 'Someone must empty their rubbish there every few hours, surely.'

'You what?' asked Michelle. 'You ever smelled that place where they keep their bins? You don't want to hang around. You dump your bag of rubbish and get out quick. He could of been there for a week.'

'Do you know who found him?' asked Roz. 'Does anyone know who he is?'

'Russell found him,' said Michelle's friend. 'He got a terrible shock. After all, he's a young bloke too, and this man's young and dark-haired. It might have been him, lying there dead, mightn't it?'

'Might be him next time,' sniffed Michelle.

'Graham's in his twenties with dark hair, too,' said Roz to Kate.

'But what would he be doing here? It's miles from where he lives.'

'You said yourself, it's only a fifteen-minute drive.'

'Are they going to bring the body out soon?' asked a voice behind them. 'Can you see what's happening?'

'Are they going to put the body in the ambulance?' asked one of the children. 'I want to see it.'

'Little ghoul,' said Roz. 'Can you push further forward, Kate?'

'I can't get through,' said Kate. 'There's someone at the door to the flats, stopping people from getting in, and there are too many people in front of me. We should have got here earlier.'

'D'you want to look at the body, then?' asked Michelle. 'You got a strong stomach?'

'Not really,' said Kate. 'But I was afraid I might know who it was.'

'Vicar's gone in to identify him,' said someone else.

'Old vicar would never do something like that,' said an elderly man with a scabby dog at his heels. 'It's not right, bringing the church into it like this. Vicar should know his place.'

'And what place is that?' asked Roz.

'In church on Sundays,' said the man. 'He shouldn't be out doing all this social work and lecturing people on being kind to beggars and down-and-outs. Whose fault is it they got no jobs? Not mine. Work-shy, that's what they are.'

'Let's go,' said Kate. 'I don't believe anyone here knows anything. They're making it up as they go along.

We'll learn more from Tim than from this lot.'

'And we'd better get back to Crossways before he does, don't you think?'

Tim knocked on the cottage door about an hour later.

'Well?' demanded Roz as soon as he was inside and before he had even removed his jacket.

'Was it Graham?' asked Kate.

'No. I've never seen the man before in my life.'

'Thank God for that!' said Roz with feeling.

'Tell us all about it,' said Kate gently. 'Start at the beginning.'

'Your friend Russell, the one with the profile and the pony tail, went downstairs to the lobby to put his dustbin out for the refuse collectors.'

'I don't remember seeing dustbins there,' said Kate. 'I'm sure I'd have noticed them. Wouldn't they be an eyesore in the entrance hall?'

'There's a utility area underneath the staircase, and it has a door – unlocked at all times, of course – and the dustbins are kept in there. It's dark and smelly and I doubt whether anyone lingers much while they're throwing their rubbish away.'

'And that's where you had to go to identify the body?'

'They'd cleared a space round him, and moved him on to a stretcher, and covered him up, except for his face. The police had already taken their photos and removed any evidence before they let me in to see him, I imagine.'

'Could you tell how he'd died?'

'I couldn't see, but I understood it was a knife attack.'

'So it might just have been a common-or-garden mugging,' said Kate. 'It was nothing to do with us and our investigations. Probably nothing to do with Donna, either.'

'Drugs-related, I expect,' said Roz. 'Isn't that what they say most crime is these days?'

'Do we believe what we're saying?' Kate asked her mother.

'I'm afraid not,' said Roz. 'This village is a maelstrom of strong emotions and homicidal impulses.'

'That might be putting it a bit strongly,' said Kate. 'But he's probably to do with the village, and with Donna, I agree.'

'Then why did no one know who he was?' asked Tim. 'No one had ever seen him before, apparently. They asked all the residents in the flats, but no one has admitted to seeing him before in their lives. And no one else in Broombanks came forward to claim him as a friend or acquaintance. That's why they contacted me.'

'So if it was a mugging, or an argument, we're left with the same question as with Donna: what was he doing here?'

'How did he get to Gatt's Hill? Has anyone found a car? Or a bicycle, even?' asked Roz.

'No. Nothing,' said Tim. 'They were talking about that.'

'And if he came to Gatt's Hill, who was he visiting? You don't just turn up here out of the blue,' said Kate. 'Apart from the view, what else is there here?'

'If he was visiting someone, why haven't they come forward?' enquired Roz.

'Presumably because they have something to hide,' said Tim.

'Where's the nearest bus stop?' asked Kate.

'Three miles away,' said Tim.

'It's not an impossible walk,' said Kate. 'A young man could do it in less than an hour.'

'No, it's not impossible. But we're left with the question *why?*' said Roz. 'You have to have quite a strong reason to take a bus out of Oxford – and I bet they don't run that frequently – then walk for the best part of an hour. And it would be uphill. Why would he do it? What is there in Gatt's Hill that's so important? What have we missed? There must be *something*.'

'Tell us more about what he looked like. What sort of man was he?' asked Kate.

Roz suddenly said, 'Wait a minute, everyone!'

'What?' they asked.

'Now that we know it wasn't Graham, can you tell me why we're so interested? What are we doing here, chewing it over like this?'

'Of course we're interested,' said Kate. 'Someone's dead and we want to know how and who and why.'

'Every man's death diminishes me,' said Tim. 'We are all part of the same universal brotherhood of man.'

'That's a nice, pious thought,' said Roz. 'But actually, we know nothing about this man. We don't even know who he is. Agreed, it's sad that someone has died. It's shocking, even, that such a thing should happen in a sleepy little village like Gatt's Hill. But what has it got to do with us? Presumably the police will follow it up and find out who the man was and what he was doing here, and this will lead them to find out why he was killed, and possibly even who did it.'

'But we don't believe it's unconnected with Donna's death, do we?' said Kate. 'Suppose this man was Donna's Raven? We've been assuming that Raven's her murderer. But maybe they've been killed by a third person

222

who wanted them both out of the way.'

'How long do you think he'd been dead, Tim?' asked Roz. 'Could they have been murdered at the same time and dumped in different places?'

'I don't think so. I'm no expert on dead bodies, but I think he'd been dead for only a matter of hours – a day, maybe.'

'So much for the horror stories by the people at the Banks,' said Kate.

'And so much for my hope that he had nothing to do with us,' said Roz. 'I just wish we could start living a normal life with regular food and lots of shopping.'

'Rubbish!' exclaimed Kate.'You've been the Holmes to my Watson, remember?'

'Perhaps you're right. Go on then, Tim, tell us more about him. Could he have been Raven?'

'I suppose so. He was in his twenties, as I said. And dark-haired, the hair cut short. Rather a gaunt face, with stubble. Black stubble: it stood out against the very pale skin.'

'The colouring sounds Celtic, Irish or Welsh. Did he have blue eyes?' asked Roz.

'Brown, I think,' said Tim. 'He could have been Irish, I suppose, but he didn't strike me like that. I know this sounds old-fashioned and politically incorrect, but I'd say he looked foreign.' He thought for a moment. 'It wasn't just his looks. Maybe it was his clothes.'

'You said they'd covered him up,' said Kate.

'They had. But I could see the top part of his shirt. That must have been it. There was something about it that looked different.'

'It's not much to go on,' said Roz doubtfully. 'But we'll have to trust your instincts since we have nothing else.'

'I assume that he had no sort of identification on him?' asked Kate. 'Did the police tell you what was in his pockets, that sort of thing?'

'They weren't taking me into their confidence, but I did learn that he had absolutely nothing on him at all. No money, no keys, no pieces of paper. Not even a length of string.'

Roz said, 'It's sounding more like a story by John Buchan by the minute. The foreign stranger turns up in an English village and keels over with a knife in his back before he can utter a useful word.'

'*The Thirty-nine Steps*,' said Tim. 'I've read that one.'

'Foreigners would stand out in this village,' said Kate. 'The villagers hurl mud and insults if you come from ten miles down the road.'

'The pub,' mused Roz. 'The waitresses at The Narrow Boat are the only foreigners I've come across here.'

'New Zealanders – Australians,' said Kate, remembering. 'Do they count as foreign? What do you think, Tim?'

'Maybe.' He didn't sound convinced. 'I thought he looked more European than that. Maybe Italian or Spanish or something.'

'Not North African?' asked Roz.

'Why? Do you think you're being pursued by vengeful Arabs?' asked Kate.

'Don't joke about it, this is serious,' said her mother.

'Sorry, but I find it difficult to take your past life too seriously.'

'To get back to our dead body,' put in Tim, 'I don't think he was North African. He didn't look like an Arab, and his skin was so pale.'

'Perhaps that's because he was dead,' said Kate, who

wasn't much of an expert on this subject but who had an opinion to express anyway.

'And I have come across another foreigner in the village, but I can't quite remember where,' said Tim.

'Male or female?' asked Kate.

'I can't place the memory. I'll leave it for the moment. Maybe it will come back to me.'

'It's time for food,' said Roz. 'There's nothing more we can usefully find out at the moment, so let's start to prepare a meal. All this talking is leading us nowhere. At least cooking has an end product that we can eat.'

'I ought to go home,' said Tim. 'I can't keep imposing on your hospitality like this.'

'Nonsense. You must eat with us,' said Roz. 'What are you going to do at home in your flat? Open a tin? Defrost a packet?'

'Yes, do stay, Tim,' added Kate. She had slipped Donna's pendant into her pocket earlier in the day, and now she took it out and looked at it. 'It seems so long ago that she was here in the kitchen, handing this to me to look after.' She passed it over to Tim.

'I'm glad you've got this,' he said. 'We mustn't forget about Donna and what happened to her. Sometimes we seem to get caught up in the chase and forget the reason we started out on it. I was really fond of her, you know.'

'We gathered that,' said Kate. 'And it's good to think that she had at least one true, disinterested friend.'

Tim didn't look entirely comfortable with this last comment.

'This second death has brought all the grief back,' he said quietly. 'Especially since I had to go and try to identify this body, too. You go in not knowing what to expect, wondering which of your friends might be lying there dead.'

'That's the trouble with death. Each new one brings back the sorrow and guilt from the other deaths in your past.'

'There's no need to get so morbid, you two. We're still The Adventurous Three,' said Roz. 'Don't worry, we'll find out who killed Donna, and why. We've only been on the case for a few days, and look how much we've found out already.'

'More than the police, certainly,' said Kate.

'Tim, help yourself to a drink from the table there. Kate and I will retire to the kitchen.'

'You can open a bottle of wine and pour us both a glass,' said Kate. 'I think we all need a drink after the shocks of the last couple of days.'

21

Roz, Kate and Tim were halfway through their salmon with dill sauce and small boiled potatoes, shiny with butter, when the phone rang.

'Hello, it's Tony Fuller here.'

'Hello, Tony,' said Kate, who had left her food to cool when she had answered the phone.

'I'm not interrupting anything, am I?'

'No, of course not.' Only my dinner, but I'm too polite to mention that.

'I've been trying to get hold of Tim Widdows, but I've only caught his answering machine all day. I did leave a message, but for some reason he hasn't rung me back.'

'I believe he's been rather busy,' said Kate, who didn't feel like going through the whole story of the dead body by the dustbins, especially since she was still hoping to return to her half-eaten salmon steak.

'I thought vicars only worked one day a week, but obviously I've got it wrong. Anyway, I was ringing him to fix the details for Wednesday's guest-night dinner in Hall.'

'At Leicester,' remembered Kate.

'Do you know your way there?'

'I think so,' said Kate, still unwilling to talk about her previous visits to the college with another man. 'And if I don't, then surely Tim will.'

'I was forgetting: of course he knows the way. Look, I'm teaching in the afternoon, and I hoped I could just cycle home to my flat to change into a suit, instead of coming all the way back to Gatt's Hill before dinner. Can I meet you both at the lodge at six forty-five? Hall is at seven fifteen, and that will give us time to gather for a sherry in the Senior Common Room before-hand.'

'Fine. I'll make sure Tim and I are there. And thank you.' Kate rang off, not wanting to prolong the conversation any further, but she had the impression that Tony would have chatted on for longer if she had encouraged him to do so.

'I've arranged for us to meet Tony in Leicester lodge at six forty-five on Wednesday,' she told Tim. 'Dinner in Hall is at seven-fifteen.'

'Oxford has a language all its own,' said Roz, wiping melted butter from her chin and chasing the last drops of dill sauce round her plate with a slice of wholemeal bread. 'More wine, anybody?'

'The lodge is the place where the porters sit,' explained Kate. 'You walk into the college through a big wooden door studded with ancient nails, past the porters, who look you over and decide whether to challenge your right to be there, then go through an archway, also ancient, into a quadrangle with a square of green velvet lawn in the middle. "Hall" is the name of the panelled, raftered, medieval room where members of the college eat every day, and also the name of the formal evening meal during term-time.'

'Thank you for the guided tour, Miss Ivory,' said Roz. 'And remember – when you're out to a posh dinner, don't soak your gravy up with your bread roll, it isn't polite. Now finish your salmon so that we can serve up the pudding.'

'Pudding? Oh, good. I never get round to making it for myself,' said Tim.

'This is something nutty and sticky that Roz learned to make during her extensive travels to exotic places,' said Kate. 'If you want to be as unsophisticated as us, you put a big glob of whipped cream on the top. And it goes very well with our single malt whisky.'

And so the three of them completed a satisfactory evening, managing to blot out, for the time being at least, the memory of the tragedies that had brought them together in the first place.

The next morning Roz and Kate got up later than usual, after their extended meal with Tim which they had followed by a number of smallish whiskies.

Yawning over her muesli and strong black coffee, Roz said, 'I wonder what the village grapevine is making of the second unexplained death. "The body in the bin".'

'That's gross,' said Kate, spreading marmalade on to toast.

'Yes, isn't it? I'm sorry about that, it just slipped out.'

'You want us to have lunch in the pub again to listen to the gossip?'

'It hardly seems worth it, does it? Shall I ring Alison Fanning? She seems to typify a certain village worthy. I'm sure if I listen to her she will speak for all of them.'

'Rather you than me,' said Kate. 'And please don't sign us up for a course in creative tatting.' She poured herself a third cup of coffee. This was more than the ration she usually allowed herself, but she felt she needed it after the previous evening's indulgence. She found the aspirin and took a couple. Maybe her head would start to feel less like a pumpkin when they started to work. She removed the empty whisky bottle from the kitchen table and put it in the recycling bin. She could have sworn it was nearly full when they got it out after dinner. Tim must have drunk more than she thought.

When Roz came back from a long phone call, she had a smile on her face.

'I'm glad the village finds sudden death amusing,' said Kate.

'She hardly mentioned the second murder. Just a brief "Oh, those awful people in the Banks, they're capable of anything, we're not safe in our beds with them living in the village", and she was off on the subject of the Hope-Stanhopes.'

'They're a big yawn.' Kate's head was hurting and she wasn't feeling charitable towards the likes of the Hope-Stanhopes. She still hadn't forgiven Emma for her awful cooking.

'No, not this time. Apparently Emma Hope-Stanhope had a major row, in public, with Hazel Fuller.'

'How did we manage to miss it?'

'We must have been off on one of our adventuring trips.'

'Were there any details? Did Alison know what the row was about?' The thought of other people coming to fisticuffs cheered Kate up.

'It was at the Countrywomen's Guild meeting.'

'I didn't think Hazel would be interested in knitting chair-backs, or whatever the last meeting was about.'

'She's not. The speaker tripped over one of her own crocheted knick-knacks and broke her ankle and so had to cancel her talk.'

'You made some of that up.'

'Only the minor details. Anyway, to continue, Hazel

230

Fuller agreed to take over at short notice and give an informative talk on "How to make the most of your investments and double your pension". She was very good, apparently. The village women are even more interested in money than they are in crochet, so the parish hall was packed. All went well until Hazel called for questions at the end of her talk.'

'I can imagine the kind of questions that Emma was asking.'

'She wouldn't stop, it seems. She started with something innocuous about Post Office savings certificates and then moved on through accusations of sharp practice on the part of antique dealers and ended up with deeply personal insults.'

'Did Alison give you any examples?'

'I think one of the milder ones was "painted, menopausal tart", but I gather that after that Emma's language was too indelicate for Alison to repeat.'

'Do we know what brought this on?'

'Emma's been very strung-out recently, and Hazel's talking about making money was just the last straw. Oh, there was one small point. When Alison was telling me about Emma's diatribe, she mentioned that one of her complaints was that she never got a decent night's sleep because of the heavy lorries that changed gear on the corner by Gatt's House and revved their engines to climb the hill to Gatts Farm.'

'Surely there aren't *that* many of them. And they pass by in the daytime for the most part. Emma must be on edge because of something else.'

'Her husband, the ladies' man, I expect,' said Roz.

'And his little friend, Wendy.'

'Maybe he's taken to playing poker again.'

After the clearing and washing-up, Kate said, 'I'm going out for a half-hour walk. Maybe the bags under my eyes will have subsided by the time I get back, and my brain might be firing on all its cylinders instead of only one.'

Certainly she did feel a little better when she returned from her walk, though that was due as much to the coffee and aspirins as to the exercise.

'There's one thing about lunch at the pub: we could check out any foreigners who might be around,' she said to Roz, who was still yawning.

'That's a long shot. Just because the dead man was foreign – *if* he was foreign – doesn't mean that he came to visit a fellow countryman in Gatt's Hill.'

'It may be a long shot, but have you any better ideas?'

Before Roz could reply, there was an impatient knock at the door.

Is this our tame vicar? wondered Kate, going to answer it. But it wasn't Tim standing there on the doorstep, it was Russell.

'You'd better come in,' she said. 'And we'll put the coffee on again.' She walked ahead of him into the sitting room. 'Look who's come to see us, Roz.'

'Who's she?' demanded Russell.

'Don't worry, she's just my mother, Roz Ivory. You can trust her.'

'Not that my daughter ever has,' said Roz, looking their visitor over.

'Are you sure? I wasn't expecting anyone else to be here.'

'Really, she's just my mother,' soothed Kate.

'I suppose she looks all right.'

Roz was wearing a slightly muted version of her exotic

wear this morning and she had dark circles under her eyes. Russell was looking even worse than Kate and Roz. After his ordeal yesterday it was possible that he had drunk even more alcohol than they had, Kate supposed. The smell of sweat and raw onions was as pungent as ever, and Russell had made a poor job of shaving that morning. His black clothes were creased, as though he'd slept in them. And he hadn't cleaned his teeth, either, Kate decided. Roz poured out coffee, which masked the other smells a little, and they waited for Russell to speak.

'Well?' asked Kate, impatient at last.

'You're trying to find out about why Donna died, aren't you?' he said.

'Only in a very amateurish way,' said Kate truthfully.

'But you've been round asking questions, haven't you? You came round to my place and asked me all sorts. You do want answers.'

'Yes, we do,' said Roz. 'And are you volunteering the answers to some of our questions, Russell?'

'I didn't have anything to do with it,' he said. 'But when the second corpse turned up there, in the flats, I'd had enough. It was horrible finding it there when I went to put my bin out. You don't expect to find a dead man by the dustbins. And murdered.' He shuddered. 'It was bad enough when it was Donna, but that was down at Gatts Farm and she was a bird, but it could have been me this time, couldn't it? So I thought I'd come and tell you what I know.'

Kate sipped her coffee and tried not to stop the flow of information.

Roz said, 'Why didn't you go to the police?'

'I don't want anything to do with the filth,' said Russell, with feeling. 'If I told them what I'm telling you, they'd be on at me for ever afterwards. Probably charge me with something. But I haven't done nothing at all. It wasn't my fault.'

Roz and Kate waited. Surely Russell would manage to tell them whatever it was he felt was so important. He couldn't just sit there for the rest of the morning.

'You know they say she died of a drugs overdose,' he said eventually.

'Ah,' said Roz.

'I believe that's true,' said Kate. 'It's what they'll find at the inquest, they tell me.'

'And you was wondering where she got the drugs from,' went on Russell. He stopped again.

'It's quite an important question, isn't it?' said Kate. 'Are you trying to tell us that you supplied her with the heroin, Russell?'

'No, not me. I don't touch the stuff no more. But I know who does.'

'Go on.' Roz was nearly whispering in her eagerness.

'Graham,' said Russell.

'*Graham?*' This was Kate. She'd been wrong about him, then. It wasn't just alcohol he'd been indulging in.

'He supplied anyone who was interested at the Banks. Not just heroin, of course. Anything anyone wanted. E for parties, quite a bit. That was popular with the younger ones.'

'And do you know who *his* supplier was?' asked Roz.

'No.'

'So it looks as though Donna might have been meeting Graham at Gatts Farm that night,' said Kate. 'If she had only tried the lighter recreational substances before that night, he might have persuaded her to give the serious stuff a try.'

'And she took too much,' said Russell.

'It's a possibility,' said Kate.

'It gives us something to think about,' said Roz. 'Thanks, Russell.'

'You won't pass this on to anyone?'

'Trust us,' said Kate. She might have told him this was bad advice she was giving him, but he seemed to accept it.

'There's one other thing,' he said, and stopped again.

'Yes?'

'I don't believe it.'

'Which part in particular don't you believe?' asked Kate.

'I don't believe Donna would experiment with anything more than a joint or a tab or two of E. She thought people who got hooked were prats.'

'That's rather the impression we got, after only a short time with her,' said Roz.

'I'd best be getting off,' said Russell. 'I've told you what I know and what I think. I'll leave it up to you now. You can sort it out.'

'Thanks. We'll do our best,' said Roz, walking with him to the door.

'And if you've any sense you won't be having anything more to do with that poncey vicar,' added Russell.

'What's wrong with him?' asked Kate, surprised.

'I don't trust him. There's more to him than meets the eye.'

'What do you mean? What do you know about him?' she demanded.

'I'm not saying no more. You just watch your step with him, that's all.'

And with this dark warning Russell left.

* * *

'What do you make of that?' asked Roz.

They had been sitting in silence, mulling over what Russell had told them.

'I suppose I believe what he was saying about Graham. And if it is true, then we may be into something much wider and more serious than we thought at first. If Donna was involved with drug dealing, then we're out of our depth.'

'I don't see that it's changed things very much.'

'Don't you? We'd be dealing with gangs – and violent gangs, at that. No wonder Graham was so frightened. He probably had very good reason to be.'

'Do you think it was Graham ringing for help the other evening?'

'Why would he ring us? I expect it was Russell, ringing from the phone box in the village.'

'Do you want to give up the investigation?' asked Roz.

Kate thought for a moment or two. 'No,' she said. 'I think I want to go and write up my notes. I don't want to forget any details of what Russell told us.'

'But you think we ought to take it to the police now, don't you?'

'We promised Russell that we wouldn't.'

'That's true. Perhaps we should carry on for a while. We can always talk to the police as a last resort. What are you smiling for?'

'I was just imagining what a policeman of my acquaintance would say if he heard what you just said.'

'You amaze me. I hadn't realized you were on friendly terms with any of the police. And what do you think about Russell's warnings against poor Tim Widdows?' asked Roz.

'He didn't have anything specific to say, so I don't think we should worry too much about it.'

'Just the usual village prejudice against a newcomer, you think?'

'Could be,' said Kate warily.

'I do hope you're right. Should you be going to dinner at Leicester with him?'

'We won't be alone. Tony Fuller and all the other college Fellows will be there. I couldn't be in safer, duller company, could I?' And Kate went upstairs to complete her notes.

22

'So that's what one wears to dine at an Oxford college,' said Roz at six o'clock on Wednesday evening. 'I had been wondering.'

Kate had put on a short black skirt, with matching tights and moderately heeled patent leather shoes. She had added a canary-yellow jacket and apparently very little else except for a plain gold necklace and a pair of outrageous earrings.

'I like the earrings,' said Roz. 'How are you getting to the college?'

'Somehow I agreed to drive us,' said Kate. 'Tim mumbled something about hating to drive in Oxford, and never knowing where to park, so I found I'd volunteered.'

'So we still don't know whether he drives a clapped-out Fiesta or a Porsche. I hope he enjoys the way you park in a crowded street,' said Roz. 'He looks as though he has strong nerves, so I suppose he'll be all right.'

'Just because I happened to have two wheels on the pavement the other day, and only an inch between my bumper and that of the next car, there's no need to be rude about my driving.'

'You haven't mentioned the angle,' said Roz.

'Was that to the horizontal or the vertical?'

But luckily at this moment someone knocked on the front door and they stopped their quarrel.

'It's Tim,' said Roz, showing him in.

'I thought at least I should come to pick you up, even if you're doing the driving,' he told Kate.

'You're looking very smart. Is that your best suit?'

'Kate! Don't ask such rude questions.'

'It is, as a matter of fact,' said Tim. 'Will it do?'

'As most of the Fellows will be wearing gravy-stained worsted, hidden under a gown dating from the 1960s, I really shouldn't worry. I, by the way, am vastly over-dressed. The usual gear for women is grey hand-knitted cardigan, tweed skirt and tennis shoes, with, of course, the obligatory MA gown.'

'Well, you two are obviously going to have a lovely evening with Kate in this mood. Send her home without her pudding if she misbehaves, Tim.'

'Pudding's the best part of an Oxford dinner! I'll behave, don't worry.'

'Come on,' said Tim. 'We'd better get going. We still have to find somewhere to park.'

They drove west into the setting sun, along the narrow country lane edged with young poplar trees, rusty with their autumn colours. The hedgerows were full of the skeletons of cow parsley and wild carrot. Dusk was falling as they drove down Headington Hill towards The Plain, and the spires and towers of the colleges rose like grey ghosts from the dark blue of the trees. As the shops and offices extinguished their lights, so the old buildings came into their own, dominating the town as they had done for centuries: the golden sandstone that crumbled with the years but could still twist Kate's heart with its beauty. One day soon she must return to this place.

Kate turned right at the traffic lights.

'I should be able to find a space in Mansfield Road at

this time,' she said, as they turned away from the city wall and passed the tall grey concrete boxes of the Science Area.

'I knew we'd be lucky,' she said, slipping fairly neatly, or so she thought, into a generous space between a couple of cars.

'Do you think we're sticking out rather a long way from the pavement?' said Tim when he had climbed out of the car.

'That's all right,' said Kate. 'It's a wide road. They'll be able to get a fire engine through there if they need to.'

'If you're happy with it,' said Tim, looking at the three-foot gap between the front wheel and the kerb.

'The back wheel's a bit closer,' said Kate. 'Come on! No one will know it was us if we walk away quickly enough.'

'Isn't it a lovely evening,' said Tim as they walked down the broad, tree-lined road towards Leicester.

'But you can't see the stars the way you can in Gatt's Hill,' said Kate, surprising herself with the observation.

'I thought you were a city girl at heart.'

'So did I. I will be again, don't worry. The straw will drop out of my hair and I will be revealed in my true urban colours.'

'Did I tell you how good you're looking in that outfit?'

'No, but thanks.'

'You always do look very attractive, of course.'

'Really?' Kate was wondering how to get the conversation back to the subject of motor cars. She still wanted to know what sort of vehicle Tim owned. 'You don't think much of my driving, though, do you?'

'It's less exciting than your mother's, anyway,' said Tim diplomatically.

'Do you drive?' asked Kate as innocently as she could manage.

'Me? I have a driving licence, certainly. But don't you think that in a city like Oxford we should all decrease the emissions of carbon monoxide as much as possible? The pollution levels in the summer in the city are above the limits set by the EU as acceptable. It's up to us as individuals to make a difference to the environment.'

'Yes, but—' said Kate.

'We've nearly reached Leicester,' said Tim. 'Now where was it we were going to meet Tony?'

'The lodge,' said Kate, knowing full well that Tim remembered. Why did he want to change the subject like that? 'We need the Parks Road entrance, don't we?'

'Yes, that's right. So you do know the college.'

'Not very well,' said Kate non-committally. 'I'm not a university person, you know.'

'Really? You could be.'

'Now you're being unusually polite.'

Tim smiled nervously. 'We're a few minutes early. Will you be warm enough in that jacket?'

'I'm fine. It's sheltered here under the archway.'

And luckily for them both, Tony arrived at that moment to rescue them from any more of their stilted conversation. We were both trying to get on to a particular and different subject, thought Kate, and neither of us was succeeding.

'Hello, Tim and Kate,' said Tony. 'So glad you could come. You're looking very lovely, Kate. I do like you in that yellow.'

'Thank you,' said Kate politely.

Tony was looking sober in a dark suit and blue shirt and tie. 'I'll just pop into the lodge to pick up my gown,' he said. 'This college is still formal about these little details, I'm afraid.'

'Don't apologize for it,' said Kate. 'It's one of the things that makes a visit to a college so interesting.'

'Right,' said Tony a few minutes later as he emerged with a black gown bundled under one arm. 'We can go through this way. It's still just light enough to see.'

And so they took the route that Kate remembered well, through the Fellows' Garden with its venerable old copper-beech tree, where she had once met a fanciable young Fellow and shared his bowl of strawberries. *But that is in the past,* she told herself. *It is over.* They walked on past a friendly gargoyle or two, who winked and smiled at her, or so she thought, and into an elegant eighteenth-century building where Tony paused and put on his maltreated gown before entering the Common Room.

'We're the first to arrive,' he said. 'Can I get you both a sherry?'

'Lovely,' said Kate, who hated sherry.

The room had been decorated since she was last there: terracotta wallpaper with a shiny pattern in the same shade, slightly darker curtains, armchairs in muted green and turquoise. She was glad that it had changed. She could pretend that she had never been here before.

The door opened and two more people came in, followed by a third. To Kate they were familiar, although she could not have put a name to their faces. All three wore gowns and therefore belonged to the college.

243

Another two followed in ordinary clothes, and Kate was relieved to see that she and Tim were not to be the only guests at dinner that evening.

'Warden, may I introduce my guests for this evening, Kate Ivory, the novelist, and Timothy Widdows, the vicar of St Michael's, Gatt's Hill.'

'You're a Leicester man, aren't you, Tim?' asked the Warden. 'I seem to remember you from some years back.'

'Yes, Warden,' said Tim, and they went into an impenetrably obtuse conversation, while Kate stood back and talked to Tony. She was relieved that she didn't have to talk to the Warden. Bill Stanton might not recognize her after all these months, but then again, you could never be quite sure how long your luck would hold.

The room was filling up with people, mostly men, and mostly wearing gowns. There were four or five guests in addition to herself and Tim, and Tony introduced her to some of the less fearsome people in the room. Conversation, she noticed with interest, was no more intellectual than it had been at the Hope-Stanhopes'. She hoped that the food, at least, would be better. But the Leicester chef was renowned throughout Oxford, she knew, and so she could look forward to an excellent meal.

Eventually a gong was struck by a college servant and they lined up in order of seniority and processed through to their places at High Table. If you didn't mind being on display, as if on a stage, in front of two hundred or more undergraduates, it was a very pleasant meal, thought Kate. There were candles in silver candlesticks on the tables. There were silver pepper pots and salt cellars, silver cutlery, silver dishes. The faces around her were well-fed and healthy-looking. These people did themselves well. Above them arched the hammer-beam roof.

Around the walls were the portraits of Wardens of the
college going back for centuries. All looked prosperous
and pleased with themselves. An undergraduate in the
long-sleeved gown of a scholar read a Latin grace and
then they were allowed to sit down and start on their
meal.

Kate spooned up pale green soup and chatted to the
companion on her left about holiday cottages in France.
Then when the guinea fowl and baby vegetables were
served she turned to the man on her right and listened to
an interesting discourse on the merits of oil-fired as
opposed to gas central heating. She was separated from
both Tim Widdows and Tony Fuller, which seemed to
her to defeat the whole purpose of having dinner with
them.

The noise from the hall below them was rising as the
undergraduates relaxed and talked loudly to their
friends. At High Table, pudding was served, and the
conversation became more general. Kate wished she
could introduce the subject of motor cars, but she
couldn't quite manage it. Finally the undergraduates
were allowed to leave, the Fellows relaxed, finished
their wine, and then they retired to the Senior Common
Room again for their coffee.

This time they sat in informal groups in the armchairs
and on the sofas. Kate, Tim and Tony were together at
last, sitting in a group with two or three of the younger
people present.

'I see you decided on the Peugeot in the end, John,'
Tony Fuller was saying to a man in his thirties with wild
dark hair and small round gold-rimmed glasses. 'I thought
you would go for something less staid.'

'Millie's talking about starting a family,' said John in a

strong Lancashire accent. 'She said I had to choose a sensible car this time.' The absent Millie must be a strong-minded woman, for John hardly sounded reconciled to his choice of car.

Now, surely I can bring Tim into this, thought Kate. She opened her mouth to ask a pertinent question, but someone else had got in first. Oxford dons were as quick to get a word in as they were to hoover up their food, she had noticed. No one spoke or ate as fast as one of these.

'It's all right for you to talk, Tony. We can't all dash around in a machine like yours!' Another man, red-haired, with a wedding ring on his left hand, was speaking now. Nice little hatch-back with toddler seats in the back, guessed Kate.

'He'll have to put the top back on now that the weather's cooled down,' said John. 'No more young women with their hair flying in the breeze again until next year, Tony.'

Kate looked at Tony. She hadn't asked herself about his car. What machine were they referring to? It sounded quite promising.

'My old man likes to indulge me,' said Tony easily. 'Mostly you'll see me on my bike around town. And if it were up to me, I'd still be driving the Fiesta I had for my twenty-first.'

'Oh, yes? Pull the other one!' said John.

'What about you, Tim?' Kate asked quickly. 'What sort of car would you like?'

Tim looked startled. 'What? Oh, I haven't really thought—'

'Don't you know about Tim?' said Tony softly.

'Know what?' asked Kate.

246

'I do believe he was even rapped over the knuckles by the Bishop at the time,' said Tony, smiling.

'Why?' She was getting tired of this game. Was this another of Tim's bungee-jumping or paragliding exploits she was about to hear?

'Dear Tim was—'

But at this moment they were interrupted by the arrival of the Warden, Bill Stanton, who made hostly noises about being so very pleased to see so many guests at High Table, and then somehow the subject had moved on, and it seemed churlish to attempt to move it back again. Perhaps she could pin Tim down on the way home when they were alone. She would certainly try.

The room was beginning to empty.

'Should we think about leaving?' said Kate to Tim.

Tim glanced at his watch. 'It's early yet, but things do seem to be breaking up. Perhaps we could have another coffee at my place when we get back to Gatt's Hill.'

'Roz and I have stocked up on single malt again,' said Kate.

They thanked Tony for his hospitality and said their goodbyes to the other Fellows in their group.

'I'll walk through to Parks Road with you,' said Tony.

'Are you going back to Gatt's Hill this evening?' asked Kate.

'I stay in Oxford mostly during the week,' he said.

'Glorious night, isn't it?' said the Warden, joining them in the quadrangle. The four of them started to stroll together towards the lodge. 'Well, Miss Ivory,' he said to Kate. 'It's always a pleasure to see you here.' As Tim and Tony moved a few yards ahead of them, he smiled suddenly and wolfishly. 'You've always had the best legs in Oxford,' he said quietly.

'Thank you so much, Warden,' she replied primly. 'I wondered whether you remembered me.'

'I always thought Liam Ross was a fool,' he said. 'Olivia Blackett wasn't a patch on you.'

'No, perhaps she wasn't. But by the time Liam realized that, it was too late.'

'It was lucky he was offered a job in the States. Life in college was growing quite uncomfortable for him. There would always have been a cloud over his reputation, I fear.'

'Did they ever find her murderer?'

'I believe not.'

'No. I thought they wouldn't.'

'And do I have the feeling that you know more about it than you're telling me?'

'How could I possibly do that?' said Kate. 'Still, I hope Liam makes a success of his life in America. I doubt I'll ever see him again.'

'I like your young vicar. Perhaps you should stick with him. You'd make a most original vicar's wife.'

'We're not quite on those terms, Warden.'

'What a pity. It's time you settled down.'

'Not even my mother would dare say that to me.'

He laughed. 'So perhaps you need me to say it instead.'

Tim and Tony had moved into their natural rapid stride and were now some twenty yards ahead of Kate and her older companion. The two younger men reached the archway leading into the front quadrangle as Kate and the Warden turned the corner. Which was how Kate saw them suddenly silhouetted against the spotlights that illuminated the public face of the college. As though remembering the other two, Tony Fuller paused before passing through the arch, and turned to see if they were still following. His gown swung out and around him, caught in the glare of the lights.

Like the wings of a great black bird.

Raven.

23

'Just calm down a bit and concentrate on getting this car away from the kerb in one piece and without inflicting any dents on that rather nice Mondeo in front.'

'But he was! I'm sure he was!'

In the face of Tim's obvious anxiety, Kate did as she was told, then pulled away from the pavement and executed a U-turn to get back into South Parks Road so that she could leave the city through its eastern suburbs.

'It would make sense, wouldn't it? It's our connection with Gatts Farm at last,' she said more slowly as she drove through St Clements and up Headington Hill.

'But what exactly did you see? A man in an MA gown. Even if that's what Donna saw and what made her call him "Raven", there are hundreds of them in Oxford. Thousands, probably. Why should it be Tony Fuller? He seems the mildest and most innocuous of men to me. And that's not a recent impression: he always was a quiet type, even when he was nineteen.'

'They're the deepest,' said Kate.

'And has anyone ever seen him with Donna?'

'No. But that makes him even more suspicious.'

'How do you work that out? You've been reading too many detective stories,' said Tim.

'And then there's his car,' said Kate.

'I've never seen it,' said Tim. 'Have you?'

'No, but—'

'I've only ever seen him on a bicycle. One of those black, sit-up-and-beg jobs. Not even a racing bike.'

'That's his cover!' cried Kate, starting to get excited again.

'Cover for what?'

'Why did his colleagues at Leicester talk about his flashy sports car, then?'

'You can't judge a man by the car he drives,' said Tim severely.

'What car do *you* drive?' asked Kate baldly.

'Er, well, there's a slight problem there,' said Tim. He cleared his throat. 'I do have a car. Yes, I do have one. It's just that three months ago I had my licence taken away for a year, and so, strictly speaking, I can't use it. I'm not allowed to drive, I'm afraid. The car's in one of the garages at the Vicarage, waiting for the penalty time to be up. And, since you seem so interested in the make, it's a Vauxhall Astra.'

'Poor old Tim,' said Kate. 'What did you do?'

'Ah, I was caught speeding on the M40.'

'You must have been going at quite a belt.'

'I was, I'm afraid. And then, when I was stopped, they breathalysed me.'

'And it was positive?'

'Yes. Well over the limit.'

'Dear, dear. No wonder the Bishop was cross.'

'I'm afraid he was. And it's so inconvenient when you live in a village with no bus service.'

'Yes, it would be.'

'I'd better tell you the rest, hadn't I?'

'It's good for the soul, or so they say.'

'I'd met Donna earlier this year, and at last I'd managed to ask her whether I could accompany her to one of her antiques fairs. I offered her a lift, which she accepted.' He paused to consider his wonderful luck. 'And then, just a few days before we were due to go out together, I had my licence taken away.'

'What did she say?'

'She laughed at me. Said something to the effect that she wasn't interested in a vicar, and a vicar without a car was a definite no-hoper.'

'How wounding,' said Kate thoughtfully. Just how wounding to a young vicar's pride would that be? Would he get his revenge by killing her? Maybe. But surely not in that particular way.

'You're suddenly very silent,' said Tim, glancing across at her.

'I was just thinking that you and Donna must have been very canny about your meetings. Not a breath of gossip about you ever reached the Fanning-Hope-Stanhope-Philbee grapevine, not that I've heard, and I have been pretty nosy about Donna and her friends.'

'Well, we were never really an item. We only had our little chats when she was working in the Vicarage garden.'

'That would explain it, I suppose.'

They were both silent as she drove away from the suburbs into the pitch-black countryside.

'Gatt's Hill,' said Kate, as she passed the first of the three streetlamps. 'Coffee at my place?' she asked.

'It is more comfortable than mine, certainly,' said Tim.

Kate parked, more carefully this time, outside Crossways Cottage. There were lights at the windows, so she assumed that Roz was still up. She was glad about that. She could try out her theory about Tony Fuller on her. She was sure that Roz would pay more attention to it than Tim had.

But Roz, after ten minutes' inoffensive conversation with them, pleaded tiredness and retired upstairs. Kate was left feeling frustrated with them both: Tim didn't believe her theory about Tony Fuller, and Roz wasn't even there to hear it.

She drank her coffee and poured them both a whisky. During dinner at Leicester she had been drinking mineral water since she was driving home, and she felt she deserved a relaxing nightcap now.

Tim took a seat beside her on the large sofa. 'We've had some interesting talks about the Church and morality, you and I,' he said.

'We have? I don't think I noticed them.'

'Oh, yes. And you do seem to have some pre-set ideas about us.'

' "Us"?'

'Those of us who are in the Church.'

'It's difficult *not* to prejudge people who wear dog collars. In spite of the way so many of you hit the headlines in the Sunday tabloids, I do think that most of you are quite conventional, don't you?'

'Conventional, perhaps. But our ideas have moved on over the years, you know. Especially in the past decade or so.'

'Are you trying to tell me you're gay?'

'Me, a pooftah! No! Certainly not!'

'Now who's showing his prejudices? There's no need to be so vehement about it. I wouldn't mind at all if you were.'

Tim continued more forcefully. 'I'm trying to tell you that ideas of conventional morality have moved on. That we no longer try to deny our sexuality.'

'Really? You're trying to tell me that you fancy me?'

'No! That is, yes.'

'Well, which is it?' Kate spoke a little wearily. She wasn't at all sure that she was ready for a new man in her life at the moment. In fact, she wasn't sure whether her friend Paul Taylor, the detective sergeant, was still there in the frame or not. She liked to think he was still waiting for her in Agatha Street if she cared to go back there. She might have urged Tim to make his mind up, but she wasn't prepared to do the same thing herself.

'Slow down, Kate. Give me a chance to say what I mean.'

'Go on, then.'

'You treat me as though I were some sort of eunuch. Well, I'm telling you that just because I wear a dog collar as you call it, I'm not. I'm the same as any other man who takes you out to dinner or—'

'Or invites me to tea?' Kate finished for him. 'I take your point, Tim. I'll think about it, really.' And I'll try not to tease you quite so unmercifully in future, she added to herself.

'Yes. Well. Thank you,' said Tim stiffly. He put his coffee cup down and drained his whisky. 'I think I'd better be going now,' he said.

'If that's what you want,' said Kate easily. 'We haven't known each other very long, Tim. How long is it? A week? Hardly that, I think. So give it a bit of time. There's no need to hurry these things, is there?'

'Yes, all right,' he said, more relaxed now. He stood up and rescued his jacket from the back of the sofa. 'But I think it is time for me to leave.'

They stood together by the gate. It was difficult not to stand and stare at the black countryside and the stars here in the peace of Gatt's Hill. Kate said, 'And you will

think about what I was saying earlier, won't you? About
Tony Fuller being Donna's Raven, that is. It would answer
a lot of our questions.'

'I'll think about it. But I can't see Tony rushing back
from Leicester College to take out some little gardener
from the village. It's too far-fetched.'

'I suppose you're right. But it seemed like a sudden
revelation when I saw him in his gown against the light
like that.'

'Sleep on it. See what you think in the morning.'

'Good night,' said Kate, and went back into the cottage.

It was a fascinating thought, sleeping with a vicar, she
mused. Presumably that was what Tim was leading up to
with his talk of rethinking conventional morality. What
would it be like? she wondered. Did he wrestle with his
conscience before sliding between the sheets? Did he
leave those dreadful sky-blue socks on? Or his dog collar?

She giggled.

It might even be worth finding out.

She was not surprised to see Roz sitting on the other
sofa when she got back into the sitting room.

'I didn't believe that one about feeling tired at ten-
thirty,' Kate said. 'Would you like a whisky?'

'Yes. Thank you. I thought I was being wonderfully
tactful. Here is my daughter, Kate, alone at last with a
man. I had better make myself scarce, I thought.'

'Ha bloody ha,' said Kate rudely. 'Though as a matter of
fact you weren't far wrong. I do believe that our innocent
young vicar was trying to proposition me.'

'Did you accept?'

'I said we needed to give it more time.'

'That means no,' said Roz in a matter-of-fact tone. 'Well,
how was your evening?'

Kate gave her a brief account of the dinner and the people at the college, and then she told her about seeing Tony Fuller in his gown and thinking he looked like a big black bird.

'You make him sound like Superman,' said Roz.

'He is, in a way. When you first meet him he's just an inoffensive, pleasant bloke. But then you start hearing about his sexy sports car and see him in his gown and think "Raven".'

'You do have a vivid imagination, Kate. No one has suggested that Tony was seeing Donna.'

'No one's managed to tell us *who* she was seeing. And Graham thought he looked rather like Tim. Well, if you didn't know them, you might say they were the same type.'

'Oxford types, you mean?'

'I suppose I do.'

'You're saying that when he saw Donna and her new man at the antiques fair, he really *didn't* get a good look at them. He didn't follow them, as we have been saying. He merely received an impression of someone like Tim Widdows.'

'Yes – Tony Fuller.'

'I understand that this would give us the connection with Gatts Farm,' said Roz, curling her legs under her on the sofa and sipping her whisky between phrases. 'But what motive would Tony have for killing Donna? He invites her to the farm, he unlocks the showroom – he would know where the key was kept, I agree – to discuss Oriental rugs or Victorian knick-knacks, or whatever was on display there at the time. Then he asks her whether she's ever tried hard drugs, and when she says no, he hands her the syringe and tells her to get on with it. When he sees how ill she is, he doesn't call an ambulance or a doctor, he just goes back to his Oxford flat. No, Kate, I can't see it.'

'What were the other motives we thought of? Jealousy. Money. Knowledge.'

'If he was Raven, why should he be jealous of anyone else? She was obviously nuts about him.'

'Money,' said Kate. 'Suppose he gambled, like Jon Hope-Stanhope, and needed money to pay his debts.'

'He could ask his father for the money.'

'And what if his father refused?'

'Then he'd ask Hazel. And what mother would refuse her only son a little money to pay off the heavies when she has so much? Anyway, he didn't sound like someone who was extravagant with money.'

'It doesn't sound likely, I agree,' said Kate. 'So we're left with the unlucky knowledge: Donna found out something she wasn't supposed to. And she was killed to keep her quiet.'

'And Tony Fuller is a mild-mannered Oxford don. I still can't see him killing anyone.'

'And so are we back to Tim?' asked Kate regretfully. 'Tim who likes to live dangerously, but whose present life gives him few opportunities?'

'Tim, who went with us to see Graham and who knows, therefore, exactly what Graham was persuaded to tell us.'

'We're going round and round in circles. Shall we give up and go to bed?'

But at that moment the telephone rang.

'I hate it when it rings this late,' said Kate, going to pick it up. 'It always means bad news.'

It was Tim Widdows. 'I've just remembered where I came across the other foreigner,' he said. 'I thought you'd still be up, so I had to let you know. It was at Gatts Farm, the morning when I was asked to identify Donna's body.'

'Who was it?'

'I don't know. It was just a voice asking me what was happening, like everyone else at the time. I didn't see him. He was standing behind me.'

'A man – another foreigner. Very interesting. Thanks, Tim. Sleep well.'

'Can I see you tomorrow morning? Don't you think we should go and chase it up?'

'If you think we should.'

And Kate went back to tell Roz what he had said.

'Does it get us any further forward?' asked Roz.

'I can't see it myself. Even if he's connected to the man who died in the Banks, I don't see where it gets us. And what's the point in walking down to Gatts Farm tomorrow morning to look for him? He's hardly likely to be still standing on the grass after all this time.'

24

Kate woke early the next morning. She had never been good at lying in bed once she was awake, so she slid out from under the duvet and went downstairs to make herself a cup of coffee. It was a sharp, misty morning and the outdoors beckoned. White vapour drifted across the fields down by the river, and the trees and a distant church tower floated above it like features in a dream landscape. Soon, now, the mornings would be dark, cold and wet, and so she should take advantage of this one while she could. She showered and dressed in jeans, T-shirt and trainers, pulled on a sweatshirt in case she was cold, and let herself out of the cottage. Cold, damp air slapped against her face.

No, she thought, pausing in the open doorway. I'd better let Roz know where I've gone. She had got out of the habit of letting anyone else know her whereabouts, but it seemed only polite. It was strange to think that there was someone in the house who would care whether she was in or not. She might be gone for an hour or two, after all, and Roz might worry. *Fat chance*, said a voice in her head, but she made herself believe that her mother had changed since the carefree, careless days of her youth. So, she wrote a quick note, saying simply, *Gone for a walk, probably in the direction of Gatts Farm. Back in time for breakfast. Love, Kate.*

She anchored the note under a paperweight on the

small table by the front door, and then left the cottage, this time closing the door quietly behind her. She walked briskly down the hill: there might even be a hint of frost in the air and she had to keep moving if she wasn't to get cold.

By the time she reached the expanse of grass outside Gatts Farm, she had warmed up and there was a film of perspiration on her forehead. She paused, jogging on the spot to keep her circulation going. What had happened behind that wall, inside that building? What had Donna been doing there, and who had watched her die? She stared into the courtyard to see if there was anything there to give her a clue about what had happened. Even at this time in the morning the gates were already standing wide open. In the centre of the courtyard stood one of the yellow vans, mud-splashed and shabby-looking compared with the usual shining vehicles that plied their way up and down the hill.

This one, thought Kate, must have arrived this very minute from Hungary, or the Ukraine. Where else did Derek Fuller say he found his furniture? Romania, that was it.

The courtyard appeared deserted, but then she heard male voices and heavy footsteps approaching from the direction of the workshops. Three figures came into view on the far side of the yard. She recognized Derek Fuller, in waxed jacket and tweed cap, but the other two men were strangers. They were large and dressed in dark clothes, with woollen caps pulled down over their ears, erasing any individuality in their appearance. The three men approached the van, and as they did so, she heard a knocking sound. At the same moment, Derek Fuller looked up and saw her standing at the gate.

For a few seconds, the four of them stood still, staring at each other. Then Derek spoke to his two companions and they came towards her. It wasn't until they were nearly on top of her, and she saw their blank expressions that Kate thought of running. Too late. By then each of her arms was in the grip of a big, strong man, and she knew she had no hope of breaking free, or of out-running them even if she did.

She found herself frog-marched, her feet only just scraping the ground, up to Derek Fuller.

'Good morning, Kate,' said Derek, when she was standing next to him.

She merely nodded in reply.

'Close the gates,' he said to one of her guards. 'We don't want any more nosy parkers watching what we're doing.'

She heard the gate clang shut behind her, and it struck her then that it sounded just like the gate of a prison.

'It's a pity Dave was delayed,' said Derek reasonably. 'He's the one who was driving the truck, by the way. Usually such a reliable man. He should have been here a couple of hours ago and then there would have been nothing for you to see or hear when you went past on your hearty morning walk.'

Kate attempted an innocent expression. 'I don't understand, Derek. What is there to see? This is one of your furniture vans, isn't it? What's wrong with that?' She opened her eyes wide and tried to breathe slowly to calm her agitated pulse.

'Nothing wrong at all,' said Derek softly. 'But you *did* hear something, Kate, didn't you?'

Kate found that the only sound she could make was an undignified squeak. 'I didn't hear anything,' she said earnestly. 'Well, just the noise the birds were making, and a bit of mooing from Sam Philbee's cows.'

'Don't pretend to be stupider than you really are. And don't underestimate *my* intelligence,' said Derek. 'I thought you heard something. And now you'd better come indoors for a little chat.'

He nodded to the two men and Kate found herself forced to follow him into the showroom where Donna's body had been found.

It was odd about the morning, she thought. If you thought of danger, you thought of night-time, darkness, or fog. You thought of footsteps behind you in a darkened street, of a knife shining in the moonlight. You never imagined that danger could come out of the crisp morning air like this. Even now people all over Gatt's Hill were hearing their alarm clocks ringing, and were stirring and wondering whether to turn over and sleep again for a further ten minutes. Kettles were humming and the smell of coffee was permeating kitchens as mothers called children to their breakfast. Nothing bad could happen at the beginning of a golden autumn day like this one.

25

'Hello, Tim, is that you?'

'Roz?' Tim sounded as though her phone call had woken him from a deep sleep. 'Is everything all right?'

'I'm not sure. I came down this morning to find a note from Kate saying that she had gone out for an early walk and would be back for breakfast. But she's not back and I'm worried.'

'It's still early, isn't it?' Tim yawned and changed the receiver from one ear to the other. He pushed his free hand through his hair so that it stood up in the way that Kate would have recognized.

'In her note, Kate says that she was walking in the direction of Gatts Farm,' said Roz.

'Gatts Farm,' he repeated.

'Do wake up, Tim!'

'Sorry. Yes. Give me ten minutes. I'll put some clothes on and be right over. Have you made the coffee yet?'

'A fresh pot will be ready for you when you get here.'

It was half an hour before Tim, dressed in unexceptional dark clothes and dosed with strong coffee by Roz, was ready to leave the cottage and start searching for Kate.

'Maybe she's fallen and injured herself and can't walk back to the cottage,' he said.

'Maybe she's discovered whatever it was that Donna

265

found out, and the same person is murdering her at this very moment.'

'You want to start searching at Gatts Farm?'

'I want to march in there with a gang of tough, muscle-bound men and demand the right to tear the place apart, but failing that, I shall make do with one medium-sized vicar,' she said tartly.

'Yes, very well. I'm doing my best.' Tim was finding these Ivory women rather hard to take. Perhaps it was just as well that Kate hadn't responded more positively to his advances yesterday evening.

'We should have listened to her,' said Roz. 'She said the answer lay at Gatts Farm. She was probably right about Tony Fuller, too. Do hurry up! We'll be too late.'

'Calm down. Slow down,' pleaded Tim. 'We don't know that anything at all has happened to her yet. She may have bumped into Alison or Emma and been invited back for a cup of coffee. She's probably sitting in a warm kitchen eating toast and marmalade, not thinking about us at all.'

'Do you honestly believe that?'

'Honestly? No.' Honestly, he was nearly as worried as Roz.

They moved to the edge of the road to let the post-office van drive past up the hill in the direction of the cottage, then walked briskly on.

'She has an unfortunate gift for barging into other people's secrets and causing mayhem. She told me about it before and I didn't really believe her. Now I do, and I'm afraid she's in danger,' said Roz.

They were silent for the next minute or so.

A car engine growled on the corner behind them and they stepped up on to the grassy verge to get out of its way. Something long, low and scarlet snarled past them and disappeared out of sight round the next bend.

'Whose was that?' asked Roz.

'I haven't seen it before,' said Tim.

'Did you recognize the driver?'

'No. The light was reflecting off the windscreen. I just noticed he was wearing dark glasses.'

Both of them thought of Raven and his flash car. Neither of them mentioned it aloud. In another couple of hundred yards they reached Gatts Farm. There was no sign of anyone around. No sign of life in the house, either.

'What now?' asked Tim.

The gate was closed. They tried the handle, but it wouldn't open. Roz rang the bell at the side. No one answered it.

'Can you see anything?' asked Roz, peering through the metal uprights of the gate. The railings were so close together that it was difficult to glimpse anything behind them. There was no welcoming *Showrooms Open* board outside.

'I think there's one of those yellow vans standing in the yard. That's all,' said Tim.

'Can you climb over?'

Tim looked up at the top of the gate. It was at least eight feet high and there were spikes and nasty-looking razor wire on top of it.

'No,' he said.

'I thought you were supposed to be so bloody intrepid!' fumed Roz. 'Why can't you get us into this place? My daughter's in there and I know that something dreadful is going to happen to her unless we get her out.'

'I don't understand why you're so upset,' Kate was saying

in as reasonable a tone as she could manage. 'What is it I'm supposed to have done?'

'I don't think you've done anything much yet. It's what you've seen and heard,' said Derek Fuller. 'And we have all noticed what a talkative little thing you are. Can't keep a secret to yourself. Now that's something we can't allow.'

'But what is it you think I've seen?' asked Kate. 'I imagine you're smuggling something into the country inside those vans of yours. What is it? Drugs? I certainly haven't seen any of them.'

'Then you're not quite as clever as I thought you were,' said Derek.

Kate was sitting at one end of the Knole sofa that she and Tim had noticed on their first visit. One of the silent heavies was still guarding her, and she knew that if she tried to get up and move away from her elegant seat, she would be unceremoniously returned to it. She didn't try. They had been sitting in the showroom for more than twenty minutes and she wanted to ask what – or who – they were waiting for, but she stopped herself, in case she didn't like the answer.

Derek sat, looking like an English country gentleman in his Barbour and tweeds. He should have looked as harmless as Jon Hope-Stanhope, but there was something a lot steelier under the mild exterior, and he was scaring her shitless. The one thing she did know was that whatever illegal activities Derek was involved with, they were bringing him in serious money and he wouldn't be giving up a sizeable income like that without an argument. Inconvenient novelists would be disposed of, without compunction. Some time later that day there would be another phone call to the Vicarage flat and Tim would be called out to identify a third body. She would have to outwit this man somehow, but at the moment he was winning the war of brains as well as of muscle.

'I can see you're making a lot of money,' she said reasonably. 'And it's probably at the expense of some poor bloody peasants in Eastern Europe. You buy their furniture for a fiver or two, you ship it out, you tart it up, and you sell it for hundreds, maybe even a thousand or more. But that isn't illegal, is it? You put a lot of work into it yourself, and you give employment to how many? A couple of dozen people – craftsmen, at that. Then there are the drivers and warehousemen. You're quite a philanthropist, I should say. I don't understand what you think I could reveal about you that would do you any harm.'

Derek didn't answer, but sat staring impassively into the middle distance as though she didn't exist.

'Don't pretend you didn't hear it,' he said eventually. 'I know you did. And I think you've worked out what it meant.'

And then, after a long wait, while Kate wondered whether she could tell him that she hadn't had her full intake of caffeine yet that morning, there was the sound of a car arriving and passing through the gates. She listened for the gates to shut, and heard the now-familiar clang. She didn't doubt that they had also been locked and bolted. Even if Roz read her note and started to wonder where she was, she wouldn't be able to get into Gatts Farm to find her. She felt like screaming and shouting, but glanced up at the impassive Muscles and knew that would be an unwise thing to do.

She heard rapid steps across the flagstones, the outer door was opened, closed again with a crash, and someone else entered the showroom. She turned round to see who it was.

'Hello, Tony,' she said, unsurprised to see him. 'Or do you prefer to be called Raven when you're in your gangster gear?'

'Shut up,' said Tony in a neutral tone. 'Well, Dad, and what is this all about? What is she doing here? And why the hell did you have to drag me away from work to deal with it?'

'Don't go getting stroppy with me,' said Derek. 'If you hadn't been playing your stupid fucking games with that girl, we'd never have got into this mess in the first place. You relied on me to get you out of the shit then, and so you can help me tidy this one up, too.'

'I do apologize for his language,' said Tony to Kate, as though they were still in the Leicester Senior Common Room.

'I wish someone would explain what's happening,' said Kate in her most plaintive voice. 'I went out for a gentle stroll before breakfast and now I seem to be in the middle of a lurid kidnapping story. And my mother will be wondering where I am by now. And so will other friends of mine.' But she wasn't even convincing herself and she stopped talking. No one was taking any notice of her, anyway.

'How much do you think she knows?' asked Tony.

'She knows very little for certain, but she has a vivid imagination and has probably put most of the story together by now.'

'What happened?' asked Tony.

'Dave got here late this morning, and left the gates open behind him when he drove the van in. That man's out, by the way. Give him his cards and pay him off. I don't want to see him again. And we found this woman was hanging around the gate, clocking everything that was going on.'

'There was nothing to see,' protested Kate. 'I've no idea what you're talking about.'

'She heard someone knocking on the inside of the van,' said Derek. 'Some stupid, impatient bastard who couldn't wait for us to come round and open up the doors for him.'

'And you think she's guessed that we're dealing with illegal immigrants,' said Tony. Kate felt that he spelt out what was happening on purpose, to let her know that the pussy-footing games were about to stop.

'It's hardly a hanging offence, is it?' said Kate.

'It's lucrative,' said Tony. 'The furniture makes hundreds. The migrants pay in thousands for their chance of prosperity in the West.'

'Romania. The Ukraine. Where was the other place?'

'Hungary,' said Derek.

'What about the drugs?' asked Kate.

'We don't deal in drugs,' said Derek. 'Deal in drugs and you find yourself mixed up with a whole new set of characters. We know what we're doing with furniture and people. Drugs are for other people.'

'If you get caught smuggling drugs, or even suspected of it, Customs will never be off your back,' said Tony. 'It's not worth the risk. We stick to the business we know.'

'I didn't think Customs were very fond of illegal immigrants, either,' said Kate. 'Weren't you ever searched?'

'I'm sure you noticed just how large some of our furniture is,' said Tony patiently. 'We've constructed some very ingenious pieces, rather like magicians' cupboards, that have fooled Customs so far.'

'Where do you keep these people when they get here? Why has no one noticed a crowd of foreigners in the village?' asked Kate, whose curiosity had still not faded, in spite of her situation.

'They arrive in the evening, after the craftsmen have left. We put them in one of the barns for a few hours, feed and water them, then ship them on before morning,' said Tony.

'That's what's supposed to happen,' said Derek. 'Some stupid bastards have been screwing up the schedules, though, and we've had to keep the migrants here for longer than we wanted.'

'I still don't understand where the heroin came from,' said Kate.

'That was an independent enterprise by Graham,' said Tony. 'He decided to use our vans to bring drugs into the country. We found out before Customs did, and stopped him.'

'We confiscated his stock,' said Derek. 'And then fired him, of course.'

'He must have found a new route,' said Kate. 'I think he's still in business.'

'He won't last long,' said Tony. 'He'll soon be wiped out by the competition.'

'And Donna?' asked Kate. 'What happened to Donna? What was she doing here?'

'That was him and his stupid fucking games,' said Derek viciously.

'Donna and I liked to spice up our encounters in various ways. We tried a little house-breaking. That was fun. We sold our loot at an antiques fair. That had an edge of danger to it, too. And then I thought it would be fun to bring her here to the farm and—'

'He wanted to screw her in his parents' bed,' said Derek. 'He's a pervert, this son of mine.'

272

'Still not a hanging offence,' said Kate equably. 'Why kill Donna?'

'One of our illegal visitors had also found his way into the house, and he and Donna met, unfortunately. I was all for buying her off, I must say. I don't like violence.'

'We couldn't risk it,' said Derek. 'I could see the cash register she called her brain registering the thousands she could take us for in return for her silence. I wasn't going to lose half the profit to a little bitch like that.'

'So you offered her some of Graham's confiscated stock.'

'Not exactly offered, no,' said Tony.

'I told him to get off back to his precious college,' said Derek. 'I could deal with the girl.'

'Someone held her down and he looked after the rest,' said Tony.

'We put her clothes on and took her out to the showroom. I thought I made rather an artistic job of her death scene,' said Derek.

And Tony isn't the only pervert around here, thought Kate.

'I pushed off to Oxford, and Dad made for the north.'

'And Hazel?' asked Kate.

'Hazel does what she's told,' said Derek with finality.

'And what about the dead man in Broombanks? I suppose he was one of your illegal visitors.'

'The same one, in fact,' said Tony. 'The silly fellow decided to leg it before we could arrange to ship him off to the turnip fields of East Anglia. He wouldn't have got far, of course. He'd have been picked up by the police, or Immigration, within a few hours. As it happened, he only got as far as the other end of the village before Dad caught up with him.'

Poor bastard, thought Kate. And what future did these people have, anyway? They probably were dumped in the turnip fields of East Anglia by the likes of the Fullers.

'One last question,' she said, hearing uneasily how prophetic the phrase sounded.

'We'll indulge you,' said Tony.

'What about Donna's pendant? The blue scent bottle. How did it end up on a stall at an antiques fair in Lower Hensford?'

'I found it. Afterwards,' said Derek. 'I didn't want it associated with Gatts Farm, so I sold it for a couple of quid to a lad in one of those stalls in the antiques supermarket in Oxford. That place is full of all sorts. No one would notice it.'

'And Chaz must have bought it from him,' said Kate.

It was becoming increasingly obvious to her that after all this true confession, the Fullers wouldn't be able to show her politely to the front door and allow her to leave. She wondered what they had planned for her. And she wondered what they were all waiting for.

As though on cue, Derek looked at his watch. 'They should be nearly through by now,' he said. 'I told them to wash the van down. We don't want it to look as though it's come straight from the mudfields of Eastern Europe.'

'There, aren't you lucky?' said Tony. 'They're busy preparing a nice clean berth for you. You should have quite a comfortable ride across Europe. Well, perhaps comfortable isn't exactly the right word for it.'

'And then?' asked Kate bravely.

'I'm sure you can imagine what happens then,' said Tony softly. 'It will be our Broombanks man in reverse. Unknown, unrecognizable foreigner found in rubbish tip in Bucharest.'

274

'And what about this end? I'll be missed. There'll be search parties.'

'And what will they find?' asked Tony. 'I might put my mind to some inventive false trail to send them off all over the country. That could be quite amusing.'

There was a knock at the door.

'Yes?' asked Derek.

'Ready to leave in fifteen minutes,' came the reply.

'Well, we'd better get you ready for your journey,' said Tony with what sounded like genuine regret in his voice.

'Have those two snoopers left the gate yet?' asked Derek. 'Check that it's clear out there, would you, Tony?'

Tony returned a couple of minutes later. 'They've gone,' he said. 'They must have returned to the cottage, or to the Vicarage for a good pray.'

'That would have been your mother and the vicar,' explained Derek. 'They didn't see anything. They didn't find anything. And they won't do.'

Roz wouldn't give up, though, thought Kate. She might have been a lousy mother all those years ago, but she was a tough old bird and wouldn't abandon her now.

'Pass me a syringe,' said Derek.

'Just a moment. What's that?' said Tony.

The showroom window, too high for Kate to see out of, looked out on to the lane between Gatt's Hill and Gatt's House. Someone was revving a car engine.

Tony crossed to the window and looked out.

'It's a bloody great Range Rover with solid steel bull bars,' he said.

There was a metallic crash outside. 'And she's charging the gates.'

It's Roz! thought Kate. I wonder where she stole the Range Rover from.

At that moment a brick came flying through the window, scattering glass all over the tasteful furniture arrangements. And an upper-class voice, female, started to shout amazingly crude insults in through the opening.

Not Roz, realized Kate, but Emma Hope-Stanhope. What was she doing here?

There was the sound of a loud report and more breaking glass.

Emma had brought her shotgun with her.

26

'That's what comes of being mean-minded,' said Roz. 'If Derek had given Emma Hope-Stanhope a decent price for her furniture, you would now be on your way to Bucharest, drugged and helpless.'

'Thanks for sharing that thought with us,' said Kate.

She, Roz and Tim were back at Crossways Cottage, filling themselves up with coffee and eyeing the whisky bottle.

'The letter from the bank manager this morning was the last straw, apparently,' said Roz. 'She hadn't realized how badly Jon was still losing at poker.'

'She shouldn't have opened it really,' said Tim. 'It was addressed to Jon.'

'Some of us are rather glad that she did open his mail,' said Kate, who thought the others weren't being quite glad enough about her reprieve from certain death.

'And what about you two?' she asked. 'I was relying on you to rescue me, and you came up with what? Zilch.'

'We brought the police, didn't we?' said Tim. 'They cleared everything up very nicely, I thought.'

'How did you persuade them to come?' asked Kate.

'Don't you remember that you told me the name of your friendly policeman?' said Roz. 'I rang Thames Valley Police and they found him for me quite quickly.'

'Doubtless after you had told a fib or two,' said Kate.

'When I spoke to him, it only took a few seconds to

277

convince him that you were in deadly danger. He seemed to think it was your natural condition.'

'What did he say?'

'I think "Bloody hell" probably covers most of it,' said Roz. 'But anyway, I didn't have to give long explanations or anything. He said he would call out the cavalry and they'd come straight over.'

'They arrived in time to remove Emma's shotgun before she did any real damage,' said Tim.

'You forget how the countryside is littered with lethal weapons for exterminating pigeons and so on,' said Kate. 'I'm glad Emma didn't walk into the Fullers' unarmed. She'd have found herself shipped off to Hungary with me if she had.'

'What happens now?' asked Tim.

'I think she's divorcing Jon. He's moving in with his friend Wendy and Emma's going to salvage what she can of her family inheritance.'

'Perhaps she could open up Gatt's House as a hotel,' said Kate. 'With her dreadful cooking and awful rudeness it could become quite a cult place to stay.'

'Actually,' said Tim, 'I was wondering what the two of you were going to do now. Are you staying here? Or moving on?'

'It's time to move on,' said Kate. 'I need to get back to Oxford. I know it's peaceful here—'

'What!' shrieked Roz.

'Well, it is now the Fullers have been carted away in the Black Maria. And I've not written a word since I've been staying here. I need to get back to the city and settle down to some work. My tenants in Agatha Street are moving out at the end of the month, and I shall move back in.'

'What about Callie's cottage?' asked Roz.

'I thought you might like to stay here until she gets back. I see there's a letter in her handwriting with a New York postmark on the table. That will probably tell us when she's returning.'

'You've got everything sorted out, haven't you?' said Tim.

'I had an opportunity to think what was important and what wasn't,' said Kate. 'It's amazing how you rearrange your priorities when you think you have only a few hours to live.'

'She's over-dramatizing again,' said Roz. 'Take no notice of her, Tim.'

Kate said, 'To continue with my plans. When Callie gets back, Roz can come and stay with me in Oxford for a while if she wants. We can get to know one another properly again: I expect it will only take a week or two before we're at one another's throats, but at least we can give it a try.'

'And what about me?' asked Tim.

'It's been lovely knowing you, really it has, Tim. And I hope we'll still go on being friends.'

'But,' said Tim. 'I know there's a but.'

'But I realized when I saw him in his lovely smart uniform, with his stern, disapproving expression and his dependable blue eyes, that I'd been missing my policeman friend Paul Taylor more than I liked to think.'

'I've enjoyed our adventuring,' said Roz.

'Me too,' agreed Tim. 'Maybe the three of us could do some more one day.'

'When you've got your licence back you can drive over and visit us in Oxford,' suggested Roz.

'I can't wait to get home,' said Kate.